CHRISTMAS WITH A COWGIRL

CALLAHANS OF COPPER CREEK BOOK 3

NATALIE DEAN

ALSO BY NATALIE DEAN

CONTEMPORARY ROMANCE

Copper Creek Romances

BAKER BROTHERS OF COPPER CREEK

Copper Creek Romances Series 1

Cowboys & Protective Ways

Cowboys & Crushes

Cowboys & Christmas Kisses

Cowboys & Broken Hearts

Cowboys & Second Chances

Cowboys & Wedding Woes

Cowboys' Mom Finds Love

CALLAHANS OF COPPER CREEK

Copper Creek Romances Series 2

Making a Cowgirl

Marrying a Cowgirl

Christmas with a Cowgirl

Trusting a Cowgirl

Dating a Cowgirl

Catching a Cowgirl

Loving a Cowgirl

Marrying a Cowboy

KEAGANS OF COPPER CREEK

Copper Creek Romances Series 3

Some Cowboys are Off-Limits

Some Cowgirls Love Single Dads

Some Cowboys are Infuriating

Some Cowboys Don't Like City Girls

Some Cowboys Heal Broken Hearts

Some Cowgirls are Worth Protecting

Some Cowboys are Just Friends

Some Cowboys Fall for Hidden Stars

Some Cowboys Come Home for Christmas

Some Cowboys Brave the Flames

Some Cowboys Fight for Love

PALMERS OF COPPER CREEK

Copper Creek Romances Series 4

Mateo & Nicole

Sophia & Cameron

Roman & Olivia

Camilla & Dallas

Isabelle & Jason

Miller Family Saga

BROTHERS OF MILLER RANCH

Miller Family Saga Series 1

Her Second Chance Cowboy

Saving Her Cowboy

Her Rival Cowboy

Her Fake-Fiance Cowboy Protector

Taming Her Cowboy Billionaire

BROTHERS OF MILLER RANCH SERIES BUNDLE

MILLER BROTHERS OF TEXAS

Miller Family Saga Series 2

The New Cowboy at Miller Ranch

Humbling Her Cowboy

In Debt to the Cowboy

The Cowboy Falls for the Veterinarian

Almost Fired by the Cowboy

Faking a Date with Her Cowboy Boss

MILLER BROTHERS OF TEXAS SERIES BUNDLE

BRIDES OF MILLER RANCH, N.M.

Miller Family Saga Series 3

Cowgirl Fallin' for the Single Dad

Cowgirl Fallin' for the Ranch Hand

Cowgirl Fallin' for the Neighbor

Cowgirl Fallin' for the Miller Brother

Cowgirl Fallin' for Her Best Friend's Brother

Cowboy Fallin' In Love Again

BRIDES OF MILLER RANCH, N.M. SERIES BUNDLE

~

Though I try to keep this list updated in each book, you may also visit my website nataliedeanbooks.com for the most up to date information on my book list.

CONTENTS

1

———

Dianna

*D*ianna let out a heavy breath as she forced herself to move forward toward Shane's friend Tristan and the little boy at his side. This was what she wanted, right? A new lease on life, something to give her purpose. She loved children and Shane's idea to try out his services with those struggling with autism had warmed her heart.

Shane was the kind of guy who selflessly continued to give and give. She couldn't think of one occurrence when he'd been involved in something just for himself. Word got around town about how he'd given jobs to those who needed money, and how his equine therapeutic center had been planned way before the country club.

He had enough money to come into Copper Creek and do whatever he wanted—and it turned out he was far more genuine than anyone she'd met in town. If she was ready to date someone, she might have swooned over him like most of the other women who lived in the area.

But the truth was, she wasn't ready for anything.

Brielle said it was because none of her sisters had been given the opportunity to explore relationships due to their father's strict rules. She didn't know what Brielle was talking about. Dianna was perfectly content to sit back and let her older sisters have all the dating fun and deal with all the drama that seemed to come along with it.

Only now, there were no rules. Her father had finally had some sense talked into him about his strict dating rules. She could date anyone she pleased. And now she felt like the whole town was staring at her and expecting her to find love at the snap of her fingers.

Well, if they expected her to fall in love with someone that fast, they would be terribly disappointed.

Her steps slowed and she avoided looking directly at Tristan. She'd heard enough about him from Shane. College friend. Single father whose wife didn't want to stick around.

He probably didn't want her pity. Not to mention, he'd brought his son here to get him some support. They'd probably both agree that the little boy was her priority.

She stopped a few feet away from the boy and got down at his eye level. "Hi, I'm Dianna."

"Mathew doesn't really talk much to anyone but me," Tristan interjected. "Even his speech therapist thought he was nonverbal for almost a whole year until Mathew warmed up to him." He offered her a crooked smile and Dianna's stomach twisted unexpectedly.

Still crouched with snow around her, Dianna smiled broadly at Mathew, who eyed her with distrust. "You know what? You're really lucky. Because I didn't like talking that much either when I was your age. You don't have to say anything if you don't want to. You're here to ride horses, right?"

He nodded but remained close to his father.

"Wonderful."

He held something clutched tightly to his chest and her focus dipped to examine it.

"Is that a Belgian Warmblood?"

Mathew's eyes widened and he pulled the horse away from his body a few inches to gaze at it before he glanced at her once more.

"Sure looks like it," Dianna said. "Around here, we have special events and those are the horses I see the most."

He hugged his horse once more but still refused to speak.

She got to her feet and gestured toward the side of the club as she met Tristan's gray eyes. "I know you probably have a lot to do to get settled, but how about we take a quick tour so you can be ready for the full day ahead of us tomorrow?" Dianna tore her gaze away from his intense stare and looked down at Mathew as Tristan placed a hand on his shoulder.

While deep and full of authority, Tristan's voice was also gentle and patient. "How does that sound? Do you want to go see the horses?"

Another nod.

Dianna beamed at them. "Come on. I'll show you around. Maybe you can even pick the horse you want to ride tomorrow."

Tristan fell into step next to her with Mathew on his other side. He leaned closer to her, his words soft as if he didn't want his son to hear. "I appreciate your willingness to help us out, but I wanted to give you a heads up that Mathew might take a long time to warm up to you, if he does at all."

A small smile touched her lips. "I'm not here for my benefit,

Mr. Wood. I'm here for Mathew. If he doesn't want to talk to me, that's fine. He doesn't have to."

His brows creased and his whole body stiffened. A frown marred his features as he said, "Isn't that what we're here for? To help him with his social skills?"

They arrived at the barn and Dianna turned to Mathew. "Hey, buddy. How about you find your favorite horse and wait by his stall for me? I'm going to talk to your dad about some of the more boring stuff."

Mathew glanced from Dianna to his dad, then reluctantly wandered down the aisle.

Dianna watched him go, then faced Tristan and folded her arms. "Equine therapy is meant to help calm the child so they can better accomplish their goals. The skills Mathew might work on can include speech, social skills, and fitness, but it also includes learning how to care for something besides themselves. We'll work on following instructions and safety. But he'll also be focused on having fun."

The longer his stare drilled into her, the more uncomfortable she became. Dianna shifted and glanced in the direction where Mathew had gone. Shane had put her through a training program so she knew what to do, but she felt like she was just making excuses. Tristan knew his son better than she did. What right did she have to tell him how this would go?

She cleared her throat and offered another smile she hoped appeared more confident than she felt. "Autism affects everyone a little differently."

"I know that."

"Of course you do. That's why you warned me that he might not even talk to me during your visit."

His features tightened. This probably wasn't what he had wanted to hear, and she prayed she was on the right track as she attempted to make her point.

"Mathew needs to trust me, and he's not going to do that if I push him. The more I put him in an unsettled position, the more he's going to withdraw. I suggest you take a step back and let me try things my way. Yes, we'll work on social skills. But that doesn't always mean speaking. It's body language and respect. Let's just see how the next few weeks go before you decide that I'm not doing what I was trained to do."

His brows creased as he glanced back toward where Mathew was standing outside of a stall, staring up at a horse that had its head over the stall door.

Dianna shifted so she stood beside Tristan. "I take it that Mathew likes horses."

Tristan puffed out a breath and rubbed the back of his neck. "That's an understatement. He named every type of horse we passed on our way here. He knows what they eat and how big they can get. He knows what events they can participate in. Honestly, if we could afford to own one in the city, I probably would have gotten him one already."

"Has he ever ridden a horse before?"

He shook his head, then met her gaze. "This will be the first time, and the only reason I agreed to come was because Shane offered to let us have ten weeks of therapy for free."

Dianna's shock must have been written all over her face because he looked away and his expression darkened.

"If we could afford something like this, I would have done it already. The truth of the matter is that our insurance only covers the kind of therapy that takes place in an office setting. But something tells me this will be better for Mathew."

She glanced over to Mathew, finding him rubbing the nose of the horse, a bright smile on his face and completely oblivious to everything else around him. "You're not wrong."

Tristan glanced at her once more, his gray eyes no longer

hard, now more curious. There was a yearning she could read in his eyes as if everything hinged on this experience.

Dianna motioned toward Mathew. "It doesn't matter if you're a child, an adult, typical or atypical—everyone has a currency. There are love languages, and hobbies, interests that pull us out of our shells. Autistic children are no different. Some like trains or dinosaurs. Mathew likes horses. I think you'll be surprised how much he comes out of his shell while he's here."

He didn't look convinced. When Tristan wasn't showing his exhaustion in his features, he was carrying it in his shoulders. He let out another sigh and raked his hand down his face. "Okay. If you think you can break open his shell, then you do what you think is best."

She smiled, a chuckle escaping her lips as she shook her head.

"What?"

Dianna stilled and stared at him. "Hmm?"

"What was that look for? Are you mocking me?"

"What? No, of course not."

The frown from before marred his handsome face. "Then why were you laughing at me?"

Eyes wide, she forced the lump in her throat down with a hard swallow. "I wasn't laughing *at* you. I was laughing—Well, I guess I found it humorous that you've been around him for his entire life and you have yet to see what you're doing wrong."

"What *I'm* doing wrong?" His voice had a bite to it that she hadn't heard before and she flinched. "I'm sorry, why don't you enlighten me, what am I doing wrong in raising *my* child?"

"For heaven's sake," she said, still quiet enough that Mathew wouldn't hear. "I didn't mean it like that. I only meant that you have this mentality that you have to make him conform to society's standards. You want him to speak to everyone he meets and behave the way *you* want him to behave."

"That's not fair. I never said anything like that."

"Not *technically*. But let me ask you this. Are you trying this therapy because you think it'll be good for him? Or are you doing it because you think it's his best shot at being 'normal'? Or at least what society deems normal."

She'd overstepped. The realization hit her like a slap in the face when Tristan's face turned a deep shade of red. She cleared her throat and looked away, feeling her own face flush with embarrassment. "The point I'm trying to make is that Mathew is different. He's never going to be what you or the world deems *normal*. People will always think he's disrespectful because society has taught them how to think. There's no such thing as 'normal,' and people need to get used to that. Yourself included." Before she said another word that could get her in trouble, she spun on her heel and strode toward Mathew.

She was off to a *great* start. Nowhere in the manual that she'd read during all of her training was there a policy that stated she could speak to the parents that way. While she hadn't exactly yelled at him, she'd basically told him he hadn't been raising his child right.

Everything she'd said she'd meant. Opposition came from all sides when it came to autism. The ironic thing about Shane hiring her for this position had come after she'd gone through her training. There were several similarities between the way her brain worked and the way a typical child with autism thought. She'd never been diagnosed, but she'd always felt a little different—she'd just managed to hide it really well by keeping her nose in books.

When she was a child, she was great at pretending to be what others considered 'normal.' She'd honed her skills, and every so often, she could pull herself together to go out with friends to the club and dance. But those moments took a lot out of her, much like she assumed would happen with Mathew.

She slowed her steps as she drew closer and crouched down beside the boy. "Do you want to know what his name is?"

Mathew gave her a sideways look, his right hand still clutching his toy horse, his left rubbing the horse's nose.

Dianna sensed more than saw Tristan approach. She tilted her head and let out a small laugh. "His name is Molasses. Isn't that silly?"

Mathew's face split into a grin and he looked at the horse again.

"I like him, too." She shot a look over her shoulder, finding Tristan's eyes boring into her. Unnerved by his stare, she forced herself to focus on Mathew. *He* was the reason she was here. And maybe after things got settled, she'd be able to find some common ground with his father.

2
———————

Tristan

Tristan had worked with several people over the years. From speech therapists to behaviorists, he'd met them all. And every single one had been recommended to him by doctors or other specialists.

But not one of them had deigned to put him in his place and tell him he was viewing his son the wrong way.

Irritation was the first emotion he noticed when she'd lectured him. How dare she tell him how to raise his son? That's what the father was supposed to do. The way she made it sound, he didn't care about his son as much as he cared about the kid fitting in.

Didn't all parents want that for their children? Mathew was in the second grade this year. And every time he was picked up from school, he didn't seem to have any friends. His teacher couldn't think of a single child in his grade who consistently played with him.

That was understandable considering the fact that Mathew didn't speak unless he wanted to, which was pretty much only when it was people he was close to. How was he supposed to fit in with the other children if he wouldn't speak to them?

All of those thoughts stomped around in his brain until he finally allowed them to slow down enough to get what Dianna was probably trying to get at.

Mathew was special in his own right, and forcing him to conform was what everyone around him did. Even his own father was guilty of that problem. A twinge of remorse sliced through his chest as he watched Dianna continue her chatting, not bothering to ask Mathew a single question. This was the first time Tristan had seen his son at ease with someone he'd just recently met.

There was something calming about her presence that he couldn't put his finger on. Maybe she had a point. Right now, she wasn't expecting Mathew to do anything but be present.

Dianna stood and motioned toward the stall door. "You can go inside if you'd like. Molasses likes to be petted. We won't be able to ride him until later, but you can see for yourself how big he is."

Mathew beamed and nodded as he moved toward her. Dianna opened the door and Mathew slipped inside with her.

As soon as the stall door closed, Tristan leaned against it, resting his folded arms over the top. His focus was glued to the woman who had somehow managed to put Mathew at ease without coaxing or bribing him. She was a natural with him.

Every so often she'd glance in his direction then her focus would dart away once more. It gave him more opportunities to really study her. She had dark hair and brown eyes. Her voice was soft but firm. And when she smiled, he saw a hint of a dimple in her left cheek.

Dianna was pretty; there was no doubt about that. But there

was more to her than that. Kind and genuine. That's what it was. Even though she had told him he was doing something wrong, he couldn't exactly fault her for it. He'd always appreciated it when someone could be blunt and tell him how it was. Mathew did the same thing. Even at the age of seven, his son didn't mince words.

Dianna placed her hands on her hips and flashed Mathew a big smile. "Well, you've been on a long trip, from what I understand. How about I show you to your cabin?"

Mathew's wide eyes bounced from Dianna to Tristan, then back. He moved out of the way and allowed Dianna to open the stall door so they could exit.

"If you'd like, we can assign Molasses to be your horse while you're here. You don't have to practice with any of the others if you don't want to." Dianna continued chattering as she walked beside Mathew and guided them out of the barn. Their feet chuffed in the snow until they made it to the sidewalk that would lead them to the cabins that had been built on the other side of the club.

Tristan's thoughts drifted from Dianna to Erika. He hadn't seen his ex-wife since Mathew was about two years old. As soon as she'd found out that Mathew was autistic, she'd bailed. It took at least three years for him to move past that betrayal. He'd thought she'd come to her senses, but when he'd gotten the divorce papers, he knew.

Erika didn't want to be part of this family.

The lingering scar from that experience made it hard to trust anyone with Mathew and even harder to trust anyone with his heart. Five years later and his whole world revolved around Mathew and his needs.

Tristan peeked at Dianna, and a ghost of a thought lingered in his mind, haunting him. If he found someone like Dianna, maybe he could learn to trust again.

He let out an audible huff just as they arrived at the front of a small A-frame cabin. The structure was probably only big enough to have one bedroom—maybe a loft area. There were at least six already built and what appeared to be space for another dozen. They had a large window at the top of the structure and two more small windows on either side of the door.

Dianna pulled out a keycard from her pocket and held it up so Mathew could see. "Do you want to do the honors?"

Mathew smiled from ear to ear and accepted the keycard without hesitation. His boots crunched against the salted sidewalk as he hurried toward the cabin and pressed the card against the reader.

Dianna followed him, her steps quick and sure. Tristan didn't have a chance to catch up with her to—what? He didn't feel like he needed to apologize, but there was a definite tension in the air that he wanted to clear. He knew he'd been tired and cranky acting earlier.

Mathew opened the door to the cabin without difficulty, then promptly returned the keycard to Dianna. Tristan leaned his shoulder against the doorjamb, watching as Dianna followed Mathew to different parts of their new home for the next few weeks. He wandered to the small living room that would only fit about four people. There was a small fireplace in the corner and shelves with books. Surrounding a coffee table was a loveseat and two chairs.

Next, his son explored the kitchen. The table was incorporated into a nook with a wrap-around bench for seating. There was a fridge, microwave, and oven, but very little storage space in the way of cabinets and counter space. Mathew hustled down the hall, and Tristan heard Dianna's laughter as she followed him.

Tristan pushed against the doorjamb, ready to shut the door to keep all the cold air out, when he heard the sound of boots crunching behind him. He glanced over his shoulder to find Shane headed toward them with what could only be a gift basket.

Smiling in spite of himself, Tristan reached for the offered gift and nodded toward the cabin. "When you said you'd have lodging, I thought you meant some kind of motel. This is too much."

"Nonsense. This is what they were built for. No one wants to go through weeks of therapy and have to stay in a hotel. It's small, but I figured you wouldn't need the additional space." Shane glanced over Tristan's shoulder to the interior of the building. "How is Dianna doing?"

Tristan nearly choked on his laugh. "She's—interesting."

Shane's eyes darted back to Tristan. "What happened?"

"Oh, nothing I can't handle."

"It's okay to tell me. She's new. But I needed to find someone local who could accommodate your schedule. Is something wrong?"

Tristan chuckled. "She's very blunt. Let's put it that way." He looked over his shoulder, making sure no one would overhear them. "Honestly, she said some things that I probably needed to hear."

"That doesn't sound good. If I need to have a word with her—"

"It's fine, really. She's not here to impress me or get on my good side. She's here to help Mathew. And it looks like she knows what she's doing."

Shane didn't appear convinced, but he didn't argue. "Well, if there's anything you need from here on out and she can't get it for you, let me know. You're my guests, and I want this experience to be a good one."

Tristan nodded. "Thank you."

His friend turned and headed back the way he'd come.

Tristan brought the gift basket into the cabin, kicked the door shut behind him, and placed the basket on the counter. Mathew and Dianna weren't back in the main area yet, but he could hear Dianna's voice. He followed the sound around to the back of the structure where there was a ladder leading to the highest point of the cabin.

Tristan quietly climbed up the ladder and poked his head over the edge to find a second, smaller bedroom with a twin bed on the far side. Dianna and Mathew were sitting in front of a small window cross-legged, with Dianna pointing outside.

"That's where we're going to exercise Molasses," she said, "before we learn riding techniques. And over there are where the trails go. I'm not sure if we're going to go riding out that way; it's really cold right now. That's the big stadium. We *might* be able to take Molasses there and teach you some tricks like jumps. We'll just see how it goes and what you're comfortable with."

Every so often Mathew would meet Dianna's gaze and smile. The boy seemed perfectly content to listen to her talk, and he couldn't tell if that was a good thing or not. Tristan moved to head back down the ladder, but his foot slipped and he thunked his head on the edge of the floor.

Dianna and Mathew glanced in his direction. From where he stood on the ladder, it appeared he'd given Dianna some form of amusement.

Mathew scrambled to his feet and hurried over to him and whispered, "Do we get to go riding tomorrow?"

Tristan's focus flitted to Dianna, who had gotten to her feet as well. She appeared more settled than when they were in the barn, which was probably a good thing. He nodded to Mathew. "I'll have to ask your teacher first. But I think so. How about we climb down and get our things from the car."

He nodded, and Tristan met Dianna's eyes once more

before he headed down the ladder. As soon as Mathew was within reach, he was able to pull him from the ladder and set him on his feet. They waited for Dianna to make it to the bottom before heading toward the front of the cabin.

She held out the keycard and offered him a smile. "I suppose you'll be needing this."

"Thank you," he said, reaching for it. His fingers grazed hers, and he was surprised to find they were warm.

The moment was fleeting and she shoved her hands into her pockets. "I don't believe there's anything else you'll need from me today. I'll be back tomorrow. We'll spend most of our time getting to know Molasses better. I'm sure Mathew will do great. Do you have any questions?"

He itched to bring up their previous conversation. But he wasn't sure how to go about it. The things she'd said were true. Society needed to be more flexible, but that wasn't how the world worked. The way he saw it, one day Mathew would need something, and he wouldn't have the tools to get it, not unless he learned how to communicate better.

Tristan opened his mouth, then snapped it shut and shook his head. They didn't need to rehash what was said. They could both be right in their own ways. He wasn't responsible for how the world treated his son, but he could darn well be the person who helped his son survive in a world that wasn't ready to love him as he was just yet.

3

———————

Dianna

Dianna poured over the book she'd picked up from the county library. Shane might have given her a brief training to help Mathew with the horses, but she wasn't convinced that she was completely ready to help the boy get to where he needed to be.

All of this was new to her. She was good with kids. And her own experiences had helped her get a good idea of how to treat Mathew. It was probably just the way Tristan had stared at her like he wasn't sure she was going to be the best fit.

Dianna *could* walk away. In fact, she hadn't been sure she wanted to take on the responsibility of this new job. She was busy enough at Slate Rock Ranch; she didn't need the extra work.

Except Constance had insisted that it would be good for her. And right now, Constance was the happiest one in their family. Whether it was because she'd found a new purpose or she finally was able to get the guy she was interested in, Dianna couldn't be certain.

Adeline was happily married, Constance was engaged, and everyone else was excitedly looking forward to more freedom in the relationship department. Everyone but Dianna and Brielle.

She placed the book aside and picked up her notebook. Everything that she'd read in Mathew's paperwork focused on his ability to communicate his needs. She hadn't heard him say a word and everything his father had mentioned in the report stated Mathew was bright and actually ahead of grade level. He just didn't like to talk to people he didn't know.

Dianna grabbed her pen and nibbled on the end. If she could figure out a way to reach him without making him feel rushed, she might be more successful than anyone else who had worked with him. Most of the specialists who had worked with him before would have focused on that goal—expecting Mathew to perform. Trying to get him to talk. Offering him rewards to try to get him to interact more.

But Mathew wasn't a circus animal. He deserved to feel comfortable with her before she asked anything of him. That was part of the problem when she'd argued with Tristan yesterday.

"Whatcha got there?"

Constance wandered into their bedroom and plopped onto her bed. "Stuff for *Shane*?" She said his name in a sing-song way, as if that would make Dianna more inclined to discuss her new boss with her sister.

"No." She lifted the book up to show Constance her reading material.

Constance tilted her head. "*Ten Things Every Child With*

Autism Wished You Knew." Her focus shifted to Dianna. "Is that for the kid?"

"Technically, it's for me. But yes. It's supposed to help me learn how to work with him better."

"I thought Shane had given you some training."

"He did. But it wasn't specific to autism. He taught me what to do to support the kid while working with horses. Most of the studies suggest that working with animals is therapeutic and the other stuff will come."

"So why are you researching? Don't you think you'll be able to work with him just fine?"

Dianna peeked at her sister. "I'm not worried about Mathew. I'm worried about his father."

That knowing smile appeared on Constance's face. "*Oh.*"

A sigh burst from Dianna's chest. "*No.* Don't even go there. He's here for his kid, and I'm here for his kid. There will be none of this '*oh*' you're insinuating."

Constance shrugged. "I just figured since you finally had the opportunity to meet someone, you might take the chance."

Dianna ignored her sister's suggestion. They'd been down this road before. Dianna wasn't interested in dating anyone and probably wouldn't be for a while. Now that the pressure was off, she didn't feel compelled to even consider a relationship so that her younger sisters would have their chance. She was more like Brielle in that respect.

Her sister dropped down onto her stomach and rested her chin on folded arms. "How long do you get to work with these guys?" Once more, Constance was interrupting Dianna's quiet space. She almost wished they could go back to the time when Constance would sneak out to be with James. But since that wasn't happening anymore, it was as if her older sister had a one-track mind—a "let's ask Dianna a thousand questions and see if she snaps" kind of mind.

"I don't know. I think Shane said that this kind of therapy is usually a minimum of ten weeks. But Tristan probably has to get back to work, and I'm sure Mathew is missing all kinds of school."

"Maybe you could help him."

"That's the idea." She sighed. Honestly, for how smart Constance was, she could be really annoying.

"No. I mean, you were really good at school stuff and you love to read. I bet you could work something out where you help Mathew with his schoolwork while he does his therapy."

Dianna lifted her head and looked at Constance. "That's actually not a bad idea."

Constance beamed. "See? Sometimes I can be useful."

"But we'd have to clear it with his father and see about getting his records. I think it could really help him to do his homework in this kind of environment." Dianna snapped her book shut and got to her feet.

"Where are you going?"

"I have an appointment to get to with Mathew today. We're not supposed to start work until this afternoon, but I think I should bring this up to Shane."

"Tell him hi for me." Constance wiggled her eyebrows, garnering another exasperated sigh from Dianna.

THE DRIVE to the club wasn't bad. The recent snowfall hadn't stuck to the roads though they were due for a good dump of snow here in the next few weeks. It always snowed hardest right before the holidays.

Dianna pulled into the parking lot and gazed through the front window at the club, completely covered in Christmas decorations. When the sun went down, this place would probably be visible from the moon. And that was alright with Dianna. She loved Christmas and everything about the holiday: stories about baby Jesus, carols, classic Christmas movies, yummy cookies and warm hot chocolate, trimming the tree, and unboxing the Christmas decorations from the attic. Each year she looked forward to the family traditions.

She smiled to herself and shook her head as she climbed out of the car and headed for the club. Mathew would love seeing all the decorations. She couldn't remember, but she thought Shane was planning on doing an official lighting ceremony, including the tree in the main window.

Dianna entered the club, always taken aback by how quiet it was before the dinner rush. She headed toward Shane's office. Her time with Mathew wouldn't begin for another thirty minutes. That gave her plenty of time to speak to him about what Constance had suggested.

She knocked quietly on the door, then pushed it open when she heard Shane's voice call out to enter.

"It's just me. I thought I'd—" Dianna stopped suddenly and her heart slammed against her chest. Tristan shifted in his seat, turning to see who had entered the room, and his reaction mirrored her own.

Shane's head lifted from where he was studying a piece of paperwork. "Dianna. Just the person I wanted to see." He wasn't smiling and based on the way Tristan was seated in front of him, Dianna could only assume they were discussing her and their first meeting yesterday.

She edged into the room, her hands behind her back. "I suppose it's a good thing I came early." Her gaze darted to Tristan and then back to Shane.

He gestured for her to take a seat. "We were just talking about how your first meeting with Mathew went."

"I can explain. I wasn't—"

"Mathew couldn't stop talking about you." Tristan's low voice cut her off.

Her head whipped around so she could gauge whether he was telling the truth. Though they'd ended things on a decent note yesterday, the particular conversation she was worried about hadn't really been settled. "Really?"

Shane tossed his document on his desk, a smile filling his face. "You made quite the impression on him."

"He really likes you," Tristan interjected.

The knots in her stomach relaxed, unraveling and allowing her to be more at ease. "I like him too." She locked eyes with Tristan, not quite sure why this meeting even needed her here if Mathew was happy with their experience yesterday.

Unless.

Unless Tristan wasn't.

A lump formed in her throat. She wasn't going to apologize for what she'd said—at least not the overall concept. She could have been more eloquent with her words. It had only taken one day for her to make a connection with the little guy. She wanted to help him see that he could trust people. He didn't have to shy away from anyone. Dianna swallowed hard.

"Is there something you needed from me?" she asked.

Shane glanced at Tristan, then back to Dianna. She expected him to take the lead with this conversation, but it was Tristan who spoke next.

"We were only supposed to be here for the month of December, but Shane seems to think we should stay here longer." His voice was flat, as if he wasn't completely sold on the idea. "But I was trying to tell him that Mathew can't miss that much school. We're struggling to keep up on the work he needs to complete while we're here."

"And I was saying there might be a way we can figure that out." Shane chuckled. "I'm not in the business of throwing in the towel just because something seems difficult. Ultimately, it's up to you, Tristan. This program is free of charge. You have to decide if you're going to see it through to the end."

Tristan took in a deep breath. He looked as though he was being put on the spot and hated it. Dianna knew that feeling, and it was the one thing she tried to avoid. Right now she had a solution, but she wasn't sure Tristan would appreciate being told in front of Shane if he wasn't prepared to stay.

She almost got the feeling that Shane was influencing Tristan's decision. Dianna glanced toward Shane. "What did you need me for?"

He clasped his hands together and leaned on the desk. "I wanted your opinion. After visiting with Mathew yesterday, what would you suggest?"

Dianna froze. This wasn't her decision to make. He shouldn't be putting her on the spot like this either. She'd had a solution if Tristan wanted to make it work, but that was only if he had his heart set on staying. "Oh, I don't think I'm equipped to make any recommendations. I'm just here to help facilitate his therapy with the horses."

"But you have a connection with him. That's been established."

She shook her head. "With all due respect, this is a decision only his father can make." There went her plan to tell Shane about her idea. He shouldn't be pushing Tristan into anything he wasn't prepared for. She could feel Tristan's eyes on her, and once again, her chest tightened. He was probably making more judgments about her regarding her responses. Dianna shot another look toward Tristan. "Ultimately, you need to do what's best for you and Mathew. If you want to stay, I've got some ideas on how to make it easier."

Dianna got to her feet. "You can let me know if you decide

that you'd like to stay. But if you'll excuse me, I'm going to find Mathew. I assume he's around here somewhere?"

Tristan nodded. "I had him set up in a booth with a book."

She offered Tristan a small smile, then glanced at Shane who appeared to be on the edge of his seat—probably curious about the ideas she'd mentioned. Neither one of them stopped her from leaving.

The moment she was out of that office, she felt like she could breathe easier. She shook out her hands as she strode down the hallway toward the main area of the club. Her focus scanned the room and landed immediately on a little tuft of black hair barely visible behind the booth chair.

Dianna strode across the room and slid into the booth across from Mathew. He startled, his eyes flying up to meet hers. A small smile touched his lips before he dipped his focus once again to his book.

She craned her neck around and stared at the pages. Bright, detailed, and colorful images of horses filled the pages. There was tiny print in small paragraphs all over the pictures. Dianna grinned. "When I was little, I liked looking at pictures of horses, too. I'd even draw them sometimes." She got up and walked around the booth. "Is it okay if I sit here?"

He nodded, not looking up at her.

The leather seat creaked as she settled beside him and pointed at the picture on the page. "That's an appaloosa. They're Idaho's state horse, and most of the time, they're spotted. Sometimes they even have striped hooves." She grinned at Mathew. "Their spots are actually a genetic mutation. Isn't that crazy?" She pointed to another picture and read the description beneath it. Then another and another until a figure approached their booth.

Dianna lifted her gaze, but she already knew who had approached. There was something about Tristan that she could sense before he even got into her line of vision. He set his gray eyes on her and she squirmed as if she had been pinned by it.

"Looks like your dad is ready to take you to your first lesson." She faced Mathew and gestured toward the book. "Let's gather your things so we can get out to the barn. I bet Molasses can't wait to see you."

4

———————

Tristan

*O*nce again, Dianna had surprised Tristan. This time in more ways than one. With the way she'd chastised him yesterday about his parenting skills, he had expected that she'd side with Shane about staying.

He hadn't decided what he wanted to do yet, but it was looking more and more like he would end up staying if only to put Mathew through the entire program. Walking away from an opportunity like this felt wrong on so many levels. He was Mathew's parent, and as such, he needed to be the one to help him in any way possible.

Right now, money wasn't a problem. He was able to work remotely and the therapy was free. Mathew's schoolwork would need to be figured out, but he'd found someone he liked as a tutor already.

The second Dianna left, Mathew asked when she'd be coming back. Their conversation revolved around how much she knew about horses, how nice she smelled, and the fact that she'd told him he could ride Molasses soon. Mathew was smitten.

When Tristan found the two of them seated in the booth, he'd half-expected Dianna to just sit quietly with him, waiting for Tristan to finish up his meeting.

Instead, she'd taken it upon herself to read to his son, connecting on a level he'd only ever seen happen one other time—with his parents.

Tristan couldn't tear his focus from her as he wandered in her wake. She strode beside Mathew all the way to the barn, chatting about the animals she had on her ranch. She was so at ease with Mathew it almost made Tristan worry that when the time came to leave, Mathew wouldn't be able to without a major meltdown.

They entered the barn and Mathew ran ahead, his hand trailing along the stalls as he went. Tristan moved up to walk beside Dianna, but the words he'd rehearsed in his head wouldn't come. He needed to break the ice somehow. They'd be working together for the next several weeks and he couldn't stand the tension that had built between them.

"I wanted to apologize," she said quietly, not meeting his gaze.

Tristan slowed his gait. "What?"

She clasped her gloved hands together, then broke them apart and let them swing at her sides. "I shouldn't have said what I did yesterday."

"But you made a good point," he said. Why was he arguing with her? She was apologizing for something she'd said. He should just accept her apology and move on.

"Oh, I *know* I was right. I just shouldn't have said it in a way that could be construed as judgmental. You're obviously a great father. Raising Mathew on your own can't be easy."

Her words rammed into him, knocking down every defense he'd managed to erect before getting the nerve up to speak to her. What was he supposed to say to any of that? "Thanks," he muttered. It was a lame response. But his mind was blank. He could blame it on the traveling they'd done or the exhaustion she'd mentioned. But the truth was, she had thrown him off balance. "Do you have children?"

A bark of laughter burst from her lips, startling him and the nearby horses.

"I take that as a 'no'?"

She shook her head. "No, I don't have children. Sometimes I forget that you're not a local."

"What does that have anything to do with being a mother?"

Dianna chuckled. "It's a long story. I don't have any plans of being a mother any time soon—mostly because I don't have plans to find and marry anyone. I have other priorities right now." Her gaze shifted to Mathew and something warm flickered across her face.

"What did you have in mind?"

Her wide gaze shot to his and her cheeks filled with color. "What? I meant my priorities are—"

"No, I mean, what did you mean when you said you had some ideas in mind to help Mathew stay?"

She worried her lower lip. The color in her cheeks deepened and she offered him a small smile. "Oh. Well, my sister pointed something out to me this morning. I'm not certified in education, but I was always really good at school. I could help tutor Mathew if you wanted to enroll him in an online school or try homeschooling."

His brows shot up. He hadn't even considered doing something like that. All of Mathew's support team was back home. Granted, this would be temporary. He could see about finding therapists out in this area if Mathew needed additional help, but knowing that they didn't have to return home right away was a very attractive option to have at his fingertips.

"Of course, you don't have to do that if you don't want to. I'm sure we could find a tutor—"

"That's a great idea. Like I told Shane, Mathew really took a liking to you yesterday."

Her brows pulled together and she nibbled on her lip once more as if she didn't believe a word he was saying.

Tristan smiled. "Seriously. Whatever you're doing, it's working. I still don't know if he'll be comfortable enough to let you tutor him, but he likes you."

She dipped her head and tucked her hair behind her ear. Whether she wasn't used to compliments or getting them made her uncomfortable, he couldn't be certain. Regardless, it was refreshing to see someone who didn't automatically act like they were better than everyone around them.

Dianna cleared her throat and peeked at him. "Well, if you'd like to move forward with that plan, I suppose you'll need to contact his school and talk to Shane."

"I'll go ahead and do that after our session. I want to be here in case Mathew needs me."

Dianna nodded. "That works too. Seeing as it's cold outside, I think we'll stay in the barn today and work on getting to know the horse and the tools we use when riding."

"That sounds like a great idea."

She hovered for just a moment before she headed toward Mathew. His son was standing outside of the stall, his eyes bright and a smile on his face. It almost looked like he was talking to the animal, but when they drew closer, he didn't hear anything coming out of his lips.

Dianna opened the stall door and let Mathew in. She shot a glance in Tristan's direction and smiled. The tension in the air had lessened and it felt more natural to be here and observe.

Immediately, she picked up a brush and held it out to Mathew. He reached for it with his free hand, his horse still clutched to his chest. Dianna dropped down to his side and gestured toward his toy. "Did you know that we have a special place for your horse? We wouldn't want him to get lost or stepped on. And sometimes Molasses likes to chew on things he's not supposed to."

Mathew's eyes widened and he glanced at Tristan.

Tristan nodded to Dianna. "Sounds like she's got a plan for you, bud. How about we find out where we need to put it."

He shook his head, clutching it even harder than before.

Uh-oh. This was it. The moment Dianna wouldn't be able to figure out what to do with Mathew. His son wouldn't be happy with that, and their budding relationship wouldn't continue. Tristan nearly stepped in, but Dianna gestured behind him.

"Behind your dad there are some aprons. I bet we can find one that will fit you and you can put your horse in the pocket. Then your hands would be free to work. What do you think?"

Mathew's expression relaxed and a smile spread across his face.

Dianna met Tristan's gaze and nodded to the hooks he'd only just noticed. "Would you mind finding the smallest one you can? We might have to tighten it up a little, but I bet we can make something work."

The aprons were leather. He imagined they were used by stable hands, veterinarians, or even trainers. His fingers trailed across the set until he found one that looked to be the shortest. It only wrapped around the waist so there would be nothing weighing on Mathew's shoulders. Tristan grasped the apron and held it over the stall door for Dianna to take.

Like before when she'd handed him the keycards, their

fingers touched. A short electrical current passed between them. His eyes met hers.

Did she feel it too?

Or was it all in his head?

Probably the latter. Hadn't she said she wasn't interested in anything besides her work right now? He was just reading into it too much.

Besides, to allow himself to get close to someone right now wouldn't be wise. They didn't live here. He was just feeling impressed by her ability to communicate with Mathew. From what Shane had mentioned, Dianna didn't have any education in working with children. She had the usual training that would be needed to work at Owens Therapeutic Horsemanship, but that was it. Her training allowed her to work with several people who needed therapeutic services.

That was why he was so interested in her abilities. If she didn't have the training, he wouldn't think she'd be doing this well. Her natural talent drew him in, making him curious about how the rest of this trip would go.

That was it.

Yes, she was objectively attractive, but he wasn't attracted to her in *that* way.

Tristan leaned against the stall door and observed as Dianna once again chatted with his son about how to help a horse trust him. "Now, Molasses is generally very trusting. He's also been trained to sense anything you need or anything you might do. That way he won't get nervous around you. But that doesn't mean that you can just do whatever you want. We still have to show him that we deserve his trust."

Dianna placed a step stool on the ground and hovered close enough to make sure Mathew wouldn't fall from it. He got to the top of the stepstool and immediately started brushing.

"Hold on, buddy. We need to go slow. Usually, a horse really likes it when you talk to them. It makes them feel more at ease. But I can help with that for now." She moved closer to Molasses's head and rubbed his nose. "Hey, Molasses. This is Mathew. He's going to brush you down so your coat can be all shiny and clean." Her gaze dipped to Mathew and she let out a little laugh. "See? Like that."

Mathew grinned, and this time his brushing was less aggressive.

Dianna must have felt Tristan's eyes on her because she shot a quick look in his direction. Their gazes locked. He couldn't tear his focus from her even if he had wanted to. Her warm brown eyes were soulful and soft. She didn't wear any makeup, and her chestnut hair was pulled back into a ponytail at the nape of her neck. She wore a knit hat to cover her ears, but she'd removed her coat at some point. She had a trim form beneath a turtleneck sweater, and she wore jeans and a pair of cowboy boots. But the one thing he liked the most was the freckles across the bridge of her nose.

She broke eye contact and pointed at the next spot for Mathew to brush. "We want to get Molasses completely brushed down. You should always brush down your horse before and after a ride. Do you know why?" Dianna didn't even wait for him to respond before answering. "When you do it before, you're making sure he doesn't have any dirt that could irritate him under the saddle. You're also making sure the tack sits properly on his back."

Mathew was soaking up every single thing she'd said.

"When you brush him down after a ride, you're soothing his itchy and sweaty skin and getting rid of any dust or dirt you might have come in contact with while on the ride." Her smile widened and she winked at him. "Besides, they like it a lot, so it's kinda like a reward for them."

Mathew returned her smile and continued to brush the horse down, then ran his hand over the animal's back.

She moved away from the horse and pressed her back against the stall door. The wood was the only thing that separated them and he could smell her floral perfume in the air. A knot tightened in his stomach. Anything he was feeling for her was all in his head. It was a known fact that impressive actions cause people to develop an attraction for others. Dianna was just exceeding his expectations, and for some reason, his heart was interpreting it in such a way that it was messing with his head.

Tristan moved away from her, edging to the far side of the door, but that only allowed for about a distance of three feet. He cleared his throat, causing her to glance his way. "You're really good with him. You make it look so easy. I don't know how you do it."

She returned her focus to Mathew. "It's like I said yesterday. I'm not putting any overwhelming expectations on him. I'm teaching him in a way that helps him learn. And I figure just because he's not saying anything, doesn't mean he isn't soaking it all in."

"But that's just it," he said. "The typical person doesn't usually understand that. Even I don't get it half of the time. Sometimes, he'll be fine one minute, then have a meltdown the next. And when he refuses to speak to someone to tell them what made him feel upset, how are they supposed to know what went wrong?"

She lifted a shoulder, her arms folded across her chest. "I guess I've just got good instincts."

5
____

Dianna

ianna could empathize with what Tristan was saying; she *could*. But when he pointed out how good she was with Mathew, it didn't feel quite right. He probably meant well. She could tell he was trying to pay her a compliment.

She should just accept it and move on.

There was just one small thing she couldn't stand. It was like an itch she couldn't scratch. Everything she was doing was just how she would have liked to be treated when she was younger. Granted, she didn't have to grow up in the public sector. She knew most everyone in Copper Creek, and she didn't feel uncomfortable around them. But had their family moved after her mother passed, she might not have fared so well. It was easy to slide under the radar here.

That fact alone almost made her want to recommend that Tristan consider moving to Copper Creek. He hadn't made any comments regarding a job to get back to, which forced her to assume that his career was likely remote. From what Shane had mentioned, his wife was out of the picture, but that was all he said.

If he didn't have anything or anyone to get home to, this place would be a great one to settle down in—especially considering that Mathew loved horses.

Tristan's presence was starting to get to her in a way she hadn't anticipated. Of course she knew he would be around during their sessions. And that hadn't bothered her in the slightest. But after their strained conversation and all the events that followed, she was becoming more and more aware of him. She couldn't put her finger on what it was. It could be the way she continued to catch him staring at her like she was going to do something wrong.

But then that didn't make sense considering how often he kept complimenting the way she was with Mathew. She thrived when everything made sense and her mind could place everything in little compartments.

Right now, her head was starting to hurt and her heart was beating a little faster than normal.

She folded her arms even more tightly than before, forcing herself to focus on Mathew and the job he was doing. "Next, I'm going to teach you about the saddle. Then tomorrow we'll go for a little ride in the arena."

Mathew gave her another smile, but he still wasn't speaking. It would come. If Tristan was right, Mathew would have about ten weeks with her. She was confident they'd have their own form of breakthrough.

They finished up their little session and Dianna walked with Mathew back to his cabin. She hadn't planned on it, but Mathew had tugged on Tristan's hand and whispered something to him. Apparently, he wanted to show her something at their cabin.

They got to the house and Tristan opened the door, gesturing for them to enter. She stood in the entry area with Tristan as Mathew skedaddled off to go get whatever it was. When he returned, he had a sheet of paper in his hand.

Mathew held the paper out to Dianna and smiled broadly.

Dianna stared at the rudimentary drawing, though it was far better than most seven-year-olds could draw. It reminded her of the pictures she used to draw when she was younger. She crouched down and pointed to the image. "Did you draw this?"

He nodded.

"It's very good, Mathew. I can tell you're a wonderful artist." She offered the paper back to him, but he shook his head. When she glanced up at Tristan, she found his eyes on her. Man, she wished she could read his mind. It was moments like this she wanted to know what he was thinking.

"He wants you to have it."

Dianna blinked. "Really?"

Mathew nodded.

She smiled. "Thank you. You know, I like drawing, too. Maybe I can bring *you* a picture."

His eyes widened and Mathew nodded again.

When she got to her feet, she only briefly met Tristan's gaze. "I'll see you tomorrow. I'll come a little early so we can figure out what we're going to do about his schooling."

"I look forward to it," he said.

Tristan opened the door for her then paused, preventing her from leaving the cabin. It was getting dark already and her family was probably eating dinner. She needed to get going if she didn't want them to eat everything and leave her with scraps.

She stared at Tristan expectantly, hoping he would get the hint and let her get past him.

"Let me walk you to your truck."

"That's not necessary. I'm—"

"Mathew." He glanced over his shoulder to where Mathew sat on the loveseat in the sitting area with a notebook and marker.

His son lifted his head and glanced in their direction.

"I'm taking Miss Callahan to her truck. Would you like to come with us?"

Mathew shook his head.

"Okay, you can stay here, but you have to stay inside."

He nodded and settled in with his notebook once more.

Dianna opened her mouth to tell him he should just stay put, but he stepped aside, motioning for her to take the lead. She could see it in his demeanor. Tristan wasn't going to take no for an answer.

She took a deep breath and let it out as she zipped up her coat and started down the path. They walked in silence, side by side. The tension in the air from earlier returned and she shoved her hands in her pockets to keep from fidgeting.

"I wanted to thank you," he said.

Her head snapped around to stare at him.

"For what you're willing to do with Mathew. I've never seen him open up this fast. You've taken a lot of the guesswork out of whether we should stay or not. I'll be making several calls in the morning to get him set up with the work he needs to do this semester." He rubbed the back of his neck and gave her a wry smile. "Just—thanks."

"We haven't even gotten into the thick of it—" she started.

"Regardless. I wanted you to know that I appreciate it— you."

She forced a smile. "You're welcome." This blatant appreciation from him felt strange and all she wanted was to move past the conversation.

They made it to her truck and he hovered as she unlocked it and opened the door. She climbed in and glanced at him once more. "Thank you for walking me to my truck."

"Of course." He still hovered, and for a second, she thought he might have something else he wanted to say. When he didn't speak up, she pulled the door shut and drove away. He shrunk in her rear-view mirror as she headed toward the main road.

"THAT'S AMAZING, Matty! I didn't know you were so good at riding!" Dianna peered up at Mathew from the side of the horse. She probably didn't even need to walk beside him because he had a natural talent for riding, but it was policy for her to stay close by in case something went wrong and she needed to intervene.

Mathew sat tall in the saddle, a riding helmet on his head and the biggest smile she'd ever seen on his face. He held tightly to the reins just like she'd shown him. So far they'd only managed to walk around the perimeter of the indoor arena, but she had a feeling he'd be up for more by this time next week, if not within a few days.

She could feel Tristan's focus on her from where he stood near the bleachers. It took everything in her willpower not to look in his direction and meet his gaze. Their meeting that morning couldn't have gone better. Tristan was all business. When it came to Mathew, he knew what he wanted. He was a good dad. It was a good thing she wasn't interested in starting any sort of relationship right now, because that was exactly the kind of guy she wanted to find. Someone who could take care of their kid the way Tristan cared for Mathew was one in a million.

Dianna swallowed hard and focused on Mathew again. "Let's take another turn. What do you say?"

He nodded.

"You know, when you get *really* comfortable with being in the saddle, you'll be able to get your horse to speed up just by pushing your heels into your horse's flanks."

Mathew nodded again, shifting in his seat.

Still no talking. That was fine. One of the first things they'd discussed was having him get used to her before urging him to do more than what he was comfortable with. She took in a deep breath and let out a sigh. According to Tristan, Mathew was very bright. He could retain a lot of information even if he had a harder time reading. He was great at math, so they didn't need to focus on that as much.

Her purpose would be to help him become more verbal and tutor him on his reading. That was simple enough. Those were her two favorite subjects.

Dianna glanced up at Mathew. "Do you know that one of my favorite things to do is read?"

Mathew glanced down at her and grinned.

"I was thinking if you'd like, we could spend some time each day reading whatever book you want, and then we could draw pictures of what we read about. How does that sound?"

His smile widened further. Mathew was such a sweetheart. It was a shame that people didn't see that part of him.

"Your father thought that you might want to start today. I figured I'd let you decide. You might be too tired after our riding lesson." She peeked at him, finding him shaking his head vehemently. "Good. I'd like to start today too. After being out in the cold for so long, I'm ready to sit in front of a fire and read a good book."

She let their ride continue for the allotted thirty minutes, then raised her hands to help Mathew down. But then Mathew's whole body grew tense. He held on tight to the reins and shook his head when she offered to help him dismount.

Once again, Dianna felt the eyes of Mathew's father drilling into her. This was what she'd trained for. She was supposed to help Mathew use his words and understand that there were moments he had to relinquish control. But there were also moments when negotiating was permitted.

"Hey, buddy. I only get to spend a short amount of time with you today. No one else is waiting to ride Molasses, so we could make one more trip around the arena. But I have to leave by dinner time. So I'm going to give you a couple of choices. You ready for 'em?"

He stared at her with surprised eyes.

"One choice is that you go ahead and get down and we go do our reading and drawing and get plenty of time to do both."

Mathew's features pinched.

She let out a soft laugh. "The next choice is that you take one more trip around the arena and we get to read, but we might not have enough time to draw."

Mathew frowned.

"It's totally up to you. What's more important?"

He shot a look over to his father. No meltdown. No tears. So far, so good. He pointed forward.

"You want to go one more time?"

Mathew nodded.

She smiled brightly. "Okay. Let's go one more time."

He grinned.

"Just so you know, sometimes we won't get to have that

choice. If someone else needs to ride Molasses for whatever reason, then we have to be respectful and let them take him."

Mathew's brow creased in the most adorable way. He frowned again, but then he did something she hadn't expected.

He nodded.

6

---

*S*omething had just happened. Tristan wasn't sure what was going on, but he knew just by the look on Mathew's face. He wasn't happy about something. It might have been something Dianna had said, but it was more likely that Mathew's reaction dealt more with not wanting to be done. According to the time on Tristan's watch, they were due to return the horse to the barn.

Tristan nearly lurched forward. Mathew could be really difficult when he didn't want to comply with the rules. He was just about to hop over the barrier that divided him from the two in the arena when Mathew pointed forward, then nodded. The horse started walking once more, and when they came closer, he waited for an explanation.

Dianna smiled at him. "Mathew has requested we take one more turn around the arena before we head back to your cabin. We'll be done shortly."

His gaze flicked to his son, finding him beaming. The tightness in Tristan's chest eased somewhat, confusion replacing the worry. Dianna was still a new person in Mathew's life. Usually, he needed to transition to a frame of mind where he accepted his new teacher's authority. This transition typically took a few weeks. Somehow Dianna had skipped this step, and he couldn't for the life of himself understand why.

What had she said?

He was still dumbfounded as they made their way toward the barn. Mathew wanted to continue riding on the way back, so that left Dianna to guide the horse with the lead rope. He walked beside her, itching to ask her what kind of magical powers she possessed to get Mathew to comply.

The question burned in the back of his throat. If he knew what she'd said, maybe he could use the same strategy with future teachers.

When he'd finally gotten the courage to ask her, praying he didn't offend her like he had before, they'd arrived at the barn but she'd moved away.

Mathew knew he was being talked about. That happened frequently when they started seeing someone new. But once they got into a routine, it frustrated him when that sort of thing continued. He wouldn't take kindly to Tristan pulling Dianna aside to speak to her about their sessions when he was present.

Tristan would have to ask her later how she'd managed to avoid a meltdown.

Over the next fifteen minutes, Dianna reviewed with Mathew how to brush the right way so as to not upset the horse. She showed him how to wipe down the saddle and how to remove the bridle. Mathew didn't speak, but then why would he? The kid was more stubborn than a mule when it came to what he was willing to do for people he didn't know well—ha, even for people he did know.

Tristan continued watching with rapt attention as Dianna laughed and put Mathew at ease. One thing that stood out was her use of a nickname.

Mathew hated people calling him Matt. He refused to work with people who made that mistake more than once. Tristan had thought it was because he preferred his given name above all else. But when Dianna used the name Matty, it didn't seem to faze him. Dianna continued surprising him at every turn. He couldn't tell if it was something special about her, or if Mathew just didn't mind the nicknames anymore.

Dianna nudged Mathew. "What do you say we head to the cabin and start a nice fire. I think we have time to read for about twenty minutes." She finally met Tristan's gaze and something strange occurred. A spark passed between them. At least there was for him.

He'd always heard what it was like when someone died. Their life would pass before their eyes in an instant, highlighting everything they'd accomplished.

Well, this feeling was kind of like that. It was brief, and not really visual. It was more of a sensation—like he knew she would play a bigger part in his life than the average person.

Tristan rolled his shoulders, hoping to shake off the strange impression. He was just impressed with her, that was all. They both wanted the same thing—for Mathew to succeed in life. Together, they might have a shot at helping his son improve to the next stage of his learning.

Dianna and Mathew brushed past him and her hand grazed his. He sucked in sharply, his whole body turning hot and cold all at once. Staring down at his hand, he turned it over to examine it. That was weird. The static electricity of this place was really different than it was back home.

The two were far enough ahead that Tristan had to hustle to catch up. He jogged a few paces then walked, the frigid air burning his throat and his lungs. Puffs of white escaped from between his lips as he kept his focus on his son and the new teacher.

Mathew's hand lifted and grabbed onto Dianna's, and Tristan froze. His feet refused to move. The distance between himself and the two walking ahead continued to grow, but he couldn't bring himself to follow. Mathew was holding Dianna's hand, allowing her to lead him back to the cabin.

Speaking was one thing, but physical touch from a near stranger? It was unheard of.

He jolted forward, his thoughts becoming clear. She had a gift, pure and simple. They made it to the cabin before he did, but it worked out since Tristan needed one more moment to soak in his newfound clarity. Tristan pushed open the door and stepped inside just as Mathew emerged from the back carrying a stack of books that he'd brought with them on this trip. Most were non-fiction, highlighting horse breeds and how to care for them.

But the one on top was different. It was a children's book about a little boy asking Santa for a horse for Christmas, and in the end, he realized horses were too much trouble and he just wanted a toy horse instead.

Dianna's eyes lit up when she picked the book from the pile. "My mom used to read this story to me when I was a little girl."

The blood drained from Tristan's face. Uh-oh. She'd said the "m" word. He lurched forward, ready to stop the inevitable conversation.

Only it didn't happen.

Dianna didn't bring up Mathew's mother. Mathew didn't get that sad look on his face.

Instead, Dianna opened the book and put her arm around Mathew as they sat close together on the loveseat by the gas fireplace. She glanced up at him once or twice and their gazes locked, but that was it.

Her voice was melodious and the longer he listened to her, the more he started to wonder what it could be like if she wasn't Mathew's counselor but maybe something more.

Tristan scowled at the thought and turned away from the sight of his son growing closer to a woman who would only be in his life for a few months. Mathew would get attached like he did on occasion, but he'd get over it. Tristan couldn't afford the same luxury. The more time Tristan spent apart from his ex-wife, the more he wished things were different. He'd loved Erika. He wouldn't have married her otherwise. But how much does a person *truly* know someone? Until that person was placed in a situation that they might not normally be in, there was no telling what side of the line they'd fall.

Erika was a wonderful person until her limits were met. Mathew's early years had been hard. More than hard, they'd pushed both Erika and Tristan to their limits. But he'd stuck around while his wife had found greener pastures.

He made it to the sink and stared at the silver lining bitterly. It had been years. Why was he suddenly so interested in living in the past? Dianna had nothing to do with any of that. She was a stranger.

Tristan peeked at her over his shoulder for what felt like the hundredth time.

A very attractive stranger who would probably report him for harassment if he fell to temptation and flirted with her.

What was he thinking? He needed to get his head on straight and focus on Mathew.

They finished their book and Dianna glanced at her watch. "Well, it looks like I can stay for ten more minutes so we can draw a picture. What do you say?"

Mathew nodded and scurried out of the room.

Tristan swiftly crossed the floor and plopped down in front of her, the coffee table the only thing separating them. "How are you doing that?"

Her brows furrowed and she took a look in the direction that Mathew had taken. "Doing what?"

"I've never seen him so compliant."

Dianna's gaze swung back to him. "What do you mean?"

"I love him, but that kid has got to be one of the most stubborn children I have ever met. I saw what you did in the arena. He didn't want to leave. But somehow you figured out a way to reach him. What did you do?"

Her pinched features grew tighter. "I guess I gave him a choice?"

Tristan huffed. "I give him choices all the time."

She shrugged. "Maybe it was giving him that little bit of extra time with Molasses, instead of cutting it off abruptly at the thirty-minute mark?" She lifted her shoulder once more and her gaze darted away. "He's a smart kid who knows what he wants. So far we haven't tested his limits all that much. I wouldn't be surprised if, at some point, you see more of his usual behavior come through. I'm new. Let him get used to me."

"But that's just it. He's not used to you by any means, and I just saw him hold your hand."

A small smile touched her lips, but just as quickly as it appeared it melted from her face. "I guess we'll just have to see how things go for the next few weeks. It could be a fluke."

He shook his head. "No. I don't think so."

She brought her gaze up to study him, and for the first time since he'd met her, he felt naked, as if she could see right through him. "Then what do you think it is, Mr. Wood? If you're so intuitive about all of this, *you* tell me."

"I haven't the slightest clue. I wish I did so I could get him to be more flexible when we need him to do something."

Dianna rolled her eyes. "Not that again."

"Not what?" he stammered.

"You're trying to change Mathew into some other kid that he just isn't. Have you ever considered that his autism isn't what's holding him back? It's you and how you're trying to fix him?"

His head reared back. Once again, she'd managed to make him look like the bad guy. All his previous notions of her being the kind of woman he would want to have in his life dissipated. Even if he was still interested, there was no way she shared those sentiments. She saw him as the villain.

Tristan held up a finger and opened his mouth, but his words never came. Mathew barreled into the room holding sheets of paper, crayons, colored pencils, and any other art supply he'd managed to stash away in his suitcase. He lifted bright, excited eyes to Tristan and sat down beside Dianna eagerly.

It was moments like this when Tristan *really* hated the strange thoughts that continued to plague him. He had never intended on living alone for the rest of his life, but he'd also given up on ever finding someone who wasn't scared off by Mathew's quirks.

Dianna would have been the perfect candidate if she didn't despise him so fully.

He spun on his heel and headed back toward the kitchen. He needed to keep his mind clear and off a certain woman who was currently sucking all the oxygen out of the air. His steps slowed when he heard her voice.

Tristan didn't dare turn around for fear that she'd catch on that he had started to pay attention. Dianna's soft humming would have put sirens out at sea to shame. The melody to the song "I'm Dreaming of a White Christmas" filled the small area. It was one of his favorite songs, and she hit every single note with perfect pitch.

As much as he knew he shouldn't turn around, he couldn't control himself. He had to look even if it meant that she stopped creating that beautiful music.

Dianna was crouched over her sheet of paper with a pencil in one hand. Mathew drew beside her, seemingly unaware of her angelic voice. And then there was Tristan, who was so fully captivated that he couldn't even drag together two brain cells to do much of anything.

7

Dianna

*D*ianna probably should have headed home after the riding lesson. Or taken her chance to escape after walking Mathew home. She definitely shouldn't have stayed to draw any pictures, because her sketch was beginning to look a lot like the man who was standing just a few feet away.

Oh goodness. What was going on with her?

She needed to keep her mind off the handsome man with the steady stare and those clear eyes. Quickly, she added more facial hair and a hat for good measure. There. Now the person with kind eyes and a soft smile staring back at her was none other than Santa Claus himself.

"Whoa."

She jumped and stared wide-eyed at the little boy seated beside her. Did he just speak to her? Dianna sought Tristan's gaze, finding him just as surprised where he stood in the kitchen. Mathew hadn't appeared to notice her change of body language as he continued staring at the picture in front of her. "I didn't know you were *that* good."

Chills raced down her spine and along her arms. She'd been told that Mathew could speak and that he was very intelligent. It was strange to actually experience it. A part of her wanted to jump up and down, grab him and make him celebrate with her. Then on the other side, she worried if she made any sudden movements he'd retreat, bursting into flight like a scared pheasant.

She swallowed and nudged the paper closer to him. "You can keep it if you like."

He looked up at her and smiled widely. "Can you draw Molasses next?"

Dianna let out a soft laugh. "I can sure try."

Quickly, he snatched a fresh sheet of paper and held it out to her.

Feeling Tristan's eyes on her, she chanced a peek in his direction. She had already overstayed her welcome. It wasn't that she had anywhere to go. It was that she needed to get out of their hair so they could get started on dinner.

She gnawed on her lower lip and brought her gaze down to Mathew. "Would it be okay if I take this home and bring it back tomorrow? We'll do some more reading, and if you'd like, we can draw some more."

His features scrunched up and his focus bounced to his father. "But I want her to stay."

As much as it warmed her that Mathew had grown fond of her so quickly, Dianna didn't feel the same sentiment from his father. There was a definite tension that continued to hang in the air whenever they were in the same room. Maybe it was the way she was a bit over opinionated about the expectations he put on Mathew's treatment outcomes. Or maybe he just didn't like anybody that much.

There was something about him that got to her. She wouldn't describe it as being uneasy. It might have more to do with the fact that despite all the irritating things he'd said, she could tell he was a good dad doing the best he could.

Not many men would stick around in the first place, and Tristan had done more than that. He'd taken on raising Mathew all on his own.

Tristan shifted, his eyes boring into her.

"Mathew, I have other things—"

"Why don't you stay?" Tristan asked.

She stiffened, unsure of why he would say such a thing.

"I'm not the best cook, but you're welcome to stay for dinner if you don't have anywhere else you have to be."

Mathew reached for her hand and smiled. "Please?"

His large, round, blue eyes were nearly impossible to turn down. How could she deny him when he asked her like that?

Dianna shrugged and let out a sigh. "Why not?"

Mathew's grin stretched even farther. "And then you can help me make Christmas cookies."

She let out a laugh. "I don't think we have time for that. But maybe we can make cookies when I come on Thursday."

"We're going looking for a Christmas tree on Thursday," Tristan interjected. "But you're welcome to come with us when we do. I'm sure Mathew would love the company."

The boy nodded. "Will you help us pick a tree and decorate it?"

She could have been knocked over with all the sudden invitations. She loved Christmas and trimming the tree, but her head was spinning and she wasn't sure how she was supposed to react. His request had her feeling pushed up against a wall. All her life, she'd liked to be able to think about things before taking action or saying yes to anything.

"Mathew, how about we see how dinner goes before bombarding her with all of these other events."

"Okay," he murmured. "But I'm still gonna invite her."

Tristan and Dianna locked eyes and she chuckled. "You're always welcome to extend an invitation, Matty, even if I can't say yes." Dianna pointed to his picture of a horse that he hadn't colored yet. "You finish up your drawing while I go see if your father needs help."

Mathew nodded and settled onto his knees.

Dianna's heart fluttered as she moved across the room and straight for the person who seemed to be making this room more difficult to read. She leaned over the island in the kitchen right as he crouched down to grab a saucepan from a cupboard. He filled it with water and placed it on the stove before turning to face her.

Tristan rubbed the back of his neck and gave her a wry smile. "I hope you know you're more than welcome to tell Mathew no. He might not like it, but we've been able to work through disappointment before."

She shot a look in Mathew's direction. "Maybe another time. I didn't want to jinx the progress we just made."

"I get it," he said.

Dianna swung her focus back to him.

Tristan continued, "I can't believe he spoke to you. It's unheard of."

Warmth flooded her stomach and she smiled. "I'm glad he likes me so much."

"It's more than that. He trusts and respects you. He thinks you're worthy of his time and energy. I know it doesn't make sense or maybe sounds harsh, but—"

She tilted her head and let out a laugh. "I know exactly what you mean, and I don't think it's harsh. These kids have such a unique view of the world, and they have to figure out how they fit in it. I would imagine Einstein had similar notions as a kid and no one was trying to make excuses for him."

Tristan stared at her like she'd sprouted horns.

"What?" She laughed.

"I don't get how you can understand him so fully. I feel like I have to break every little nuance down into pieces people can grasp. Even his therapists back home have to get used to him and vice versa before they can make any progress. But you make it look so effortless."

Dianna broke eye contact and turned around so her elbows rested on the island instead. "I guess I just have a specific sort of empathy."

His footsteps chuffed against the tiled floor as he walked around the island and stood beside her. "Whatever it is, I think you've found your calling."

She gave him a funny look. "Why do you say that?"

He didn't meet her gaze; his focus locked on Mathew as he continued his drawing. "I can't really explain it. You're just so..." He sighed and shrugged before he looked at her. "There's something different about you."

Goosebumps erupted on her arms and she moved to rub them away.

"Shane said that you're a recent hire and that you're just doing this to help out during the holidays."

She nodded. "My family's ranch is pretty busy, but I was able to get my father to agree to my working here for the holiday season. It's better than spending every waking moment with my sisters."

His lips quirked into a grin. "Well, maybe you should consider doing this full-time. Have you thought about going to school to become a therapist?"

Dianna's whole body stilled. She hadn't thought about that at all. She liked to work with animals. And she was obviously good with children—but she felt like she connected to Mathew more just because she had similar tendencies as a kid. There was no guarantee she'd be this good with other children. What if her connection with Mathew was an anomaly? Failure didn't sit well with her. Stomach knotting, she ignored the question and prayed he didn't notice her lack of response. "Do you have any family?"

Without missing a beat, Tristan nodded. "I've got a sister. She's married and has three kids. You said you have sisters?"

"Six."

He let out a low whistle. "It's all coming together."

"What do you mean by that?" Dianna meant for her tone to sound offended but couldn't hide the amusement she felt. She already had a few ideas of what he could be inferring.

"You're good with kids. You must have several younger than you whom you've spent a lot of time with."

"*Oh*, and here I thought you might be suggesting I only stayed because I didn't want to go home to a house full of hormonal women."

Tristan laughed.

It wasn't just a dry chuckle meant to make her feel good. It was a deep, warm, and smooth laugh that only added to the tremors she felt by simply being a few inches away from him. She could feel the heat emanating off him, and all it would take was to scoot slightly in his direction for her to get to experience it.

While he watched Mathew, she got a few minutes to examine him without being caught. His jawline was sharp and unlike the cowboys who resided here, he opted to be clean-shaven. His eyes were gray with hints of blue underneath—probably where his son got his coloring. And the mussed sandy hair made him look like he belonged on a beach somewhere, not in the mountains covered in snow.

He could pull off the fur-lined leather coat with the best of them. Tristan was tall and lean and... he was looking right at her.

Dianna tore her eyes away from him and glued them to the floor, shifting ever so slightly away from him without being obvious that was her intention. It was probably too late. She shouldn't have allowed herself to get caught up in her study of him. No wonder she'd drawn him. He was a handsome specimen.

Her face burned with embarrassment. How could she have been so stupid to get caught checking him out?

Tristan shifted, moving away from her and around the counter, but his distance only served to make her feel chilled. The warmth that had flowed from him was gone and as her blush faded, she couldn't prevent the shiver that racked her body.

"I hope you like macaroni and cheese because that's the only thing Mathew will eat."

"Do you have any tomatoes?" The question slipped from her lips before she could prevent them. Her sisters had always thought she was weird for mixing the two items together, but it was the only way she could stomach the pasta dish.

"I think so," Tristan drawled. "Why?"

The flush started to crawl up her neck once more and she gave him a half-smile. "I cut them up into cubes and mix them in."

He wrinkled his nose and laughed. "I've never heard of that before."

"I want some too," Mathew piped up from his place at the coffee table.

Tristan's brows lifted. "But you hate tomatoes."

"Not in my macaroni," he insisted.

"You're not going to eat them," Tristan shook his head. "How about we don't waste our food."

Mathew glowered. "I want tomatoes. Dianna gets them, so I want them."

Dianna mouthed the word "sorry" to Tristan, relieved when he waved her off with a dismissive hand.

"I'll cut some for you, but how about you put them on the side and try it one bite at a time."

Before Mathew could argue, Dianna interjected. "That's how I want mine tonight."

"Me, too," Mathew agreed.

Tristan's gray, unwavering gaze met Dianna's once more and that strange current flowed between them. He was probably just glad that she was being a buffer.

He wasn't looking at her like that because he liked her. And the fact that her thoughts had already gone to that extreme meant she was spending too much time here. Getting involved with a client was a bad idea.

A *very* bad idea.

$$8$$

Tristan

Tristan could tell Dianna was uncomfortable. He should have provided an out for her to leave, but instead, he'd fed his own selfish desires. When Erika left, there hadn't been one day where he felt like he wasn't drowning. Having Dianna around gave him the first opportunity to get a gulp of fresh air. He felt like he could breathe again.

And *that* was nice. More than nice.

She wasn't even here for him, she was here for Mathew. The thing was, Mathew was becoming more at ease, with less meltdowns. Tristan figured things were becoming easier, simply because Mathew was allowed to just be himself, without the pressures of school and therapists trying to mold him into something he's not.

Plus with Dianna around, Tristan could finally take a step back and let someone else take the reins for a little while.

It was selfish.

The more he thought about it, the more he realized he couldn't continue asking so much of her. She was someone who was assigned to Mathew. It wasn't like she was doing any of this out of the goodness of her own heart. She was being paid by Shane.

He let out a sigh as he put Mathew's dishes in the sink. True to form, Mathew had refused to try the tomatoes, but that didn't stop him from requesting that he get a scoop on his plate just like Dianna. He insisted on sitting next to her, which forced Tristan to sit across from her at the small kitchen table.

Throughout the whole meal, she hadn't met his gaze. Though at this point he wasn't sure what he would do if she caught him staring. He still couldn't get over how quickly she was able to win Mathew over.

"Thank you for dinner." Her soft voice yanked him from his thoughts and he nearly dropped the glass he was rinsing out. She offered him her plate and another glass. "Do you have a container where I can save the extra tomatoes?" The corners of her mouth lifted into a grin. "Or would you like me to toss them?"

He chuckled, though it sounded strained even to him. This dance they were doing with each other was probably all in his head. He needed to knock it off. "I think it's safe to say that Mathew probably won't eat them later."

She nodded, then left his side, returning with a few more of the dishes they had at the table. Without comment, she grabbed one of the dishes he'd placed in the side of the sink filled with water to rinse what he'd just cleaned.

"You don't have to—"

Dianna gave him a pointed look. "I was raised in a home where everyone did their part. You had to when there were so many. I can dry the dishes. It's not a big deal. Then I'll slip out, and you can have the evening to yourself."

You make good company.

The words were on the tip of his tongue. He could ask her to stay, get to know her better so he could prove to himself that he wasn't supposed to be feeling anything toward her, especially not interest.

But he couldn't get his heart to slow down. All he could think about was what if things were different and he'd met her by chance at a supermarket or somewhere else? Would they have made a connection? He already knew she was amazing with Mathew.

Stop it. She's not interested in you like that.

He needed to leave the poor girl alone. If only his heart and mind could follow suit. He'd have no problem. But here he was. With his heart feeling like it was jumping rope in his chest.

Tristan nodded once and together they did the dishes.

A few times, he caught her stealing a glance at him. He shouldn't feel elated by such a thing, but he was well beyond following the rules his head insisted. Tristan shifted and cleared his throat. "Did you take any lessons—drawing, I mean?"

Dianna shot one more look in his direction and shook her head. "I've always loved drawing. I think it's just the way my brain decodes the world around me." She placed a dry plate to the side and grabbed another one. "What about you? What do you do in your spare time?"

He chuckled. "I think it's pretty clear I don't get much time to do anything besides taking care of Mathew. He can take a lot out of me."

She arched a brow. "That doesn't mean you should let your own interests take a back seat. Surely there has to be something that you enjoy doing. Perhaps when he goes to bed?"

"I suppose I like reading. That's probably where he gets it." A smile tugged at Tristan's lips. "His mother wasn't really interested in anything like that. She was more of the athletic type."

Something in Dianna's features shifted as if a light had left her face. "Does Mathew see her often?"

Tristan's chest tightened. He'd stepped right into that one. Of course if he mentioned Erika, there would be questions. "How much has Shane told you about my situation?" He hadn't meant for it to happen, but his voice had hardened. It was hard not to feel disillusioned while discussing his ex-wife.

"You don't have to tell me if you don't want to," she offered. "I just thought—"

"It's fine," he bit out.

"It sure doesn't sound fine."

He let out a heavy sigh and put the dishcloth back in the sink. "It's been years. And honestly, I'm over it. But it still makes me—" He jumped when her hand reached out to touch his forearm.

"It's perfectly normal to be angry. I'm mad and I didn't even know her." Her voice was quiet, and he couldn't tell if it was due to not wanting Mathew to overhear them or if it was something else.

"Thanks," he murmured thickly. That's all he could say. He wasn't the type of person to use his past hardships to gain favor or sympathy. Dianna didn't need to see him as a victim.

Even if she did, it shouldn't matter.

He glanced down at where she still touched him and she followed his gaze. Immediately, she withdrew her hand to pick up another dish. Her arm brushed against his, causing a strange reaction to ripple through his body. He was tempted to scoot closer to her so they could touch once more.

Tristan hadn't dated anyone since Erika left. His reactions to Dianna had to do with that. And he hated that it was getting harder to focus on keeping things professional. He cleared his throat and shifted his weight from one foot to the next. "Tell me more about your family."

She smiled softly. "What do you want to know?"

"Are your parents as good as you when it comes to kids like Mathew?"

Dianna pressed her lips into a firm line. "Not particularly."

His brows lifted. "Oh? I'm sorry."

She lifted a shoulder. "It's not what you think. My mom passed away when I was pretty young. And my dad was very strict."

"Your father raised all of you on his own?"

The only response he got was a curt nod.

"Wow. That must have been really hard."

She gave him a pained smile. "You know? I think it was harder than he let on. Up until recently, he didn't want any of us dating until our older sisters were married."

A bark of laughter escaped his lips. Upon seeing the seriousness in her eyes when he glanced at her, he sobered. "I thought you were kidding."

Dianna turned back to the dishes she was working on. "Nope. But you have to admit, raising seven girls on his own in this day and age wasn't easy. And there are more concerns than making sure we're raised to be respectful and hardworking. My father had to worry about each of us plus every man who might be interested in us."

"I guess I never thought about that." Tristan's thoughts shifted to Mathew, and suddenly he developed a deep appreciation that he didn't have to raise a girl on his own. He wouldn't know the first thing about raising a little girl. Doing hair, worrying about her hitting puberty...

Heat crawled up his neck and he shoved those uncomfortable thoughts aside, grateful she couldn't read his thoughts.

"So what changed his mind, if you don't mind my asking?"

"Hmm?"

"Your father. You mentioned that he had that rule up until recently. What changed?"

She put the final glass down, then tossed the dish towel over her shoulder as she leaned her hip against the counter. "Well, my oldest sister got married, and then my second oldest sister refused to be pressured into getting married. Then Constance, my sister who's just a little older than me, fell in love and..." She shrugged.

A pastel pink color bloomed in her cheeks, making her appear as though she'd just come back from a hike. Her skin practically glowed.

"Anyway, now that his rules are no longer in the way, I guess my sisters have all started going on dates. Now he gets to deal with *that* series of unfortunate events."

"And you? Are you currently seeing anyone?" The question was probably too personal and he really didn't need to know the answer. Part of him didn't want to know. The whole time he'd been fixated on her, he hadn't considered whether or not she was dating. Someone as pretty and smart as she was could definitely be in a serious relationship.

For a moment, time slowed down and he held his breath even though he told himself it didn't matter if she was dating anyone or not. He wasn't really allowed to date her.

"No. I don't see the draw to dating right now."

"Really?" he blurted. "Why not?"

Dianna would have been within her rights to shut him out. The kinds of questions he was asking her were highly inappropriate. But instead of pushing him away, she offered a smile. "Well, you of all people should understand. I don't mean to be rude, but look what happened between you and Mathew's mother. Personally, after meeting you, I have a feeling that the fault lies with a specific party. And that happens a lot. Sometimes the fault is found on both sides. I guess I would rather not go through that sort of situation."

Why did he feel let down?

Dianna wasn't dating anyone and that meant she was free to spend more time with him and Mathew. He wasn't supposed to initiate any sort of personal relationship anyway.

But what if he could? She probably wouldn't be interested in dating him even if the rules weren't in place.

Not only that, but she made a good point.

She cocked her head to the side and shoved her hands in her back pockets. "But that doesn't mean I don't want to make as many friends as I can."

"I'll be your friend."

They both turned, finding Mathew standing a few feet away.

Dianna laughed. "Boy, you're quiet."

He held up a sheet of paper and beamed at her. "I drew you another picture."

"Oh yeah?" She reached for the page and turned it over, then gave Tristan a sideways glance. "It's a lovely picture, Mathew. How about you tell me about it."

Mathew stood on his toes and pointed at the image of two taller people with a smaller person. "This is dad. This is me. And this is you." All three individuals were holding hands and smiling. "Over there is Molasses. But he's not part of our family."

Tristan stiffened as he peered closer at the image. "Mathew—"

"But maybe one day we could get a horse that's just for me." Mathew turned his face toward Dianna, then to his father.

Tristan dropped down so he could be at eye-level with his son. His heart ached, twisting in all kinds of knots. This was a new development he hadn't been prepared to discuss. Mathew had never been interested in what made up their family besides having a father and a set of grandparents. He'd only known Dianna for a few short days and already he was putting her in pictures—pictures that depicted what he appeared to want in his family.

"Buddy, this picture is really nice. But Dianna is just a friend. She's not going to be part of our family."

Mathew frowned, his smile dissolving from his face.

Dianna edged closer to him and placed her hand on his shoulder. "But you know what? Friends can be like family, too. If you want to call me your family, I think that would be an honor. But after Christmas, you're going to head home and I have to stay here."

Mathew's frown deepened and he shook his head. "No."

"Math—"

"You said I could ask Santa for anything. I want a mom."

Tristan's eyes widened and understanding washed over him. "Santa is really special, but sometimes he can't get you what you want. Remember when we talked about his elves and how they make toys at their workshop?"

"But Santa is magic so he can make it happen," Mathew insisted.

Prepared to die on this hill, Tristan reached for Mathew's hands, but Dianna cut him off.

"One year I had this beautiful little pig. She was the runt and she got really sick. I asked Santa and prayed to God that my pig would get better."

Mathew's eyes had turned red and he wiped at his nose with the back of his hand. "Did she get better?"

Dianna met Tristan's eyes briefly. "No. My pig died."

A tear tumbled down Mathew's face. "But Santa is magic. And God is supposed to answer our prayers."

"And sometimes they both have to make a hard decision.

My little pig was suffering. She needed to go live with God in heaven. He knew that was the right thing to do even if I didn't agree with him."

"Why can't I have a mom?"

"One day you might," Dianna insisted. "You will never know until it happens. But not even Santa or God can make people do something they're not ready to do. Like when you didn't want to talk to me right away. That was your choice. When you finally do get a new mother, she's going to be made just for you. And you'll meet her right when God thinks you're ready, not a second sooner."

"How do you know?"

"Because she'll *choose* you. She'll love you so much that she won't be able to bear living without you."

Tristan gaped at Dianna. This conversation had taken a turn. Should he be upset that she'd turned this into a spiritual lesson? Was he impressed that once again she'd handled a situation that could have turned ugly? Both thoughts passed through his mind as Mathew rubbed his eyes.

"I want a mom now, though."

"I know, kiddo. It's hard to be patient. But you know what else? If you can be patient right now, you're developing strong muscles. And I bet when you *are* ready, you'll be able to show off those muscles to whoever is lucky enough to earn your love."

He gave her a funny look. "I can't show those kinds of muscles."

She laughed. "Okay, you got me. But you could draw her a picture and show her just how wonderful you are from the inside out."

9

———

Dianna

Dianna tossed her hat onto her bed and collapsed onto the mattress with a groan. Constance looked up from where she sat at her desk on the other side of the room, then returned her focus to the book she was flipping through.

An exaggerated groan escaped Dianna's lips and she rolled over onto her stomach to get a better view of her sister.

Without looking up, Constance said, "Let me guess. You need me to ask you how work went today with that hot guy and his kid."

"Their names are Tristan and Mathew."

"So I was right," she said dryly.

"Yeah."

"Okay. What happened?"

"You're not even paying attention," Dianna said, dropping

her head onto her arms. "I listened to you complain and talk about James when you were sneaking around with him. Now you have to give me some advice."

Constance lifted a brow, her gaze darting to Dianna briefly. "From what I recall, you didn't like hearing me talk about my romantic exploits any more than you wanted to share yours."

"I didn't *have* romantic exploits," Dianna said, a groan following.

"And now you do?"

"*No*," she drawled, lifting her head up to look at her sister. "I mean, I don't know. Yes?"

Finally, Constance snapped her book shut and the smile Dianna had been expecting filled Constance's face. "I knew it. I told James you weren't going to last long. Only I thought you might end up having a crush on Shane."

"Shane? Eww, no. He's my boss."

"*Hey*," Constance said with mock offense. "Technically, James was my boss when I started to develop feelings for him."

Dianna smooshed her face into her blankets, her voice muffled by the duvet. "That's different." When she sat up, she found Constance eyeing her with an expression that wasn't easy to read. "*What*?"

"You tell me. You're the one who wanted to talk about this. So talk. What's going on? Has he hit on you?"

"What? Of course not. Tristan is a gentleman."

"Gentlemen can hit on women."

"Not when there's a line of professionalism that needs to stay in place."

Constance rolled her eyes. "So that's what you're upset about? He's *not* hitting on you?"

"*No*." Dianna groaned once more. "I've got these feelings and these thoughts flying around my head like bats."

"Halloween was two months ago, sis."

Dianna gave her sister a dirty look. "I'm being serious. I didn't think I was interested in anything romantic. But the more time I've been spending with Tristan and his son, the more I find myself fantasizing what it would be like to be part of their family."

Constance's mouth dropped open.

Clambering to her feet, Dianna reached into her back pocket where she'd painstakingly folded the picture that Mathew had drawn for her. She tossed it frisbee-style at her sister. "Look at that." The folded sheet of paper bounced off Constance's knee and fluttered to the floor.

She reached for it and carefully opened it, then met Dianna's eyes with a frown. "He's married?"

"*No*. That's a picture Mathew drew of me with his family."

"Aww, that's sweet."

"No, it's concerning," Dianna insisted. "I can't date Tristan. I can't let myself fall for him. And now Mathew is getting too attached far too early for it to be healthy."

"Why?"

"They're going to move back home after their therapy plan is over."

"So, why can't you date him while he's here?" Constance flung the folded sheet of paper toward Dianna. "Because I fail to see why that is something that can't be changed."

Dianna dug her fingers into her hair as she rolled over onto her back and stared at the ceiling. "Have you already forgotten that there's a degree of professionalism that needs to be maintained?"

"What does Shane say?"

Dianna stiffened. "Why would I ask him?"

"Because he's your boss and has the final word. Unless there's an HR department out there at the country club."

"I'm not going to date him, Constance."

"Then why are we having this conversation? You're really confusing me."

"Because I think I want to date him."

"So date him."

Dianna threw her hands down at her sides, allowing her fists to bounce against the mattress. "You're not being very helpful. You need to tell me what to do so I don't make a mess of everything. I don't want to lose my job, and I don't want to hurt Mathew."

"Then don't date the hot man."

She glowered, rolling over. "No offense, but I'm not going to ask your opinion after this. You don't have a clue what to do."

"Of course I don't. This is your life, Dianna. You have to go—"

"Never mind," she muttered as she climbed off the bed. "I'm going to ask someone else."

"No one else is engaged," Constance called after her.

Maybe that was her problem. Constance had already found her man and she'd snagged him. The rest of her sisters, except Adeline, were single and actively dating. Maybe one of them would be able to tell her what she should do.

Okay, none of them would be able to give her the answer that she wanted. Or they would, but it wasn't the answer that she needed—and that was how to construct a wall between herself and Tristan so she didn't end up doing something stupid.

It was decided. She'd go to work and keep her mind off the handsome man who treated her like she was more important than just some therapist who was assigned to his kid. It was like she'd said. They could be friends.

She'd been telling the truth. Relationships made her wary. The fact that he could understand her reasoning had made it that much harder to compartmentalize the emotions stirring within her. She'd done harder things. By the time Mathew and Tristan were done with their therapeutic services, everything would be settled and she'd be better for it.

10

Tristan

"I hate you." Tristan stormed into Shane's office and slouched down into the chair facing the desk.

Shane lifted an amused smile to his friend. "What happened this time?"

"I think I need a new therapist."

Shane's features sobered and he put the paperwork in his hands down. "Did something inappropriate happen? Did Dianna—"

"It has nothing to do with her. In fact, she's great. *Too* great." He gave his friend a pointed look. "I don't know what to do. Mathew loves her."

"Isn't that a *good* thing?"

"Of course it's a good thing." Tristan shot out of his seat and paced the room. "It's wonderful. I have never seen Mathew take to someone so quickly."

"I'm sorry for my confusion. But I fail to see what the problem is."

"I like her, too."

It took a few moments for Shane to catch on to what Tristan was getting at. Tristan stopped his pacing and the two of them stared at each other until Tristan couldn't stand it anymore.

"If I were interested in dating, she would be the kind of person I'd be looking for."

"Again, Tristan, I fail to see the problem."

His mouth fell open. "What are you suggesting?"

"What are *you* suggesting? You can't just come into my office, bounce around the room, claim you're starting to develop feelings for the girl, and tell me that I need to fire her. That's not how this thing works. I could get sued for something like that." Shane leaned back in his office chair and steepled his fingers together at his lips. "I feel like you're hinting that you want me to do something."

"I thought I made it clear. I don't think I can work with her."

"With all due respect. This isn't about you. This is about your son. And if she's made a connection with him, then you ought to let him keep the person in his life that makes him feel safe."

Tristan raked his hand through his hair and let out a sound that resembled a groan and a growl all at once. "He drew her a picture the other night."

"That sounds sweet."

"You didn't let me finish. It was a picture of the three of us as a family and he insisted he wanted her to be his new mother."

Shane laughed.

He actually threw his head back and laughed.

"It's not funny. Do you even understand what's going to

happen in a few weeks when I tell him we have to go home and we can't take her with us? He's going to be devastated."

"Well, what did she say?"

"She handled it perfectly." Tristan sighed. "She told him that one day he'll get his new mother and she will be made just for him. And he'll know it's supposed to be her because she'll choose him."

Shane had the decency to appear shocked at what Tristan had said. His mouth fell open and his eyes widened. "That's actually really intuitive."

"I know."

"I don't think I'm paying her enough."

Tristan's head snapped up. "What?"

"Well, initially I hired her for temporary work for the holiday with the possibility of an extension. She insisted she just wanted to volunteer. So I told her to name a price. I wasn't about to have her do an entire ten-week program without some kind of compensation. She's gotten a couple checks from when she was in training, but none of them have been cashed. I'm beginning to think she isn't going to cash them at all." He shook his head as if in disbelief. "But you don't have to worry about that. I told you this program would be free to you. And that's what it's going to be."

Dianna was volunteering? That's what Shane had made it sound like. No, he couldn't be right. Dianna spent most of her days in his presence working with Mathew. Why wouldn't she accept the money?

Because she was a selfless human being who didn't deserve to be on this planet. She was meant to be in heaven with the other angels.

It was getting harder and harder to shove aside those stray thoughts. He glowered at Shane. This was his fault, too. He could have hired someone who wasn't nearly as pretty or as warm. He would have gladly taken a male therapist.

Okay, that was a bald-faced lie.

After he'd met Dianna, he knew in his heart of hearts that Mathew needed her in his life. It wouldn't be fair to rip her away just because he couldn't control his thoughts. Feeling Shane's gaze on him, he glanced up. "What?"

"You do realize that I don't have that rule, right?"

"What are you going on about?"

"The made-up rule that states you can't date the therapist I have assigned to your son. Granted, it might not be wise, but when it comes to matters of the heart, nothing ever is."

Tristan's mouth fell open. "Are you actually suggesting what I think you are?"

"Do you think I'm telling you to ask out Miss Callahan?" He leaned into his chair again and let out a laugh. "You wouldn't even be considering it if you knew who her father is."

"I've heard about him."

"From whom?" He laughed again. "Dianna? You realize that a child's perception of their parent is always going to be skewed, right? This is Dianna we're talking about. Out of all the Callahan sisters, she's got to be the most even-tempered."

Tristan huffed.

"What?" asked Shane.

"She's definitely great with Mathew, but she's had a few moments with me that weren't so even-tempered."

"Then you must have really peeved her off. I'm telling you. That woman wouldn't talk bad about anyone. Maybe you should go into town and ask around. I think you'd get a much clearer picture of what you would be up against if you decided to move forward with this fascination of yours."

"I'm not scared of her father if that's what you're inferring."

"I wasn't inferring that at all. But I do think you can make some *good* stupid choices."

Tristan shook his head and held up his hands. "Wait, so back to this dating thing. You're actually saying I should go for it."

"Sure. As long as you keep it away from Mathew. This goes without saying, but if that kid is already getting attached to her, then you don't want to confuse the kid further if this relationship of yours doesn't work out."

Shane made a good point. The thing that was holding him back from asking her out shouldn't be the working relationship they had. It should be how it would affect Mathew.

Tristan got to his feet. "I still hate you," he muttered as he left Shane's office, his friend's laughter following him out the door and down the hallway.

They were only going to be here for a max of ten weeks. He needed to weigh the pros and cons. He'd never jumped into a relationship this fast. Even with Erika, they'd taken it slow. And with what Dianna had mentioned the other night about not having an interest in a relationship, he couldn't be sure she'd even say yes.

If he asked her out and she turned him down, would both of them still be able to maintain a certain professionality?

All of these questions weighed on his mind, and not one of them would be answered today. He was taking Mathew to pick out a live Christmas tree on the far reaches of Shane's property. It would be the first one they picked out and chopped down together. Tristan enjoyed celebrating Christmas with Mathew, but they usually didn't have the time or resources to do many fun activities like this. He was so grateful to Shane for this opportunity. And maybe he could release some of this pent-up energy he had humming through his body like a live wire ready to crackle at the first contact that was made with it.

He headed down the steps of the country club and nearly collided with none other than Dianna. Her genuine smile filled her face, contagious from the very first second the corners of her mouth lifted. "Hi, Tristan. I left Mathew at the cabin. I knew you'd be headed over that way in a minute. How did your meeting with Shane go?"

"Good."

She fidgeted, shifting her weight as she stood on the step just below his. "I told Mathew to find his snow boots and gather his gloves and hat. I'm sure he'll be ready for you when you arrive.

"Would you like to come with us?" The words burst from within him like a bolt of lightning that could no longer be contained. "Mathew has been begging me to convince you to come. I know you just had dinner with us a few nights ago, but—"

"I'd love to."

"You would?"

She grinned. "Picking out a Christmas tree here is a tradition that not even I can pass up."

11

Tristan

Tristan stayed about a foot away from Dianna as they walked through the snow along a well-marked path. Shane's property stretched a lot farther than he'd realized. They were supposed to head out to an oversized sleigh that would be pulled by a couple horses. The driver would take them into the woods that grew on the outskirts to the north of the country club.

The air felt colder somehow, farther away from the buildings and the lights from the country club. Clouds overhead made the evening sky dimmer than it usually would have been at this time of day. They probably had only about an hour left of sunlight before it wouldn't be very wise to chop down a tree.

A breeze picked up, tugging at his coat and the cowboy hat he wore at Mathew's insistence. Dianna wore a knit hat beneath the hood of her down coat, but she still looked like she was freezing. Perhaps after they brought the tree back, they could get some hot chocolate and sit by the fire.

His hand tightened around the axe that Shane had shoved in his hand before wishing him luck. At first, Tristan had been confident that he could chop down the tree. But by the way Shane had chuckled and reminded him the driver would be more than happy to help, he wasn't so sure.

Dianna clasped her gloved hands together and kept her gaze on Mathew, who wandered ahead of them. He stopped every so often to touch a tree branch covered in a dusting of fresh snow before moving on to the next one. It was hard not to stare at Dianna's serene expression. Even if he tried, he wouldn't have been able to imagine someone looking like they belonged so perfectly in a place like this.

It was enough to make him want to move out to this area. The people were kind and welcoming when he managed to get to town. He looked forward to spending time with Dianna despite not knowing if she'd end up biting his head off for saying something she disagreed with. He adored her passion.

He took in a deep breath and let out a heavy sigh. What was he thinking? Moving out here wouldn't work. It wasn't just him he needed to think about. Mathew's well-being mattered the most. There was no telling how Mathew would do if Tristan uprooted his son to make him stay here. He'd have to make new friends, get used to new doctors and therapists, and that was if Tristan could find a place to live. Sure, Mathew had taken a shining to Dianna, but there wasn't even a guarantee she'd be sticking around after this season.

One more peek in her direction, and his stomach tightened. The thought had been tempting, but his logical side knew better and that was why after the holiday, they'd head back to the city.

When Tristan and Dianna arrived at the sleigh, Mathew

had already climbed inside and perched on the back edge with one of his toy horses.

Tristan gestured toward the horses on the other side of the sleigh. "Didn't you want to sit over there?"

His son shook his head. "Molasses isn't over there."

Tristan glanced over at the animals. Sure enough, Mathew was right. Molasses wasn't one of the horses leading the sleigh. He made his way over to his son and sat down. "I guess Molasses had other things to do today."

Mathew shook his head. "No. Molasses doesn't do jobs like pulling sleighs."

"Oh yeah? How do you know?" Tristan bit back a smile, his eyes meeting Dianna's as they shared a brief, chest-tightening moment.

"Because Molasses is *show* horse," Mathew said with a matter-of-fact tone.

Tristan chuckled and his eyes found Dianna's again. It was small, but something passed between them. Right now she was one of the only people who could appreciate the little moments like this one. Mathew was special. He might not act like society expected him to, but he was intelligent. Sometimes Tristan thought his son was smarter than he was. The kinds of conversations Mathew could have was way beyond his age level. And the ideas he came up with when trying to figure something out... was pretty incredible.

Dianna took a seat on one side of Mathew and Tristan sat on his other side. It was momentary, like flashes of a falling star, but in that second as Dianna met his eyes, he could imagine this was what a life with her could be like.

Wishful thinking, that's all that it was.

Maybe not even that.

There was a part of him that hadn't quite come to terms with being a single parent even after all these years. He rested his hand on the back of their makeshift seat, behind Mathew, and when the sleigh lurched forward, Dianna's arm flew to grasp the back of their wooden seat. Her hand grazed his and her eyes darted once more to meet his. Quickly, she returned her hands to her lap but not before he noted the way she pressed her lips together like she wanted to hide a smile.

He cleared his throat and settled against the uncomfortable seat. If it wasn't completely inappropriate, he might have tried asking her out. If she wasn't his kid's therapist, and if he even had the time to date, he wouldn't have thought twice about it.

The snow-covered woods passed by them, the scenic view the perfect backdrop for the holiday. The bells attached to the reins jingled as the horses trotted along the path. The farther into the woods they got, the stronger the scent of the pine became. Mathew snuggled closer to him, resting his head against his side.

Though Dianna wasn't looking at him, her smile grew a little more. Tristan secured his son to his side by wrapping his hand around Mathew's shoulder.

"Do you pick out a live Christmas tree every year?" Dianna asked over the sound of the horses and bells.

He shook his head. "Usually I put up a small artificial tree and we make homemade ornaments."

A stunned expression flashed across her face. "Really?"

"Why is that so surprising?"

She shrugged. "I just—"

He wasn't sure with the cold, but he could have sworn she blushed.

"That sort of thing is usually something that kids do with their mothers." She dipped her head and let out a soft laugh. "That sounds terrible, doesn't it?"

Tristan laughed with her. "It's not *so* terrible. I probably overdo it trying to fulfill both roles for Mathew." His voice was soft, so much so that he didn't know if she even heard him very well.

Her hand reached out and touched his forearm. "I think it's wonderful—not that you should feel obligated to do such a thing—but there's not a doubt in my mind that Mathew knows how much you love him."

Mathew nodded and craned his head around. "I love you, too, Dad."

Dianna tossed back her head and laughed. For Tristan, it was the most beautiful sound he'd heard in a long time.

"There's no getting anything past him, is there?" she said.

"I don't believe there is." Tristan chuckled, then kissed the top of his son's hood-covered head.

The sleigh slowed and came to a stop. The driver turned around, flashing them all a smile. "Any tree with a red ribbon is up for grabs. If you need help, let me know."

Mathew jumped up from his seat and hurried toward the sleigh steps. "Come on, Dad. Come on, Miss Dianna. We hav-ta get a tree. It's gettin' dark." He clambered down, jumping with both feet into a pile of the freshly fallen snow.

Tristan's gaze locked with Dianna's for what felt like the millionth time. He gestured for her to take the lead. She scooted past him, careful not to make contact with him. After their accidental touching before, it appeared she wasn't as interested in him as he was in her. One more reason for him to get his head on straight.

He climbed down from the sleigh and watched as Mathew hurried ahead. "Stay on the trail, Mathew. I don't want you to get lost." He walked side by side with Dianna, but he kept about two feet between them for her sake. "What about you?"

She peeked at him. "What about me?"

"What traditions do you have this time of year?"

Dianna smiled. "We get a fresh tree every year. I like

reading by the fire every evening in December." She looked up at him. "I love making Christmas treats to share with friends and family. But I don't get a chance to do that as much these days."

His brows furrowed until realization dawned on him. "Please don't tell me that I'm keeping you from—"

She laughed. "Of course not. Things around my family have been pretty busy. Need I remind you of my father lifting his rules for his daughters."

"*Right*. The dating rules."

"Bingo." She laughed again, but this time it sounded more nervous than the previous ones. "So with that in mind, you can imagine that the traditions we usually partake in haven't happened."

"Well, you're welcome to make Christmas sweets over at our place. I'm sure Mathew would love that."

She glanced at him once more. "Perhaps we could make some cookies while I work with him on his educational goals."

His insides practically sang with jubilation, but immediately he squashed the hope he'd created. "I only have one request."

"Oh?"

"Sugar cookies."

"I wouldn't dream of leaving those out."

"Dad! Dad! This one. I want this tree."

They turned to find Mathew jumping up and down, pointing at a tree he stood beside. "It's perfect, right?"

The tree was only about two feet taller than Mathew making the top branch only reach five and a half feet. It would be easy for Mathew to decorate all on his own if he really wanted to. Tristan nodded. "I think you picked the perfect one."

Mathew beamed and stepped back. The process of cutting it down took more time than Tristan expected, and at one point, he thought Dianna might offer to step in and help. But finally with the right angle, he was able to get the axe to hit it just right. The final crack split the air and the tree fell with a heavy thud against the snow-packed earth.

Mathew jumped up and down, cheering excitedly. His energy was contagious and Tristan couldn't fight his own enthusiasm.

Tristan gave the axe to Dianna and grabbed the trunk of the tree. "Let's get this back to the sleigh and maybe when we get back to the cabin, we can get some hot chocolate."

"Yay!" Mathew hurried over to Dianna. "You'll come for hot chocolate, right?"

She sent a cautious look in Tristan's direction, then brought her focus back to Mathew. "If you really want me to."

Mathew nodded vigorously. "Then maybe we can make some ornaments, too." Before she could respond, Mathew ran ahead, faster this time. It was harder to keep up while dragging the tree behind him.

"Thanks for coming," Tristan said softly. "I appreciate it."

"I don't feel like I helped very much," Dianna said. "You and Mathew did all the work."

"You underestimate how calming your presence can be." The words escaped his lips before he had a chance to examine them or consider how they might sound to Dianna.

She kept her focus on Mathew. "It's funny that you say that. I haven't seen many blowups with him." She was quick to continue, her voice tighter. "Not that I don't believe you. I guess I've just noticed that Mathew doesn't need as much help as I expected."

"You're right. He hasn't had as many meltdowns as he usually does. And I equate that with you."

She slowed her pace.

"I mean it. There's something about you that speaks to him.

It's like he can see something that I can't." That wasn't true. Tristan could see a great deal about Dianna that impressed him. Mathew probably just connected with Dianna on a different plane.

"Thanks," she whispered. "It's nice to hear that."

Before he could say anything else, Mathew scurried back toward them. "Do we have marshmallows? I want marshmallows in my hot chocolate."

"If you don't, I'm sure we could track some down at the country club. They've got to have some in the kitchen, right?" Dianna moved away from Tristan when Mathew grabbed her hand and tugged her forward.

"And whipped cream? I want whipped cream, too."

She laughed. "A guy after my own heart. That sounds delicious." The volume of their voices lowered the farther away they got. Mathew didn't release her hand as they continued walking, choosing to swing her arm back and forth as he skipped beside her.

There it was. The moment he'd dreaded since he'd met this woman. His heart knew what it wanted, and it wanted Dianna. Shane wasn't averse to it. That left Dianna. Would she even consider anything romantic with him?

Not likely, especially after what she'd told him about her interest in relationships.

It wouldn't hurt to ask, though.

Would it?

Somehow he didn't think that Dianna would make things awkward between them if she turned him down. He certainly wouldn't. Mathew's experiences here were too important.

But maybe he'd give it a few more days.

If he could wait that long.

12

———

Dianna

"I'm so sorry. My truck is broken down and I'm going to be a little late. Do you think you could have Sean or someone else help the Woods with Molasses? Mathew needs his practice this morning. It's part of his routine."

"Of course. Thanks for letting me know," Shane hung up without saying goodbye.

Dianna stared at her phone, a sense of trepidation flooding her chest. She wasn't able to track down anyone to check her truck to see what might have happened to it. Already her anxiety had elevated with the change in her schedule, but even worse than her own emotions was how Mathew would cope with her being late.

She grimaced as she hurried toward the house. Adeline, Constance, and Brielle were all gone. And the rest of her sisters were busy. The only option she could see was to saddle a horse, but she'd be *really* late if she did that.

Dianna burst through the front door and kicked off her tennis shoes. She headed for the storage closet so she could get a decent pair of boots, nearly bumping into Grace. Her youngest sister let out a yelp and her eyes widened.

"Geez, Dianna. Where's the fire?"

"Are you doing anything right now?" Dianna asked, putting her boots on.

"I was gonna—"

"My truck won't start. I think it's too cold. Can you take me to the country club?"

"I mean, I guess I could."

"Great." She grabbed Grace's wrist and tugged her toward the front door. "I'll get a ride home. I'm late for my shift and that little boy I've been working with isn't going to like that I'm not there."

Grace shuffled behind her, nearly tripping over her feet. "I'm sure he'll be fine."

"You don't get it. He needs me. More than anyone will understand." Of course Mathew's father would understand. But besides him, Dianna knew deep in her gut that Mathew relied on her and if she wasn't there, he might really upset him.

"You said this kid was seven?"

"Yeah."

"Well, he's gotten along just fine so far. Do you really think that you're the only one who can help him? His father is there. We don't have to rush. Let me at least get some shoes on."

Dianna looked down at her sister's feet and huffed. "Well, hurry up. I need to get out there. It's not just about him. This is my job, and I—"

"And Shane doesn't strike me as the kind of guy who wouldn't understand when your car has problems. It's gonna be just fine."

Dianna sighed with exasperation. This was one of the many

instances when people didn't understand her or what was important. She'd long since realized that this wasn't something she'd ever be able to explain.

She hurried outside. While she stood beside her sister's truck, she shifted her weight, hopping from one foot to the other. Dianna checked her phone, gaining only a small amount of relief from the fact that neither Shane nor Tristan had called her. Not yet, anyway.

When Grace emerged from the house, Dianna had to bite her tongue to prevent herself from yelling at her sister to pick up the pace. It wouldn't do any good. It never did.

The whole way there, she attempted to remain calm. Yes, what Grace had said was true. Mathew had done just fine before they had met. He had coping skills and his father to advocate for him.

So why couldn't she shake her nerves? He wasn't her son. For all intents and purposes, she shouldn't care until she was on the clock.

But that just wasn't who she was.

Mathew was a sweetheart, and she'd already grown close to him. It wasn't hard to foresee just how much she would miss him when they left.

She closed her eyes briefly and took a deep breath. It wasn't just Mathew she'd miss. The other night when they went looking for a Christmas tree, there had been a connection between herself and Tristan which resulted in her losing sleep for the next few days. Each time she arrived for her meeting with Mathew, she had avoided looking directly at Tristan unless it was absolutely necessary.

It was a strange feeling, to say the least—like she and Tristan were two magnets being pulled together. She couldn't tell if that was something he was interested in, and for the sake of Mathew, she'd opted to pretend none of those feelings were present.

Her job was to take care of the boy, not fall in love with his father.

Dianna said a quick thank you for the ride as Grace pulled into the parking lot. Then she launched from the vehicle toward the path that would lead her straight for the barn. She heard the screaming before anything came into view.

The hairs on the back of her neck stood on end and she quickened her pace. Finally, two adults, a child and a white horse came into view. Mathew was on the ground, the screams coming from him. Tristan hovered over him, his expression a mixture of embarrassment and frustration. He glanced up as she neared.

She almost thought she saw relief in his eyes, but she couldn't be certain. The man holding the reins of the white horse looked at a complete loss. He said something to Tristan, who shook his head and raked a hand through his hair.

Dianna already knew what the problem was. It was very likely that Tristan knew the problem too, but it didn't appear he was telling the ranch hand.

Breathless, she skidded to a stop. Before Tristan or Mathew could say anything, she stepped between the ranch hand and Tristan. "What do you think you're doing?"

He held up the lead rope. "Mr. Owens told me I needed to get the Wood family a horse."

"No."

"No?" The ranch hand glanced nervously between Dianna and Tristan. "I'm pretty sure he told me to get them a horse."

"He wouldn't have told you to get them *a* horse. He would have told you to get them *their* horse." Dianna placed her hands on her hips. "Mr. Wood and his child are here for therapy sessions. They get to have the same horse every practice. Where is Molasses?"

The man glanced back toward the barn. "I think he was being looked at by the vet."

"Then that's what you tell the Wood family. Their horse would be available momentarily."

"But—"

She pinched the bridge of her nose. At least now, Mathew's meltdown was starting to subside, or at least not be as bad as it was. She lowered her voice and moved closer to the ranch hand. "This little boy struggles with change. He needs to work with the same horse he's been with."

"I didn't know about that."

Dianna let out a sigh. "Well, next time you should double check. I appreciate your help while I was gone, but this isn't the kind of experience we should be offering our guests. Would you mind taking this one back and getting Molasses once the vet is done with him?"

He nodded. "Of course, ma'am." He touched the brim of his hat and turned around.

She took a deep, steadying breath before she faced Mathew.

Tristan stepped forward. "That wasn't neces—"

Dianna held up a finger and crouched down on Mathew's level. "Hey, kiddo."

He wiped his hand across his face, rubbing his nose, then he blinked at her. "Hi, Miss Dianna."

"Can we talk about what just happened?"

Mathew frowned and cast his eyes down. "Okay."

"What made you feel so upset just now? Was I right in guessing it was because they brought a different horse?"

He didn't answer.

"You know I would have been here soon to get the right horse for you."

Mathew glanced at her. "But I wanted Molasses."

"I know you wanted Molasses. And that cowboy brought out the wrong horse. But do you think maybe he didn't know all the rules? He was just trying to do his job. When you got upset instead of telling him what you wanted, you weren't giving him the chance to fix things. Sometimes we get so caught up with what we think we're going to lose that we don't take a minute to calm down and come up with a solution."

This seemed to capture Mathew's attention. He glanced at his father, then back to Dianna.

"Do you think next time you would be willing to slow down and use some skills I can teach you?"

He nodded.

She smiled brightly at him just as the ranch hand reached them with Molasses being led by his rope. Mathew sniffled and got to his feet. Dianna accepted the lead rope and held it out but didn't relinquish it to Mathew yet. "Before I teach you a skill, how about you teach me one."

Mathew's brows creased, pulling together with confusion. "What do you mean?"

"If I was upset about something that wasn't going as I expected it to, what would you tell me to do?"

His eyes darted to the side and he stuck out the tip of his tongue. "Maybe count to five?"

She grinned. "That's a very good one. But it's hard to remember, isn't it?"

Mathew nodded once more.

Dianna tilted her head slightly. "How about we come up with a code word that will help you remember to count?"

His eyes brightened. "Like a secret code word?"

"Exactly. It can be something only you, your dad, and your teachers know. What do you think?"

He grinned. "What's it gonna be?"

"That's totally up to you." Dianna smiled and finally chanced a look in Tristan's direction. Her heart leapt into her throat. His serious eyes delved into her as if they could see past all the walls she'd built around herself over the years. She wouldn't be surprised if he pulled her aside and told her he knew all her secrets.

She swallowed hard and turned her focus back to Mathew. "Just make it a good one. Maybe one that will make you happy so when I have to say it or if your dad has to say it, then you can remember right away what you're supposed to do."

His cute little furrow deepened and he pressed his lips together into a tight line. The three of them stood like that for a few moments until Mathew's head snapped up, a smile lighting his face. "I think it should be Molasses."

She laughed. "I think that's a wonderful idea. Molasses makes me smile too." She held out the reins and nodded toward the arena that was a few yards away. "How about you lead Molasses today?"

If it was possible, Mathew's smile grew even larger. He held the reins reverently as he started toward the building. Dianna let him get a few paces away before turning toward Tristan. "Now, I know what you're going to say—"

"I don't think you do." His voice was gruff but not angry.

Dianna blinked and folded her arms. "Okay. Then tell me and I'll let you know if I was right."

He moved forward, closing the small gap that had been the buffer between them. She sucked in a soft breath, not expecting him to invade her personal space like that, but it was probably so Mathew didn't hear what he was about to say. Tristan's focus darted to where Mathew continued toward the arena and then back to her. "I don't know how you do it."

Her brows shot up. "Pardon me?"

"You came charging in here like a mama bear ready to

pounce on that cowboy for doing the wrong thing, but you did it with a poise and assertiveness that few people possess. I half-expected you to put him in his place, but you didn't. You were able to explain to him what was going on without being demeaning."

"Well, he wouldn't have learned anything if I made him feel small, now would he?" she quipped as she lifted her chin and fought the blush that threatened to make an unscheduled appearance.

"I don't think you're understanding where I'm coming from. I didn't want you to put him in his place. He didn't do anything wrong, not really. It was obvious he didn't know what to do just as much as I didn't. He brought a horse out like he was told to do, and it just happened that it wasn't the one Mathew wanted."

"Oh."

He took a deep breath and exhaled; the warmth of it fanned against her cheeks and goosebumps rose on her arms beneath her coat. "Then just when I thought you couldn't surprise me anymore, you go and do it again."

As much as she wanted to, she couldn't tear her eyes from him. He held her captivated with his discerning gaze, pinned against what she thought she knew and what he was now trying to help her understand.

"I was ready to jump in and tell you that Mathew needed to learn how to cope with disappointment. He is too old to throw fits like that, especially when he had a decent second option. You might not like it, but that's how I want to raise him. I'm not going to be around for his entire life, and he needs to learn how to figure things out when they don't go as planned." His voice softened, filling with awe. "You knew exactly what to say to reach him on a level where he didn't feel judged or unloved."

Chills ripped through her body. Everything he was saying made her feel seen. She couldn't explain it. Perhaps it had something to do with that magnetic pull they shared. Her mouth felt like it was full of dirt, dry and closing up without any way to respond to him. Dianna could only think of one thing to say. "Thank you?"

He chuckled, and the sound felt like hot chocolate and fleece blankets on a cold winter morning. "I wanted to ask you something, but I wasn't sure how you'd respond."

She swallowed hard. "Okay."

"I was hoping that you might—"

"Miss Dianna!" Mathew's voice called from near the entrance to the indoor arena. "I can't open the door!"

She swiveled her head around, taking a step away from Tristan in the process. The moment had felt all too intimate—at least to her. For all she knew, he was going to ask her about Mathew or for recommendations on how to reach his son in a more effective way.

He most definitely wasn't going to bring up the possibility of wanting to explore something personal. She shivered and shook her head as she sent him an apologetic glance. "Sorry," she murmured and jogged away.

13

———

Tristan

Tristan's heart pounded, hitting different beats and tempos and making him wonder if it wasn't trying to compose a new rendition of "The Little Drummer Boy." It had been but a small moment—a surge of confidence that had drawn him closer to Dianna.

In the back of his mind, there was an itch, a warning that he shouldn't lose sight of why he was here. Mathew was their priority. They both knew it.

And yet his heart roared with the idea that Dianna could be what had been missing from his life. He couldn't get over the way she'd handled the situation with the wrong horse. If he'd been waiting for a sign to do something, it had been that.

Tristan heaved a sigh and trudged across the frozen ground toward the arena. Dianna and Mathew had already entered the building, leaving him to continue beating his thoughts sense-less. He couldn't help but feel like time was running out.

What was it that people always said? He'd miss one hundred percent of the chances he didn't take?

He entered the building and headed for the usual area where he liked to watch. His eyes locked onto his son and Dianna, and a swelling of pride filled his chest. But it was more than that; a twinge of longing seemed to dance within him. This was what he wanted and if he didn't do something about it —force himself to fight for something this important—he'd lose his opportunity.

He'd stepped around the subject since meeting her. When he'd been younger, things were different. He was different.

Whenever he met someone new and wanted to get to know them better, he'd ask them out on the spot. Somehow that part of him had changed, and he wasn't sure he liked it.

He found himself watching Dianna more than Mathew, enthralled with how well she worked with him and how gentle she was with the animal. Really, there should be nothing to hold him back from taking that first step.

Nothing except that latent fear that it wouldn't work out and Mathew would be hurt.

Tristan shook the thought from his mind.

Dianna wasn't like that. She wouldn't just leave because things were hard. He could tell. If a relationship with her didn't work out, it would be for something understandable.

Her eyes found his and he smiled, reveling in the way she dropped her gaze. Her cheeks flushed. He might be out of practice, but that reaction seemed more telling than she probably wanted it to be.

The next half-hour went off without a hitch. Mathew was on his best behavior, and it was easy to forget what had transpired before Dianna had arrived.

Once they were done, they returned Molasses to his stall and headed for the cabin. Dianna sat down at the table with

Mathew to help him with his assignments while Tristan moved into the kitchen to make them a snack.

The tension continued to build with each glance that passed between himself and Dianna. The weight of the air pressed in on him until it was almost suffocating. He placed a cup of hot chocolate on the table in front of Mathew, then kissed the top of his head as he moved over to Dianna and held out a mug toward her. Her fingertips brushed his and a thrill shot through him.

"Thank you," she said.

He nodded, then returned to the kitchen area to put away what he'd gotten out. The next hour dragged on as he recited in his head over and over what he wanted to say to her, how he wanted to ask her.

Once Mathew completed his work, he hopped down from the table. "I'm going to draw."

Tristan smiled. "Have fun."

Mathew disappeared down the hallway, leaving Tristan alone with Dianna. He made his way over to the table and sat down in the seat Mathew had vacated. "Thank you for working with him."

She lifted her hot chocolate to her lips and took a sip. Her fingers curled around the mug and he could have sworn she hid a smile behind the edge of the cup. "I've really enjoyed working with him, too."

He shifted in his seat. "You mentioned that you've never worked with kids like Mathew before."

"That's correct." She placed the mug on the table and turned it in her hands. "I've always liked kids. But I've never worked with them in an official capacity."

Tristan blew out a slow breath. "Well, you could have fooled me."

Her smile returned. He could feel the warmth resonating

inside him attempting to make an appearance to show the world just how ridiculous he felt he was being. This small talk was excruciating. He should just let it all out and tell her exactly what has been on his mind.

"Regarding what we were discuss—"

"I should probably get—"

He cut himself off and stared at her. "Oh. Right. You must have a lot to do."

Dianna shook her head and let out a small laugh. "No, but I think I've overstayed my welcome enough for one day."

Tristan leaned over the table, praying he didn't look as desperate as he felt inside. "You're not." Clearing his throat, he leaned back and raked a hand through his hair. A strained laugh tore from his chest and he looked away. "What I mean to say is that you're always welcome to stay as long as you'd like." Geez. Why did his statement sound so immature? He wasn't some hormonal teenager. He was a man who could tell a woman what he wanted, for heaven's sake. He opened his mouth to continue what he'd started to say, but she rose from her seat.

"You're very nice, but really, I think I should head out."

He rose from his chair and followed her toward the door. "Let me walk you out to your truck."

Her features faltered and her face bloomed with a shade of scarlet only she could produce. "Shoot! I completely forgot. I didn't come in my truck."

His brows furrowed. "You didn't? How did you get here?"

Her shoulders slouched and her hands dropped listlessly to her sides. "My sister drove me—rather unhappily, I might add. I should probably go see if Shane can take me—"

"Of course not. I can take you. It's not far, is it?"

She shook her head. "Only about a five-minute drive if we don't run into any cattle blocking the road."

"Does that happen often?"

Her grin returned. "More often than avalanches." She nodded toward the hallway. "Do you think Mathew will mind? He's probably not going to be thrilled about being interrupted from his drawing."

"I'm sure he'd love to see where you live. That sort of thing is right up his alley." Tristan fidgeted again. "But maybe you'd like to stay for dinner before we take you back?"

The hesitation was evident on her face. This was when he would hit himself upside the head and tell himself he knew better. Someone like Dianna wasn't going to be interested in a guy who had a kid and couldn't even get the courage to just ask her out.

"I think we're out of macaroni and cheese, but I got some hot dogs if you're up for it."

She laughed. "Well, how can I say no to that?" Dianna grabbed her phone from her pocket, then returned it. "You know what? It doesn't look like anyone is asking me to get home for anything. Maybe I could make those cookies I've been promising Mathew."

Dinner went quick, and there weren't any moments when Tristan could speak to Dianna about his intentions. They started making cookies, but Mathew quickly lost interest and wandered off to play.

Tristan leaned his forearms on the table as he watched Dianna roll out the sugar cookie dough. "Can I ask you something?"

Her hands slowed and she looked up at him. "Of course." There was that hesitation again, adding to the insecurity he felt growing. He had to think quick if he wanted to say something that didn't sound completely crazy. "How do you know if the dough is going to turn out like a soft cookie or a crunchy one?"

Okay, that was the wrong thing to ask. Dianna stared at

him, her expression blank. "That's what you wanted to ask me?"

Did he hear a note of disappointment in her voice? No. It was only his imagination. He chuckled for lack of anything better to do. "Yep. I can never get my cookies to turn out the way I want them."

"And what way do you want them to be?" she asked softly.

"Well, I grew up with my mom making me these really wonderful cookies. They were melt-in-your-mouth delicious. Soft, but not too sweet—unless you put frosting on them, which I always did." He smiled at the memory. "But I can never get the cookies I make to turn out the same way. I always get the crunchy kind that resemble crackers more than they do cookies."

She looked down at the dough she rolled out, then back up to him. "Come over here."

He straightened and hovered where he was for a few moments before moving around the counter and standing beside her. Her perfume was overtaken by the scent of flour, sugar, and a faint hint of almond. Without giving him any warning, she grasped his wrist and brought it to the ball of cookie dough that sat in the mixing bowl.

"Okay, now poke it a little bit." She didn't release him. Instead, she pushed his finger into the dough enough that when he pulled it out, some of the dough got stuck on the tip.

He made a face. "No wonder Mathew didn't like touching this. It's too sticky."

She snickered. "Not really. By the time you toss out your flour and roll the dough flat, you'll end up losing all of that stickiness. It will cook really well and maintain that soft texture you were talking about."

Tristan frowned. "You're telling me that the reason my

cookies always turn out miserable is that I put too much flour in the recipe?"

Dianna released his hand and lifted a shoulder. "That's not the *only* thing. The recipe has to have a few things in it to help with the baking process."

"Really? Aren't all the recipes the same?"

She laughed again. But he didn't feel like she was making fun of him. It was more of a laugh like he'd said something funny and she was joining in on the joke. "Of course not. Recipes are like people. There are so many different variations that each cookie will come out likewise. Some people use vanilla, and some people use almond extract. Some people use a lot more flour than I do. Whatever recipe your mother gave you, I would wager it has a few things in it to help make them soft. Do you happen to have that recipe?"

He shook his head. "It's back home."

"Well, I would wager that it calls for something like yogurt to help the dough stay softer. But more than that, I bet it also tells you to cook it at a higher temperature, like three-hundred and seventy-five degrees."

Tristan shook his head. "Okay, *that* I have a hard time believing. Wouldn't that just cook it faster and you'd end up with a harder cookie?"

"Not necessarily. If you have a higher temperature, yes, it will cook the treat faster, but it will also prevent the oven from drying out the cookies. And if you undercook them slightly, they still continue to cook even after you pull them from the oven."

He hadn't moved from his position beside her. The more she talked, the more he realized that he couldn't continue skirting the issue at hand.

"...that's why your cookies aren't turning out as well."

"Go out with me."

Her expression slackened.

Great. Had he just blurted out those words?

Of course he had. Because he wasn't some suave, debonair suitor. He was a bumbling fool who had allowed himself to fantasize far too much over a woman who very well could be disinterested in him.

"I mean—that's not what I was going to—"

"Tristan," she started.

He could hear it in her voice. That was the tone a woman used when they wanted to let a guy down easy. He'd heard it before, but only a handful of times.

And he wasn't about to let it get to him now.

"Hear me out, please," he said quickly.

She snapped her mouth shut and stared at him expectantly.

"I'm going to be here for the next month. Mathew adores you. I think you're wonderful. Would it really be so bad if we spent some extra time together?"

Dianna opened her mouth, shut it, then opened it again. "But what about the conflict of interest? I probably shouldn't be involved with my client's family in that way."

"I think it's pretty clear that you shouldn't be dating your client." His lips quirked into a grin. "We can both agree that you really *shouldn't* date him."

A soft snort burst from her lips and her hand clapped over her mouth. "What about Shane? I'm sure he has rules against this sort of—"

"Shane practically wished me luck."

Her eyes widened. "He did?"

Tristan nodded, his arms folding tight against his chest to keep them from shaking with his nerves. "He did. The way I see it, the only one standing in the way of me kissing you right now, is you." He didn't think it was possible, but her eyes widened even more. Her mouth formed a small "o" but she didn't withdraw from him. They stood like that in the kitchen, her hands covered in cookie dough and flour, and all he could think about was the fact that she hadn't immediately turned him down when he mentioned going on a date.

Dianna gnawed on her lower lip, her eyes darting in all kinds of directions as she shifted her focus toward the cookie dough and commenced to roll it out before using the star-shaped cutter to create about half a dozen cookies to place on the cookie sheet. "I'm going to have to think about it."

That wasn't a yes.

It wasn't a no, either.

It was a maybe. And it was more than he'd had when she arrived for their therapy appointment earlier today.

He nodded, unable to fight the smile on his face. "Sure."

14

———

Dianna

*D*ianna groaned and flung her body on the bed in her room. She stared at the ceiling, angry that she'd allowed herself to fall into this mess in the first place. She wasn't relationship material. She couldn't be entrusted with someone else's heart, no matter how much her own heart yearned for that very thing.

"What's the matter with you?"

She gasped and sat up, finding Brielle standing in the doorway. Her older sister eyed her with curiosity. "Getting tired of that job that Constance dragged you into?"

"No. Of course not." Dianna scooted to the edge of the bed. "I'm wondering if I've made too many mistakes over the last couple of weeks."

"What kind of mistakes?" Brielle wandered into her room and sat on the edge of Dianna's bed. "I've made several in my lifetime. Perhaps I can help you figure out a way out of this one."

Dianna peeked at her sister. Brielle had dated several men over the years. She'd been the one to sneak out when their father's rules had still been in place. Perhaps Brielle had a point. "Tristan asked me out."

"You're going to have to give me a little more than that. I have no idea who Tristan is."

"Mathew's father."

"And Mathew is..."

Dianna rolled her eyes. "If you don't want to help, just say so."

Brielle laughed. "Kidding. So the kid's father wants you to go out with him."

"Yeah."

"I fail to see the problem."

Dianna's head spun around to face her older sister. "You're not serious."

Brielle shrugged. "He's a handsome guy with a kid. Isn't that sort of something you've always wanted?"

"Well, sure, but—"

"Then where's the problem?"

"He's Mathew's *dad*. Isn't there like some kind of code that says I shouldn't date a client?"

"Mathew's the client. Tristan isn't." Brielle laughed.

Dianna groaned. "It's one and the same if you ask me."

"Oh, come on, Dianna. It's not and you know it. Tristan is the kid's father, and he has nothing to do with hiring you or paying you. He's there to make sure his kid gets the best care. You're getting paid by someone else entirely. Think about it. If there was ever an opportunity to make a mistake that just might turn out great, this one is the jackpot."

Dianna frowned at Brielle, trying to come up with something smart and snappy that would completely break the foundation of her sister's argument, but she couldn't think of a single thing. Scrambling for *anything* to say, she muttered, "That's rich coming from the person who refuses to get into a committed relationship."

Her sister wagged her finger. "Uh-uh. That's an entirely different issue. I'm single because I *choose* to be. I'm not going to settle down if I can help it. None of the guys here are worth the trouble. You might have found a good one, but that's because he's not a local."

Dianna rolled her eyes. "You know what I think? You're scared."

Brielle snorted. "I'm the furthest thing from scared. I don't need a man to complete my life."

"Neither do I."

"Okay, but for whatever reason, you want one."

"I want what?" Dianna couldn't help it—she laughed.

"You want a guy. Or maybe not *a* guy but *that* guy." Brielle nudged Dianna and her features softened. "Just because I don't want to be tied down doesn't mean that you shouldn't want it. I've always loved the idea of finding someone who could mean as much to me as Mom did to Dad. I might not act like it, but I am a romantic." She expelled a sigh and her eyes grew distant for a few moments.

Dianna studied her sister's contemplative expression. Maybe she made a good point. Tristan was her type. He was a good father, smart, and he came all the way out here just to get his son the kind of treatment he needed.

On the one hand it was easy to be with him. Then there were those moments she thought her heart would explode from their proximity. A smile touched her lips.

"Ha! *There*. See? I *knew* you liked him."

Dianna jumped. "I wouldn't go *that* far. I barely know him."

Brielle pointed at her. "But based on that little grin you were wearing, I can tell there's part of you that *wants* to get to know him better. It's okay, Dianna. For once in your life, don't stick to all these preconceived notions that you have to follow rules that don't exist." She got up from her seat and faced Dianna with her hands on her hips. "You've always been a rule-follower. Maybe you need to do something daring and just have some fun. No one would blame you."

She nibbled on her lower lip, laying back down on the bed. "What happens when his therapy sessions are over and he moves back home? I—"

"You're not committing to a *marriage*; you're saying yes to a date. For heaven's sake. You might go on a date and realize that you don't even like each other and the only thing you have in common is the way you care about his kid."

Brielle made an excellent point. There were no absolutes. Tristan wasn't asking her to marry him. That was laughable. How had she managed to get into her own head and make such a big deal about this?

She knew why.

This was part of her own spectrum tendencies. She just needed to stop overthinking everything.

Dianna sat up on her elbows, propping herself up to get a better look at her sister. "Fine. I'll do it under one condition."

Brielle tossed her head back and laughed. "I don't care one way or the other if you decide to date him or not. I have nothing riding on this."

"Really? Because sometimes it feels like you live vicariously through those of us who are dating. You have all this advice, and yet you refuse to do anything about your own loneliness."

"I am *not* lonely," she said, not very convincingly.

"Maybe you are, maybe you aren't. But something tells me you might want to fall in love *more* than any of us, and you're just as stubborn and maybe even more scared than any of us, too."

Brielle scoffed. "I don't have to prove anything to you."

"I wasn't asking you to."

"Then what was the condition you were referring to?"

Dianna straightened, folding her legs beneath her and offering her sister a sneaky kind of grin. "Shane's hosting a Christmas party this weekend. I'll go with Tristan, but you have to go with Shane."

Brielle's eyes narrowed. "He's not my type."

"Rich billionaire who has a history of being charitable?" Dianna's voice dipped into an exaggerated tone. "*Right.* I've seen the way you glance at him whenever you two are in the same place. If I had to guess, I'd say the reason you haven't asked him out is because you're worried he'd actually be someone worth risking your heart for."

Brielle scowled, indicating that Dianna had hit the nail on the head, which only made Dianna's smile spread wider. Brielle threw her hands into the air and huffed.

"He hasn't even asked me to go. I can't just show up to a party he's throwing and tell him I'm his date."

"I've got that all figured out. He told Tristan about the party and Tristan asked if he was bringing anyone. Shane said he wasn't. I'll just message Tristan right now and tell him that we can set him up with someone."

Brielle sighed. "Fine. I'll go on one date with the guy, but that's it."

"Maybe."

"Not maybe. I'm not interested in Shane. Like I said, he's not my type."

"Then what is your type?" Dianna pressed.

"I don't know. I'm all over the place."

Dianna chuckled. "Maybe you don't have a type. Maybe

everyone is your type and you just haven't clicked with anyone. *Maybe* you just need to kiss him under the mistletoe and then you'll figure out that he's the one."

"I've kissed plenty of guys, Dianna. I'm guessing that's not the problem here."

Dianna shrugged. "And maybe it is."

"Well, if you think that spending a few hours with a guy like Shane is enough to make him my soulmate, then you're sorely mistaken. I can't see myself as being the good little housewife who hosts parties and drapes on the guy's arm so he can show me off. I have too much pride for that."

Another shrug and a sly smile. Dianna didn't care if Brielle found love or if Shane was that person. Secretly, she didn't want to attend a big event without having someone there she could use for support. Adeline already said she and Sean were busy. And Constance was spending that evening with James's family. Dianna wasn't as close to her younger sisters, which was ironic considering that she was the middle child. Regardless, she had better relationships with her older sisters.

She climbed off her bed and headed over to where she'd left her phone on the dresser. "I'll tell Tristan." Shooting a quick glance in Brielle's direction, her lips twitched upward again. "And I'll make sure he doesn't tell Shane *who* he's going to be on a date with."

Brielle groaned. "What kind of party is this?"

"It's a Christmas party."

"Yeah, I get that. But what *kind*? Is it formal? Do I need a pretty dress? Or is it casual and I can wear one of those ugly sweaters?"

Dianna paused. "I'm not sure."

"You're not sure? Come on. That's one of the first things you need to find out when you get invited to something like this. If it's a bunch of people who are on the upper end of society, that would dictate the kind of party he's throwing. I doubt he'd be serving deviled eggs and fruit cake. Somehow Shane strikes me as the kind of guy who serves up caviar and kuidaore."

Dianna snorted, but it wasn't a small or cute one. The snort that escaped her mouth was loud and sounded more like the pigs she tended to out in the corral. She got a dark look from Brielle.

"What?" her sister demanded.

Shaking her head, Dianna let out another laugh. "Nothing."

"It's not nothing. What were you laughing at?"

"It's just—where did you hear that word?"

"Caviar? You know what that is."

Dianna shook her head again. "No. Kuidaore. Where did you hear that?"

"I don't know. Someone I probably went on a date with. Why? Do you even know what it means?"

She nodded. "Yes. Do you?"

Brielle folded her arms and shifted her weight from one foot to the next. "Of course I do. It's a fancy dish."

Dianna snickered again. "Kuidaore isn't food. It's a Japanese term that basically means you ate yourself into bankruptcy. The literal translation is to ruin yourself in extravagance by food."

"See? Isn't that what caviar is? It's an extravagant food and if you eat too much of it, you'll go bankrupt." Brielle's face flushed. "So what if it isn't an actual dish? It's still food related. And I wouldn't be surprised if Shane were the kind of guy who would buy all that fancy stuff and go bankrupt in the process."

"Actually," Dianna held up a finger, but Brielle's irritated look was enough to put a stop to her explanation. Most billionaires were very stingy. They were careful with how they spent their money, and Shane fit the bill on that one. He was one of the more down-to-earth people she'd ever worked with. He used his money wisely and accounted for every dollar. She didn't see him filling the country club with food that no one would eat. He probably wouldn't serve deviled eggs either, but that was beside the point. Dianna shrugged. "Okay, so we're set. You'll come to the Christmas party as Shane's blind date, and I'll tell Tristan that I will go with him."

Her heart fluttered slightly at the thought. To be with Tristan in a manner that didn't involve his son triggered a new kind of anxiety in her chest. It didn't necessarily feel bad. It was new. And being such, she had to figure out a new way to cope with it so it didn't consume her mind for the next few days.

Brielle huffed and stormed from the room. "I don't even know where you come up with these kinds of words."

"I didn't," Dianna called after her. "*You* did. I just knew what it meant cuz I read a lot."

Her statement fell on deaf ears. There was no way her sister would have heard the last part. At least their little interaction had brought some humor into Dianna's evening.

15

"Don't you worry about a thing, Mr. Wood. I'm great with kids." The young woman in front of Tristan couldn't be more than sixteen years old. She was the younger sister of someone who worked the drink bar at the country club, and Shane swore she'd be a good fit.

Her sister would be working tonight's party. With Tristan staying on site, he wasn't too worried about any emergency occurring. Still, Mathew hadn't come out of his room yet to meet her, and he wasn't sure that his son would appreciate a new face.

He cleared his throat and glanced over his shoulder. "Mathew, the sitter is here."

Mathew appeared in the hallway. He didn't look upset, but he didn't seem all that excited either. His eyes landed on Kimberly, then darted to Tristan. "I don't want a babysitter. I'm not a baby."

Tristan moved across the room toward his son and knelt down. "We talked about this. If there's an emergency, I need to know that there is someone who can handle it."

"I'm old enough to take care of myself," he muttered.

Tristan bit back a smile. "You're very smart, kiddo. But there are still a few things you have to learn before you can be in charge of yourself. Miss Dianna will be at the party. What do you say if I bring her here before you go to bed and she can read a book to you?" He hadn't cleared it with her yet, but based on how often she'd read Mathew stories up until this point, he was sure she'd be up for the task.

Mathew's demeanor brightened almost immediately and his eyes widened. He lowered his voice into a whisper. "Are you going to marry Miss Dianna?"

Tristan grimaced. He should have known better than to bring up Dianna when he was all dressed up and ready for a night out. Mathew was smart and more than attentive. He could figure out what was going on even if Tristan had done his best to hide it.

Standing, Tristan patted his son's shoulder. "I don't know."

"But you're going on a date with her."

"Yes, and sometimes that just means we're going to be friends."

"But if you kiss her, then you get to marry her."

He chuckled. "Just because you kiss someone doesn't mean you get to marry them. There's a lot that goes into a decision like that." Sometimes it was hard to remember that Mathew was only seven years old, especially when he asked questions like that. "Now, you be good for Kimberly and remember to listen to what she says. You don't have to go to sleep until nine, and I'll make sure Dianna comes to read to you."

Mathew offered him a small smile and glanced back at

Kimberly, who stayed by the door. "Fine. But I'm not going to talk to her."

"You're in charge of your own destiny."

Mathew rolled his eyes.

Tristan laughed. "It's okay if you don't want to talk to her. I already told her you may not be up for chatting much and she said she's perfectly fine with that. I'll see you in a few hours, bud." He left the cabin and headed for his car. She'd offered to meet him at the country club, but he'd insisted that he wasn't going to make her drive, especially since her truck was out of commission and at the shop. She'd offered the rebuttal that her sister was going to come and they could carpool together.

He'd put an end to that real quick when he told Shane he wasn't to allow his blind date to drive herself to the party. Once Tristan picked up Shane, they could go get their dates and then be ready for when the guests began to arrive.

Shane was already waiting by Tristan's car when he got to the parking lot. His friend glanced at his watch, then up to Tristan. "You're late, which means I'm going to be late, and I'm never late."

"Well, there's a first time for everything." Tristan unlocked the car and they both climbed in.

"Okay, now that it's the night of, are you allowed to tell me which sister Dianna is setting me up with? I'm guessing she's not going to be one of the youngest sisters. Mr. Callahan would have my hide if I even looked at one of them." He laughed, but it was strained. "The only one I can think of is Eloise. She's the next one, right? They were named in alphabetical order so that has to be it."

Tristan lifted a brow, the corners of his mouth quirking with amusement and climbed into the car. "And if it wasn't?" The ride to the Callahan's ranch wasn't that long. They might even get there before Shane figured it out.

Shane chuckled. "Well, it's not Brielle. Everyone knows this isn't her thing."

"How well do you know Brielle?"

"We've talked a few times when she's come by for one thing or another. Definitely not worth the trouble, if you know what I mean." Shane settled back in his seat. "The stories that circulate around that woman." He whistled. "You could fill several books."

Tristan held back a chuckle, but still, a sound came out that gave him away. Shane stiffened and turned toward him.

"You didn't."

"I didn't do anything." Tristan feigned mock innocence.

"Please tell me you didn't let Dianna set me up with that woman."

Tristan peeked at Shane. "What's the matter? Are you scared?"

Shane folded his arms like he was a child. "I'm not scared of going on a blind date. Do I want to have to deal with the gossips in town who insist on making something out of nothing? No."

"Who says it will turn out to be nothing? Maybe the two of you will hit it off and you just didn't realize how good you could be together."

Shane let out a snort. "You wouldn't be saying that if you knew her. You're still new. *And* you only have your experience with Dianna to compare things to. Those Callahan sisters all have their quirks, but Brielle is the one that takes the cake."

Tristan glanced at him once more out of the corner of his eye. "Dianna had mentioned that her father had been pretty strict when she was younger."

He let out a derisive laugh. "That's the understatement of the century. At one point I had nearly considered asking Brielle out—before Zeke had changed his rule—and I quickly learned you can't just go on a date with her and not suffer some kind of consequence. I missed out when her older sister found Sean. Brielle? Nope."

"I'm sure you're exaggerating. Maybe you should stop listening to the gossip yourself and try to get to know her one-on-one."

Shane took in a deep breath and let it out. "You're lucky we're friends."

"I know."

"And if anything goes wrong with her tonight, I'm blaming you."

Tristan chuckled. "Everything will go just fine. You'll see."

"Not if we don't get back on time. I need to greet my guests."

They pulled up in front of the house and Tristan shut off the engine. "Then let's round up our women and get back."

Shane gave him a blank look.

"What?" Tristan asked.

"You're starting to sound like a country boy."

He pushed open the door and Shane did the same. They stared at one another over the top of the car. "What is that supposed to mean?"

Shane's face broke into a smile. "You're sounding more and more like the cowboys out here. You're not planning on making this move permanent, are you? Because that would be great."

Tristan's hand covered his wrist over his watch, and he spun it around absently. "I don't know."

"I knew it. You've totally grown attached. You like it here." He paused and peered at Tristan with narrowed eyes. "You're falling for her."

Stiffening, Tristan looked toward the house. "There's a lot about this place that would be good for Mathew. I can see us settling down here. And yes, I'd be lying if I said that Dianna doesn't play a part."

"A *big* part. That's why you've invited her to the party

tonight." He waved his finger at Tristan. "And you were playing it off like it wasn't a big deal. Come on, man. We're friends. She's my employee. You should have told me. I could have given her a little push—"

Tristan's head snapped around and he gave Shane an unyielding stare. "Don't you do a single thing. I don't want you meddling in this. If it's meant to be, it will happen."

Shane seemed to be considering him for a few moments before he nodded. "Fine. But she's not Erika. She's not going to just abandon you. Remember that, okay? Don't let your concerns about that mess up anything that you might find with Dianna."

"Who said I was worried about Erika?" He scoffed. "Erika has nothing to do with this. She's been out of our lives for several years."

His friend shrugged. "Just a hunch, I guess. People in general seem to find any reason to sabotage something when they don't feel they deserve it." He walked around the car. "And you deserve to be happy more than anyone I know."

The front door to the house opened and light spilled out onto the porch. There were two silhouettes standing in the doorway, but only one of them captured Tristan's attention and made it hard for him to breathe.

Dianna was a vision in a deep crimson dress that came to her mid-calf. The fabric swirled around her knees in the front, then draped lower in the back. She held her coat draped over her arm and her gaze locked onto his. Her hair was swept up into a pile of curls on top of her head and he didn't dare move in case what he was looking at disappeared.

Shane dug his elbow into Tristan's side and let out a low chuckle. "I think it's customary to help the lady with her coat." He didn't waste any time. Shane moved forward and hurried up the steps toward his date. Brielle wore a white dress that came to her knees. There were lace embellishments, and it was easy to believe what Shane had said. Tristan could see her attracting trouble wherever she went.

By the time Shane had reached the top of the stairs, Tristan had jolted into action and hurried to meet Dianna before she came to him. "You look..." He shook his head and gestured toward her dress. "You look amazing, Dianna."

She smiled and moved closer to him. Her fingers adjusted his tie and her lashes fluttered before she lifted her gaze to meet his. "You clean up nicely yourself." Her hands traced down the breast of his jacket, resting near his lapel.

Chills swept down his spine and up again, but it wasn't because of the cold weather. He couldn't believe how lucky he was to be out on this date with her after everything he'd been through in his life. In a perfect world, tonight would be the first of many. He could already imagine what life would be like with her by his side.

"Come on, guys. Stop ogling each other and let's get going. I'm sure Shane has a lot to do." Brielle looped her hand through Shane's arm and gave him a flirtatious wink, to which Shane gave Tristan a meaningful look.

Tristan gazed down at Dianna, wishing they didn't have an audience. He would have liked to pull her close and finally break the tension that had continued to grow over the last several days. He wanted to kiss her, letting his lips rove over the soft curves of her shy smile and show her how he really felt inside. Instead, he reached for her wool coat. "May I?"

She nodded, allowing him to take the coat and hold it up for her. She slipped her arms into the sleeves, and before she turned to face him, he trailed his hands down her arms. When she did face him, her expression was guarded. Had he misread the signs she'd been giving him?

"We should probably get going," she whispered.

He nodded. "Right." There was plenty of time for the two of them to have a quiet conversation later. Even as he'd said the word, his feet refused to move.

The car horn honked loud and long, then another short burst. Both Dianna and Tristan jumped and faced the car, finding Brielle leaning forward from the front seat with a wide grin on her face as she honked the horn once more for good measure.

Dianna grimaced. "Sorry."

Tristan chuckled, shrugging as he laced his fingers within hers. "She's not *my* date. Maybe you should be apologizing to your boss."

She flinched again and laughed. "Maybe you're right."

16

———————

Dianna

 ianna fidgeted as she stood beside the large Christmas tree in the main area of the country club. There were tables and chairs set up around a small-ish dance floor, but the DJ hadn't completely finished setting up. People were arriving in a trickle, and she was just glad that she wasn't the one on a date with Shane.

Brielle was playing her role perfectly. If pressed, Dianna would have said that Brielle loved the attention far more than she'd let on. For all her complaining over having to be on a date with Shane, she sure seemed to be enjoying herself.

Her arm clutched Shane's tightly and she didn't move from his side. She played the dutiful date of a wealthy man well.

"Seems like they're getting along, don't you think?"

Dianna jumped and faced Tristan. Her heart refused to slow even as he offered her a glass of eggnog and turned his attention to the couple who were welcoming the newcomers.

She took a sip of her drink and nodded. "I knew she'd be a good fit. Not because they'd make a good match but because if anyone knows how to play a part, it's Brielle."

Tristan moved beside her and suddenly her mind went blank. All she could think about was how good he looked and how nice he smelled. She must not be a strong person if it only took a few weeks to change her mind about relationships. If there was anyone she wanted to try one out with, it was Tristan.

His arm brushed against hers and those pesky goosebumps exploded all up and down her arms. She shivered, which only drew his attention.

Goodness gracious.

Tristan removed his suit jacket and she sucked in sharply, trying to hold in a cough as she shook her head and waved him off. None of that worked. Before she could tell him it wasn't necessary for him to give her his jacket, he'd draped the item over her shoulders. His adorable smile reminded her of Mathew. He looked so proud of himself.

"Thanks," she murmured. The silence between them continued to grow as they watched her sister and his friend like a couple of awkward teenagers on their first date.

"What do you do for work?" Dianna asked.

"Besides drawing, what else do you like to do?" Tristan asked at the same time.

They stared at one another before they both laughed.

"You first," he insisted.

She cleared her throat and glanced at him quickly before turning her focus to her drink. "I love to read."

"Yeah?"

Dianna nodded. "There is nothing like escaping into a good book."

"What do you like to read?"

Heat seared her cheeks and she bit down on her lips, pressing them together. She shook her head.

"Oh, that means it's good. Now I'm curious."

Dianna let out a soft laugh. "I'm kinda a big nerd. You might change your mind about me when I tell you."

Tristan faced her. "I guarantee there is nothing you could say that would make me think poorly of you."

She peeked at him. "You first. What do you like to read?"

He tossed back his head and laughed. "I feel like if I say anything other than classic novels, you're going to be disappointed."

Dianna shook her head. Much like his sentiment, she didn't think there was ever going to be a possibility that he'd make himself appear in a bad light. "I don't have anything against any reading material. The way I see it, the majority of people don't read for pleasure these days. So if you like to read even a little bit, you're already on the right side of things."

"Fair enough." He leaned his shoulder against the wall they stood beside and tilted his head to look at the ceiling. "My favorites cover a wide range of stuff. I like Stephen King. *Ender's Game* is another favorite. But the ones I like the most have to be crime thrillers."

She squinted. "Really? I didn't peg you for that kind of stuff."

"But at least I read, right?" There was amusement in his eyes that made every muscle tighten as her stomach turned over and remained upside down.

"Right," Dianna murmured.

"Okay, your turn. I'm guessing that you're just placating my son when you read the stuff he's into."

She laughed. "I like those kinds of books. I love horses too you know. I'm always up for learning. *But* my guilty pleasure is epic fantasies."

Tristan's eyes narrowed. "You mean stuff with witches and knights?"

The blush returned to her face. There was a wide audience for such stories, which was why several movies had come out over the years. She nodded, hating the way her face gave away her embarrassment. She was supposed to be this person who was smart and a good influence on his son.

"What's so bad about that?" He shifted so he was closer to her.

Too close.

His voice lowered so that only she could hear it. "Like you said. Anyone who reads is already a step above the rest of us. And from what I understand, those books are the hardest reading material out of all the fiction genres."

She couldn't stop staring at him. Tristan had phrased that so perfectly. He'd made her feel validated, even if it was for something so insignificant as her reading choice. None of her sisters read as much as she did. They were all too busy with their chores and spending time out in the fresh air. Dianna finally looked away, unnerved by the way he continued to inspect her. "Well, I guess I'm glad you approve. I have to admit, I've always been a little self-conscious about what I enjoy reading."

He tucked her hair behind her ear with his finger. "Never feel ashamed of what makes you happy."

It was a small gesture, but one that resonated within her nevertheless. Dianna swallowed hard. She didn't want all this focus on her. She needed to change the subject or her anxiety might get the better of her. "Your turn."

"My turn?"

"You haven't told me what you do for work."

His hand dropped to his side. "Right. Well, I do computer

coding for the company where I work. It's nothing special. They tell me what they want and I make it happen."

Her brows lifted. "That's impressive."

Tristan shrugged. "It's a job. I can do it without much thought and usually when Mathew is otherwise entertained. It works with my availability, and they give me a lot of flexibility when it comes to projects coming due. I wouldn't have been able to come out here with Mathew if I didn't have the job I do."

"It sounds amazing." She'd never considered doing anything related to computers, mostly because of the family business that needed her. "When I was younger, I thought working with math and numbers might be fun."

"Fun?" He chuckled. "You must have *really* been a nerd."

She gasped and gave him a little shove. "If I'm a nerd, then you're a geek."

He nodded with a smile on his face. "That's fair. I guess we're a match made in heaven then, don't you think?"

Dianna stilled. This wasn't where she had anticipated this conversation going. But now that it was here, she didn't know what to say.

Tristan held up a hand. "Don't worry. I'm not expecting anything. We're just here to have fun." Then he grimaced. "Oh, and Mathew wants you to visit so you can read him a bedtime story."

It was funny. Mathew's request was all it took to make Dianna relax. That sweet little boy's face flooded her mind. Maybe it was how much she admired him for thriving in this world the way he already had. Or it could be that little voice in her head telling her that he only got this far because of the man in front of her.

If there was anyone who could accept her quirks for what they were, it would be a guy like Tristan.

"I think that sounds like a wonderful idea."

By now the majority of the guests had arrived. The refreshments were served on a large buffet table, but there were also several servers bringing out small snacks on trays. Brielle hadn't left Shane's side, and there were more than a few women who eyed her with jealousy.

The DJ put on "I'll be Home for Christmas" and Tristan held out his hand toward Dianna. "Would you like to dance with me?"

She stared at his offering. "I don't really dance."

"There's a first time for everything." He gave her a crooked grin and there was no way she'd be able to decline his offer.

Dianna placed her hand in his and let him lead her toward the dance floor. He took one hand in his and placed the other on the small of her back, pulling her gently against him. His scent wrapped around them like a warm wool blanket on a snowy morning. He smelled like peppermint and coffee, and up until this point she hadn't realized just how much she liked that combination.

She rested her chin on his shoulder, swaying to the music, her pulse thundering in her ears as if dancing to the beat.

For all her pushing against finding love, she couldn't help but let her thoughts linger on the man who held her in his arms. Had she been fighting a relationship because she truly didn't want one? Or was it more than that? Was she fighting it because she was scared that she wasn't meant to have one?

With her father's rule no longer being held over her head, she had the opportunity to make that choice without worrying how it would affect her younger sisters.

The longer she thought about it, the closer she came to one single realization.

She didn't want a relationship.

Dianna wanted a future.

A future with Tristan.

She squeezed her eyes shut, fighting the emotion that threatened to burst from inside her. It wasn't a sadness she tried to hold in. It was something different. Something foreign. There was a possibility that she could end up just as happy as every couple currently dancing tonight.

Even Brielle seemed to be enjoying herself, allowing Shane to spin her around the dance floor. Maybe her sister had finally found the person who had eluded her all these years.

Dianna grinned at the thought. All it had taken was getting set up with a man who Brielle had insisted wasn't worth it.

The music came to an end and the DJ switched the music to something more upbeat. "Rocking Around the Christmas Tree" blared through the room. Tristan still held her close, his mouth right next to her ear so his whisper only served to refresh the goosebumps that had settled down. "Would you like to go for a walk?"

She nodded, rubbing her nose with the hand she'd placed on his shoulder. Before she could pull back to look into his eyes, her focus shifted toward Brielle and she froze.

Brielle leaned against a doorjamb, her hands holding the frame behind her. Shane was incredibly close to her, his lips curled into a flirtatious smile that was only rivaled by Brielle's. He pointed up and she tilted her head, then laughed. Mistletoe hung overhead, plain as day.

Without warning, Brielle wrapped a hand firmly around Shane's neck and pulled him in for a kiss.

Dianna gasped, causing Tristan to pull back. "What?" He turned around, looking for what had startled her, but by then Brielle and Shane had slipped down the hall and disappeared.

A soft giggle bubbled up from Dianna's chest. "I think I successfully ended Brielle's insistence on remaining a bachelorette."

Tristan frowned. "What? How do you know?"

Dianna looped her arm through Tristan's arm and propelled him toward the back door. "I'm not going to jinx it."

"Come on, you can tell me." Tristan grinned. "I can keep a secret."

She laughed again. "It's not about secrets. It's the fact that Brielle has dated so many people here that it's surprising she hasn't been out with Shane before now."

Tristan looked over his shoulder. "Shane? Do you really think those two could make it work?"

Dianna shrugged. "Who knows? But I'm not going to jinx anything, so stop asking." She rested her head on his shoulder, sidling up next to him. If Dianna could find love when she didn't think it was possible, and if Brielle could find love unexpectedly, then maybe Christmas magic actually existed.

She snickered to herself. Magic wasn't real. As much as it was nice to believe in that sort of thing, the fact remained that Christmas magic was only real when people were willing to put forth the effort to make it happen. People might be guided by God to do the right thing, and it might happen a lot more during the month of December, but that's all it was.

Still, it was a nice thought.

They stepped out into the cold and wandered down the back steps. The trail they walked on would lead them near the barns, paddocks, and corrals, then toward the cabins. Their steps were slow and neither one of them spoke.

The silence should have felt strained, but for once, Dianna hadn't been more comfortable in the presence of another person. Tristan's hand tightened around hers and he pressed a kiss to the temple of her head.

"So, we're really doing this?" Dianna asked.

Tristan slowed and stopped completely. They stood in the middle of the trail, far enough from the country club that people wouldn't be able to see or hear them. The only light that shined on them was that of the moon overhead. "If that's what you want." He placed his palm on her face and brushed her cheek with his thumb. "This isn't the first time I've had these feelings about you. If it were only up to me, I'd pull you into my arms and kiss you senseless. You'd know without a shadow of a doubt how I felt about you and the extent of my interest."

"Aren't you worried that your interest in me has more to do with your son than—"

He shook his head vehemently. "Don't get me wrong, you are amazing with Mathew. I'm constantly in awe of you. But this is so much more than that. I want to see what my life could be like with you in it."

She blinked, her whole body vibrating with an energy she'd never before experienced—not with high school crushes, not with anyone. "Then why don't you?" she rasped.

"Why don't I what?"

"Kiss me."

17

———————

Tristan

Tristan didn't move. There was no way he'd heard her right. Dianna had put up so many walls; she wouldn't just drop them like that, would she? Not only had she told him it probably wouldn't be smart to start something, but it was also in the way she carried herself. He didn't know how she did it, but she could keep him at arm's length without doing or saying anything.

"You… want me to kiss you?"

She stepped closer to him, pulling his suit coat tighter around herself. Dianna tilted her face toward him. "You've been telling me that the only thing holding you back from kissing me has been me. Well, I'm not standing in your way anymore."

He exhaled, his breath coming out in white puffs.

Dianna tilted her head, her eyes narrowing. "You *do* want to kiss me, don't you?"

"Well, yeah. I just wasn't expecting—"

"For heaven's sake," she said in exasperation as she slipped her hands around his neck and pulled. His jacket slipped from her shoulders to the ground in a heap. Her lips were soft and, at the same time, blistering against the frigid air that encircled them. She kissed him tenderly, exploring his mouth with hers.

Tentatively, he held her close, telling himself she must be freezing and they could preserve their body temperatures. But deep down, he knew otherwise. They molded together, one heart and one mind, two people who cared about the same things.

If he had thought Erika was meant for him, there wasn't a doubt in his mind that he had been terribly wrong. Dianna stirred emotions within him that he hadn't felt before—certainly not with Erika.

If he could memorize one moment from his life, this would be it. Tristan's emotions boiled over, taking with them his common sense and logical mind.

Tristan came to his senses and pulled back, putting a good two feet between them. His eyes dipped to the coat and he lurched toward it. "You must be freezing. Here." He wrapped the coat around her and, once again, made sure to put enough space between them that he wouldn't be tempted to lose control like that again. His relationship with Erika had been fast, too. And up until this point he hadn't connected that it might have ended so abruptly because he hadn't realized who she really was.

It wasn't that he thought Dianna would do something so treacherous as leaving her own son. But he wasn't sure he was ready to risk everything on something so new. They should take it slow.

Dianna touched her lips with the tips of her fingers and stared at him.

He couldn't tell if she was upset or if there was something

else going through her mind. That was one more drawback to how well they knew one another. Or the lack thereof. Tristan gave her a half smile, taking in a deep breath and letting it out. "You okay?"

She nodded.

"You sure?"

Dianna pulled the jacket around her tighter and said, "I never knew a kiss could feel like that."

"Is that a good thing?" he asked. He wasn't sure if he was ready to hear her tell him that this wasn't going to work out.

Her gaze darted up to meet his and the hint of a smile touched her lips. "I've never been kissed like that before." She touched her lips again, her smile deepening. "You were my first."

Tristan couldn't help it. His eyes widened and his mouth fell open. "You've never—are you sure?"

She arched a brow. "I think I would know if I had been kissed." There was that familiar tone in her voice—the one that said she was disappointed in him, the one that said he should know better than to say such things. She'd used it on him when she'd lectured him about how he wanted Mathew to be treated. "Is that going to be a problem?"

He took a step toward her, the pressure of his chest squeezing the blood from his heart so he felt lightheaded. Cupping her face with his hand, he dipped his face lower so it came within inches of hers. "It was a pleasure to be your first." He grazed his lips against hers briefly, for good measure. "How about we go visit Mathew, then come back here for a little snack."

Dianna nodded, the smile returning to her face. "I'd like that."

There was a light snow covering on the ground from last night's snowfall. They were about halfway to the cabin when the first snowflake of the evening drifted to the earth beneath their feet. It was big and fluffy, resembling a down feather more than a snowflake. A second and third followed in its wake until the entire area was being dumped on by the clouds overhead.

Dianna laughed, tilting her face to the sky and closing her eyes. She brought up her hands and turned around. "I love the snow. Especially at Christmastime."

Tristan watched with fascination as her hair was adorned by the fluffy flakes. When she brought her focus to him, she looked like a snow queen with a crown of ice. He shivered as a fresh wave of chills assaulted him. "Come on," he held out his hand, "I'm certain Mathew is waiting on us."

The snow was still dumping, coating the entire property in a thick layer of white. By the time they made it to the cabin, they were both soaked to the bone. They stepped inside and immediately Mathew came barreling out from the hallway, his sitter on his heels.

"Miss Dianna!" He threw his arms around her, then jumped back and looked her up and down. "You're wet."

She laughed. "That's because it's snowing. Did you see it yet?"

His head whipped around to stare out the window, then he darted around a chair and collided with the window ledge to stare outside. "I can't see anything."

"Then let's get out there." Dianna glanced at Tristan. "If it's okay with your dad."

"Dad! Can we? I want to see the snow."

"Sure, bud. But we have to get your coat, gloves and boots on. I don't want you getting sick."

Mathew pouted. "But you guys were out there without—" He shot a look in Dianna's direction, and once again, Tristan's heart stuttered with shock. It was almost like he wasn't looking at his son. The boy before him had been taken over by another entity. One who argued less often. Mathew snapped his mouth shut. "Okay." He took off toward his room and returned with a pair of snow boots, a hat, and gloves.

Tristan had never seen Mathew dress so quickly. They were out the door in what felt like mere seconds. Mathew flew to the snow quickly piling up in the small yard. The only one who stayed behind to watch inside was the babysitter.

Mathew crouched down and gathered a snowball in his gloved hands. Then he waddled with his legs apart, rolling it until it came to his knees. Excitedly, he gestured toward the ball. "Miss Dianna, come make a snowman with me! Please?"

"Oh, I don't think Miss Dianna can come out into the yard, bud. She's not wearing the right kind of shoes." Tristan offered Dianna a reassuring smile. He didn't expect her to catch her death either.

Dianna glanced from Mathew to Tristan. "I saw an old pair of cowboy boots by the front door. I'll try those on."

"I don't think those are for... wearing."

She was already inside and pulling on a pair of worn, cracked cowboy boots that were probably only there for decoration. When she didn't return immediately outside, Tristan moved toward the door. But then it shut and Dianna was out, wearing the sitter's coat. She beamed at Mathew. "See? I'm all ready now."

Dianna shoveled her way through the quickly growing snowfall and made her own ball with her bare hands. She rolled it until it was an appropriate size and then placed it unceremoniously on the ball Mathew had made.

"Your turn, Dad!"

Both Mathew and Dianna turned toward him expectantly. Already he could tell he wouldn't be able to get out of this one. If Dianna was willing and able to put on some stranger's boots, then he could join in on the fun. Memories like these would be the building blocks for Mathew's childhood.

He threw his hands in the air and laughed. "Oh, alright." A few minutes turned into a half hour, and three snowmen later, they stood back and admired their work. The snow still continued to dump around them, but no one seemed to care. Mathew hugged Tristan around the legs and he rubbed the top of his son's head, displacing the snow that had accumulated there.

"Dad?"

"Yeah?"

"I'm cold. We should go inside."

Tristan chuckled. "I think you're right." They headed inside and the babysitter sat up from where she was looking at her phone on the couch. "Mr. Wood? My parents said the roads are getting pretty bad. They want me to head home if that's okay."

"Of course." Tristan removed his soaking coat. "Thank you for coming." He pulled out his wallet and paid her, then walked her to the door. After she had safely gotten to her car, he returned inside to find Mathew in a fresh pair of pajamas sitting in front of the fire. Dianna had changed too.

The familiar t-shirt and flannel pajama pants practically drowned her. Tristan couldn't move from his place as he stared at the scene before him. Dianna and Mathew sat on the floor, reading a copy of *The Night Before Christmas*. Their decorated tree and the flames from the fire were the only sources of light in the room.

Peace.

That's what this feeling was.

Dianna fit in his life like the missing piece of a puzzle. She was the part of him that he hadn't realized he'd lost. And it appeared that Mathew could sense it too. He snuggled up in her lap, turning the pages as she read them.

Tristan didn't dare move closer for fear that the scene before him would disappear like a mirage in the desert.

But his clothes hung heavy and wet on his shoulders, and the fire looked so inviting. He kicked off his shoes as quietly as he could, then slipped past them to his room. Tristan found an additional pair of pajamas and grabbed the crocheted blanket from a rocking chair that sat in the corner.

When he arrived back in the living room, Mathew was still in Dianna's lap, but this time she was reading to him from that book on horse breeds. His son's eyes drooped and he climbed out of her lap to lay on the floor, resting his head where he'd just vacated. She ran her fingers through his hair almost absently as she continued to read. "The average height of a Clydesdale will usually exceed eighteen hands. And most will be around six feet in length. It is not uncommon for this breed to weigh more than one ton." Her eyes flicked up to meet Tristan's and she smiled before she continued. "The hair around their hooves is called feathering. This trait is believed to have evolved naturally and is one of the strongest in the Clydesdale horse breed."

Tristan moved quietly behind her and draped the Afghan around her shoulders before he took a seat on the couch. Dianna's voice was soothing and melodic, and it was easy for him to sit back and just enjoy her narration.

Mathew's eyes drooped closed and he yawned. Before Dianna finished reading about Clydesdales, Mathew had lost consciousness. Soft snores hummed through his son's nose. Dianna carefully closed the book and put it aside.

"Thank you," Tristan whispered.

She glanced at him, still tracing her fingers through Mathew's hair. "For what?"

"For *this*. For playing in the snow even though you weren't dressed for it. For being there for him." It was all so much.

Perhaps it was *too* much. He couldn't help but feel like he was being ridiculous as his feelings for her continued to grow more serious. "I don't think we've ever had so much fun during a snowfall as we did tonight."

"I'm sure you've made plenty of wonderful memories," she said quietly. She shifted, taking care to adjust her position without waking Mathew. "I don't remember much of my mother before she got sick and passed, but I do remember the holidays. She was always willing to do whatever it took to make Christmas special." Dianna offered him a pained smile. "I don't think she could ever tell us 'no.' Drove my dad completely crazy."

"I'm so sorry."

She shook her head. "I was pretty young. Probably close to Mathew's age, actually. I *do* miss her—what I can remember, anyway—but it's been so long..." She lifted tear-filled eyes. "You ever get the feeling that there's more out there?" Her face flushed bright red. "I'm a very logical person." She paused and chuckled. "As you might have noticed. But sometimes..." She got a far-off look in her eyes. "Sometimes I feel like she might be watching me—helping me get through parts of my life that I find more difficult than others." She sighed, her focus shifting to Mathew. "I don't know. Maybe that's crazy."

"I don't think it's crazy at all." He waited until she looked at him. "I'm of the opinion that there are far too many miracles for there *not* to be something bigger out there. I guess that's why I believe in the Good Lord above. I'd like to think that we're here for a reason, and one day we'll be rewarded for our efforts."

The only sound reaching him was the crackle of the fire behind her. Shadows danced on the walls as the flames flickered. Tristan shifted his focus to his son, then got to his feet. "I'll put him down and then I can walk you back to the club. I'm sure Shane would be happy to drive you home."

She glanced toward the window. "I wouldn't want him to have to leave his guests." Dianna seemed to hesitate before setting her gaze on him. "Would it be okay if I crashed on the couch tonight and we can evaluate the roads in the morning?"

"Absolutely." The words burst from inside him before he had a chance to rein in his enthusiasm. Her idea was likely better anyway. Trying to get back to the club after the dumping that occurred over the last hour didn't look at all appealing, especially considering they were finally warm and dry, save for their hair. Plus he wouldn't want Mathew to wake up and him not be there. Even if it was only for a few minutes. Tristan scooped Mathew into his arms and smiled at her. "I'll be right back."

He moved toward the bedroom and Mathew let out a heavy sigh. "Daddy?"

"Yeah, kiddo?"

"I really like Miss Dianna."

"Me too, bud."

"Can she be my new mom?"

Tristan's chest tightened. His stomach rolled and knotted. "We've talked about this, buddy. It's not as easy as that."

"But I asked Santa for a new mom."

Tristan carefully placed Mathew on his bed in the small room. Pain sliced through his heart, splintering it with each breath he took. "When did you do that?"

"I wrote him a letter when we got here and gave it to that nice man."

Tristan's brows furrowed. "Do you mean Shane?"

Mathew yawned and rolled over. "Miss Dianna would be the perfect mom."

He had no argument there. He just couldn't guarantee such a thing was possible. Tristan sat on the edge of the bed and ran a hand over his son's head before kissing his damp hair. "Good-night, buddy." He didn't know how long he stayed there, staring at his boy, but when his thoughts cleared, he eased off the bed and quietly closed the bedroom door.

Upon entering the living room, he found Dianna curled up on the couch, the knit blanket covering her body. Her eyes were closed and her breathing was heavy. After the strain she'd put on her body while playing in the snow in less-than-ideal clothing, it wasn't a surprise she had fallen asleep so easily.

Tristan watched her for a moment, doing his best not to imagine a future with her the way Mathew had suggested. Neither one of them could afford another broken heart right now. He moved to the edge of the couch and pressed a soft kiss to her cheek, growing still when she let out a soft sigh. Thankfully, Dianna didn't stir any more than that. He gathered another heavier blanket and draped it over her sleeping form, then put out the fire and returned to his room.

18

———————

Dianna

Dianna's nose itched and she scrunched it up.

Something light grazed it. She sniffled, then rubbed it.

"Dad, she's waking up."

"Mathew, I told you to leave her alone."

"But she's waking up."

Her eyes fluttered open and she gasped, finding Mathew's bright blue eyes staring at her.

"You slept a long time," Mathew said.

Dianna blinked a few times. It was dimmer than she would have expected it to be for a Saturday morning. Then again, kids like Mathew didn't typically sleep in. She yawned and stretched her arms over her head just as Tristan came into view with a steaming mug.

He held it out and offered her an apologetic smile. "Good morning."

She sat up and accepted the cup. Her fingers curled around the warm ceramic and she breathed in the scent of peppermint tea. That's why he smelled like that.

Mathew hopped up onto the couch beside her and held out her cell. "Your phone keeps buzzing."

Her eyes flew wide and she nearly dropped her drink in her lap. "Oh my gosh. I forgot about Brielle."

Tristan's brows furrowed. "I let Shane know that you were staying here for the night."

She gasped, her eyes darting to Mathew then back to Tristan. The implication of what he'd just said could have meant anything depending on how he'd phrased it to his friend. "You didn't tell him that we..." She glanced at Mathew again; the words *slept together* were on the tip of her tongue, but she knew better than to assume that. Tristan didn't seem like the type to brag about his exploits with women.

Tristan stared at her, his face a mask of confusion. He couldn't possibly be unaware of what he might have started, could he?

Mathew reached for a book from the coffee table. "Will you read to me?"

Tristan sighed. "Hey, bud? How about you get breakfast first. Then you can see if Dianna is ready to read to you."

"Okay." Mathew climbed off the couch and headed for the kitchen.

"In answer to your concern. No, I didn't make it sound like anything sordid was occurring, though I don't think Shane would believe it if I had."

She nearly asked him why he would assume such a thing, but he answered for her before she could.

"This place is only so big and there's a seven-year-old boy living here. Not to mention, I heard plenty about your family dynamics. I wouldn't dare press you into anything of that nature."

Heat bloomed in her face, filling her cheeks, racing down her neck, and settling in her stomach. Dianna looked away and brought her mug to her lips to take a sip of the scalding liquid that probably would have felt hotter if her face wasn't already burning up with embarrassment. "Thank you," she whispered.

"That being said, Mathew is right. Your phone has been very active this morning, so I would suggest calling whoever it is that is clearly worried about you to assure them of your well-being."

There was no way this blush would leave her face any time soon. She should have known better than to think her absence would go unnoticed.

Tristan glanced toward the kitchen and then brought his steady gaze back to her. He tucked her hair behind an ear and gave her a quick, adrenaline-inducing kiss. "You don't know how much I wanted to do that since I woke up this morning," he said softly.

Her gaze followed him as he stood and headed for the kitchen.

"Okay, bud. What's for breakfast?"

"I want what Dianna's having."

"You don't like peppermint tea."

"No. I mean I want what she wants. Miss Dianna?"

"Yeah, bud?" She didn't dare turn around. She could feel Tristan's gaze drilling into her and she wasn't quite ready to scrutinize the next step their relationship had taken yet.

"What do you want for breakfast?"

"What is your dad going to make?"

Mathew sighed. Tristan chuckled and moved around in the kitchen.

"What are you making, Dad?"

"How about pancakes?" Tristan offered.

"I don't want pancakes."

Dianna's mug hid her grin as she got to her feet and headed toward the kitchen. "Mmm. Pancakes sound yummy. But only if I get to eat mine with honey instead of syrup."

Mathew made a face, and it took everything in her power not to laugh. He wasn't thrilled with that idea. "I want pancakes. But I still want syrup."

"Sounds like a plan." Tristan moved toward the fridge, but not before another intense gaze passed between them.

For a few moments, she took in the scene before her in the kitchen. All of this was just surreal. One second she was on a date, sharing her first kiss with the guy, and the next she was woken up by his son.

Dianna gripped the mug a little tighter, attempting to quell the rapid beats of her heart. This was okay. Everything would be okay. She'd been here multiple times before. Nothing was amiss.

But something didn't feel right.

Too fast.

Too new.

She placed her mug on the coffee table. "Actually, I'm gonna go."

"Right now?" Tristan deposited the pan he was holding on the stove.

Mathew stared at her with confusion.

Dianna nodded. "I'm sure I can get a ride from someone. If I can't, I'll borrow a horse."

"That's ridiculous. I can take you." Tristan moved over to where his coat hung on a coat rack and slipped his arms into the sleeves. "Mathew, get your boots."

"*No.*" She said it too quickly, but as she did, she closed her eyes and held up her hand. When she opened them, Tristan was in front of her, holding her upper arms.

"Hey. It's okay. I can take you," he said.

She shook her head. "It's not that. I just—I need to clear my head—alone." Her gaze darted to Mathew and her heart melted. When she brought her focus back to Tristan, she gave him her best reassuring smile. "Everything is fine. I'm fine. Just let me catch my breath for a bit, okay?"

He frowned. "But—"

"Dad."

They both turned to Mathew.

"Remember when I need a break sometimes?"

Goosebumps erupted on her arms and she rubbed at them furiously. This kid, who wasn't even eight years old, knew exactly what she was going through. It might only be a temporary understanding, but there it was.

Tristan swung his focus back to Dianna and his hands dropped. "Sure. Okay." He rubbed the back of his neck, putting some distance between them. "Would you like to come by tonight for dinner? With all of us?"

She swallowed hard, not sure if her anxiety attack would be settled by then. But then one more look at Mathew and it was like that small innocent face could ground her, reminding her she could do hard things. Dianna nodded. "How about we do dinner and decorate some Christmas cookies."

Mathew's face brightened and he nodded vigorously. "Can we, Dad?"

"Of course, bud. How about you go brush your teeth while I walk Dianna to the club."

Without complaint, Mathew darted toward the bathroom.

Tristan didn't close in on her, something she was grateful for. Instead, he tilted his head and narrowed his eyes. "You okay? I didn't overdo anything, did I?"

"What? No. Of course not. It's totally all me." She rubbed her arms again. "Sometimes I put myself in these situations and don't realize how they're going to affect me. I'm fine. *We're* fine. Promise."

A line formed between his brows.

She moved forward and placed her hand against his cheek, fighting against her instincts to run and find shelter. "Last night was the most fun I've had in a long time. I'm glad we did it."

He covered her hand with his own, then turned his face and kissed the inside of her palm. "Good. Me too."

Chills raced from where he kissed her down her arm and along her spine, causing a flurry of sensations.

"You're certain you don't want me to take you home? It's not that far."

Dianna nodded. "I'll call one of my sisters. You cook some breakfast for Mathew, and I'll see you later tonight." She shifted to head toward the door, thinking how nice one more kiss would be. But she knew better. She needed to regain control of the situation the best way she knew how and that was by taking some time to herself.

And possibly distracting her racing thoughts by cornering Brielle and finding out how last night went for her.

GRACE'S TRUCK pulled up in front of the club and she shifted in her seat as she rolled down her window. She gave Dianna an incredulous look. "Do you *know* how much trouble you're in?"

Dianna grimaced, darting toward the truck and climbing inside. "Is Dad mad?"

Her sister gave her a blank look. "Dad? I don't think he's realized you're not home. No, it's Bri. She's livid."

"Brielle's mad? What happened?"

"I don't know, but when she found out you called me to pick you up, she started stomping around the kitchen and slamming cabinets. Dad went to town early this morning, so thankfully she didn't wake him up."

"I still don't get why *she'd* be mad."

Grace's focus swept over Dianna's outfit and a small frown marred her features. She didn't say anything, but Dianna could tell she was curious as to what exactly had happened.

Dianna sighed. "I assure you, anything you're concocting in your head is going to be ten times worse than what really happened."

"What *did* happen? No one could get ahold of you last night, and with the snow..." She peeked at her sister once more before driving out of the parking lot. "We were worried, Dianna."

Guilt washed over her. She hadn't thought about how worried everyone would be.

Dianna glanced at Grace and mumbled, "I'm sorry."

"You should be. You can't just disappear like that without a word. None of us know this guy. The only saving grace was that Brielle was on a date with your boss and *Shane* seems to know Tristan well enough to put us all at ease."

Shoulders slumped, the exhilaration from the night before had all but dissipated. There would be no talking about the amazing experience she had. Everything was overshadowed by her poor choices.

She sat in silence, mentally preparing herself to be lectured by Brielle, too. Though that didn't seem all that fair. Brielle was the queen of disappearing acts around here. She could pick out a guy, spend the whole evening with him and come home after everyone was asleep without caring a lick about what her sisters thought.

The more Dianna thought about it, the more disgruntled she became. By the time she got to her room, she'd slammed three doors and stomped every step she could. Why did the rules get to be different for Brielle and not for her? She should be able to do what she wanted without the threat of her sisters putting her into a corner and telling her she was a bad person.

She yanked open the door to her bedroom, then let out a surprised scream. "Brielle! What are you doing in here?!"

Brielle sat on Dianna's bed, her ankles crossed and a book open on her lap. She didn't even react.

"*Brielle.*"

Her sister looked up from the book and snapped it shut. "I don't even know what you like so much about these books."

"I asked you a question."

She put the book aside and sat up straighter. "Well, that's ironic. I have a question for you too."

Dianna sighed. "Fine. Just lay it on me. Tell me how terrible I am for making you worry and—"

"Did you kiss him?"

Her head snapped up, gaping at Brielle. "What?"

Brielle scooted to the edge of the bed, a smile filling her face. "You kissed him, didn't you?"

"I—well, yeah—but—"

"Okay. So tell me the truth. Are you an item? Or are you taking it slow? Because I could see it go either way." Her eyes narrowed. "Or are you following in my footsteps and you're not going to let it go any further?"

"Wait, so you're not upset? But Grace said you were slamming cupboards and stomping around this morning."

Brielle tilted her head. "Was I? Oh yeah. That's probably because Shane sent me a message this morning thanking me for a wonderful night."

"And that made you *mad*?"

"Not *that*. The stuff that came after it. He said he didn't want to start anything serious."

Wait a minute. Brielle was upset that a guy *didn't* want anything serious? Her head ached and she shook her head. "I don't get it."

"Shane said he had a great night but that we were too different, and he wished me luck."

"He *said* that?" Even to Dianna that sounded harsh.

"Right? I mean, I agree with him. There's no way *I* would want to be locked into a relationship with him. Do you see me being the doting wife? Ha! In his dreams."

Dianna shuffled across the room and sat on the edge of her bed. "Okay, so you're *not* upset."

Brielle groaned. "Why aren't you getting this? He's not allowed to break up with me."

"But you weren't together in the first place."

"That's beside the point. No one breaks up with me because I'm the one who breaks up with them." She waved her hand through the air. "None of that matters because I'm in here to figure out what's going on with you and your date. You didn't come home. That took guts. What would you have done if Dad caught you?"

Dianna sighed. "I don't know what I'm doing."

"Do you like him?"

"Of course I do."

Brielle scooted beside her and nudged her shoulder. "Do you want to see him again?"

"I'm going to see him tonight."

"Then what's the problem?"

Dianna stared at her hands. "I'm scared."

"Oh. Well, that's normal."

A huff burst from her chest. "How would you know? You've never had a long relationship." The room dropped a few degrees in temperature and Dianna suddenly realized how that probably sounded. "I didn't mean—"

"No. You're right. I haven't risked anything. But let me tell you something. The things you want the most are the hardest to get and the most worth the effort. If you like this guy, if you like his kid, and you're happy when you're with them, then take a chance." She bumped Dianna's shoulder with her own. "And I'll stand with you one hundred percent of the way. Just do me one favor."

"What's that?" Dianna croaked, emotion in her throat.

"Please don't set me up with any more guys—especially Shane."

Dianna let out a tight laugh and Brielle gave her a side hug. She hadn't expected it, but Brielle had managed to put everything into such simple terms that helped her realize she was on the right path.

19

———————

Tristan

At one moment Tristan felt elated, overjoyed that the other night had gone so well. It may be unwise, but there were moments when he could see himself and Dianna together with Mathew as a family.

And then the doubt crept in. He didn't know what her reaction was this morning. She'd seemed a little off. At first he thought it might have to do with waking up in a strange place, confronted by Mathew. But it was more than that.

Mathew had figured it out. That much was clear.

For some reason he could tell that she was nervous and she needed a break.

There was this ghost of a thought in the back of his mind. It hovered there, and he couldn't quite see the whole picture. Tristan knew when he finally did, he'd be able to better understand what made Dianna tick.

Well, there was plenty of time for that.

Tristan spent the afternoon outside with Mathew, letting him play in the snow on their day off. While his son made snow angels and threw snowballs, Tristan's thoughts drifted to the way it felt to hold Dianna in his arms.

It had been perfect.

More than perfect; it just felt right.

He had two options at this point in time. He could ruin his day by worrying about Dianna and what she might be going through, or he could trust her and enjoy the time he had with Mathew until she came back.

"Dad!" Mathew hurried over. "Did you see how far I threw that snowball?"

Tristan smiled. "Sure did, kiddo."

"Do you think Miss Dianna will play with me outside when she comes?"

"Probably not unless you want to skip decorating cookies."

Mathew's eyes widened and he shook his head. "No. I want to decorate cookies."

Tristan looked down at his watch. "It's getting pretty late. How about we head inside and I'll start making dinner."

"Can we have mac and cheese?"

"'Fraid not. I think Miss Dianna would prefer eating something different."

Mathew pouted. "But I don't want something else."

"I know. Remember when we had that talk about making sure our guests feel welcome?"

"Yeah," Mathew mumbled.

"Well, what do you think Miss Dianna would want?" Tristan could sense Mathew's frustration bubbling. He'd be really narrow on his choice of food lately. The kid could eat macaroni and cheese for a whole month straight and not get tired of it.

"Mac and cheese."

Tristan chuckled. "Tell you what, I'll make some mac and cheese for you just this once, and if Miss Dianna wants to eat it with her dinner, she can make that decision."

Mathew's whole body relaxed and he smiled. "She will. I know it."

"Well, how about you help me come up with something that she might like to eat *with* it."

His son cocked his head and his eyes drifted to something in the distance. "I know! How about a cheese quesadilla?

Tristan grimaced. "How about steak?"

Mathew wrinkled his nose. "Yuck."

Tristan sighed. "Eventually, you're going to have to try something new."

He clamped his mouth shut and shook his head.

Tristan ruffled his hair, then motioned toward the cabin. "Come on. Let's get you warm. Maybe you could draw a picture for Dianna. I bet she'd like that."

A SOFT KNOCK at the door tore Tristan's gaze from the skillet he was cooking at. "Mathew! Will you get the door?"

Mathew jumped off the couch and hustled to the door. He pulled open the door and disappeared as he launched himself outside.

He heard Dianna's laughter before he saw her. She waddled into the cabin, with Mathew attached as he hugged her tight around the middle. "Okay, buddy. Let's get in far enough that we can shut the door before all the cold air gets in."

Mathew darted toward the couch.

Dianna glanced in Tristan's direction. She smiled at him, tucking a strand of hair behind her ear. "Hey," she said timidly.

"Hey." His stomach swirled and he itched to go running

toward her much like his child had. But instead, he stayed back. After this morning, he didn't want to do anything to cause her any anxiety. He didn't have to wait long.

She wandered over toward him, a small smile on her lips. She leaned against the counter, her elbows resting on the vinyl countertop, and she tilted her head. "Smells good."

He beamed. "How do you like your steak?"

"Medium."

Tristan checked on the macaroni. "Wouldn't be dinner without this. You don't have to have any if you don't want—"

Dianna laughed. "I'm not *that* picky." The humor in her gaze dissipated, and his nerves shot out of control. But before he could say anything, she spoke. "About this morning."

This was it. Here was the moment he'd been dreading since he started cooking. Either she wasn't interested or she wasn't ready to deal with the baggage he had. He should tell her he was okay with waiting. He could be patient. But that sounded like a lot. Telling her that would only scare her off.

Dianna traced her finger along the designs on the counter and her gaze dropped.

"Look, I get it—" he started.

"I just wanted to apologize."

Their gazes met and they smiled. He flipped his steak then moved closer to her, touching her arm briefly. "You don't have to apologize."

"Oh, I know."

That wasn't the reaction he'd expected.

She let out a shy laugh. "I didn't do anything wrong. But I wanted to apologize because I don't want you to get the wrong idea."

His brows furrowed. He didn't like where this was going.

"This morning I wasn't prepared to deal with everything. I have this—*thing*—about needing to analyze everything from every angle before I can even begin to deal with it." She finally looked up at him. "I was never officially diagnosed, but I have some autistic characteristics."

Tristan didn't move. This wasn't as big of a reveal as she probably thought it was. And it didn't bother him in the slightest. He just didn't want her running off in case he didn't respond in the way she was hoping he would.

She stared at him as if she were just as frozen as he was. "Well?" she said.

"Well, what?"

"Aren't you going to say something?"

"Do you want me to say something?"

She let out a frustrated sigh. "I just told you that I have a condition that makes me see the world differently, and it's obviously going to continue affecting any relationship I will have with someone. If you can't bother—"

"Dianna," he said in a low voice, moving closer. "If you're expecting me to make excuses and tell you I'm no longer interested, you need to change that thought immediately."

Her mouth shut and her eyes widened.

He gave her a crooked grin, then placed his palm against her cheek. If only she knew how amazing she was. "The way I see it, no one is exactly the same, right? No one's relationship is typical by definition. We would both have to learn how to deal with each other's quirks."

A ghost of a smile touched her lips. "Really?"

"Really."

She took in a deep breath and let it out. "I know I'm not an easy person to—"

"Hey," he whispered. "No one is. People don't fall in love and stay together because it's easy. They stay together because it's worth it."

Her expression faltered.

And his heart stumbled.

What had he said that caused her to react that way? He went over the words in his head but couldn't figure out what might have triggered her current concerned expression. "What did I say?"

"You said love."

"Yeah?"

Dianna didn't move away from him. That was one good sign. But she did break eye contact. "Are you saying you're falling in love?"

He could say no. But deep down he knew that was a lie, and he wasn't about to get caught in something like that. The truth of the matter was that his feelings were stronger than he'd expected them to be. Maybe he was a fool for allowing his heart to go rogue. Or maybe his instincts were right on. Only time would tell, and he wasn't willing to risk losing the possibility of finding someone as perfect as Dianna. He took a moment to study her, making sure he'd be able to see even the slightest change in her demeanor. "Yes."

He'd always thought that the phrase "time stood still" was a ridiculous analogy. How could time stop? There were always other things going on. Never would there be complete silence.

But that is *exactly* what happened. He couldn't hear his pulse roaring in his ears. He didn't feel his heart beating wildly in his chest. She didn't move. Everything around him faded away as he waited for her response.

Then she blinked. That was the first indication that he hadn't taken them through some kind of wormhole.

"Is that okay?" he asked, his voice catching.

"Your steak. You should probably flip it over."

The sizzling on the stove reached his ears before the smell of his charred steak. He spun around and flipped his steak over, then chuckled when he met her shocked expression. "You didn't answer me."

"What?" She blinked again.

Tristan let out a groan. "You're not going to make me ask again, are you?"

She looked away and her cheeks filled with a pastel pink color before she met his gaze again. For a minute he thought she still wasn't going to respond. She worried her lower lip, then nodded. "I think I'm okay with it."

A grin stole over his face once more. "I think I'm okay with it, too."

The skillet popped and sizzled and his eyes widened as he turned comically toward the food. He'd be lucky if their dinner didn't end up in the trash for being too burnt to consume.

Dianna moved closer, leaning against the fridge as he cooked. She glanced over to Mathew and lowered her voice. "How do you think he's going to handle it?"

Tristan glanced over his shoulder and shrugged. "Remember when he drew that picture of us?" He chuckled as he put together that memory with what had occurred last night and then this morning. "I think he's going to be very excited."

Her gaze darted over to Mathew again. It was small, like the flutter of dragonfly wings, but he noticed something shift in her countenance. She was pleased with the idea of Mathew caring enough to want her in his life. When her eyes cut to Tristan's once more, she moved closer. He nearly didn't hear her whisper. "You don't think he's going to think I'm replacing his mom, do you?"

Tristan was almost certain that Mathew thought that. Granted, he didn't know much about his mother as it was. He would only be able to recognize her due to the handful of pictures Tristan still had lying around.

The problem with telling Dianna any of this was that this

could be the one thing that scared her off again. The relationship was still too fresh for any talk of marriage. It was natural for her to worry about him though. He rubbed the back of his neck and focused on the food. "I think Mathew likes you well enough that he's not going to be thinking about that all too much. You're still Miss Dianna."

She seemed to accept that explanation. "Do you mind if I go over there and draw with him while you finish up here?"

"Go for it. The food will be done in a little bit. But I'm sure he'd love to have the extra attention. In fact, you probably spoil him more than you realize."

Dianna snickered. "Well, it's Christmas. He deserves to be spoiled." She leaned up on her toes and wrapped her arms around his neck before she placed a firm kiss on his lips. Her touch sparked the fire inside him once again. He didn't have much of an opportunity to react to her. And when she released him to wander across the room, his eyes followed her with awe.

No matter how he spun it, she was exactly what he'd been praying for. If he had put all his preferences on a list, he wouldn't have been able to find a more perfect option. It was funny how things like that worked out just when he needed them to.

Once the food was done, they shared their meal. Clean-up was quick, mostly because Mathew wanted to get right to Christmas cookie decorating. Dianna taught them how to mix the dough just right so it was the best consistency for soft cookies. Then, while they cooled, she prepared the frosting.

Mathew had a blast decorating but lost steam around the twelfth cookie. It was getting late and his mood had shifted to something stereotypically ornery. He got frustrated with how the gingerbread man was turning out and ended up throwing the butterknife on the floor.

Dianna jumped, but Tristan moved in quickly. "Hey, bud.

It's getting late and we had an early morning. How about I tuck you in." He reached for Mathew's hand, but his son tore it away from him.

"No! I'm not tired."

Tristan and Dianna exchanged glances and she moved closer. "Mathew, the cookies will be here in the morning. You can decorate some more then."

Mathew glowered at her. "I don't *want* to go to bed."

"Don't you think you'd feel better if you got some extra sleep? I know we don't have a ride scheduled for Sunday, but we could probably still head out early if you'd like." Dianna was truly the level-headed one.

When Mathew's shoulders relaxed and he climbed down from the chair where he sat, it almost made Tristan wonder what he'd done up until this point with his son. Dianna was showing him up. Would it get to a point where she might even think he wasn't capable of controlling Mathew?

That was ridiculous.

Once again Tristan was letting his concerns and frustrations get the better of him. Dianna had no reason to think that Tristan was anything other than a good parent. Granted, she didn't have any reason to think he was great either.

He shoved those disparaging thoughts aside. He couldn't afford to get into his own head about any of this. Mathew needed to get ready for bed, and Dianna was still putting cookies into the oven.

Tristan mouthed the words "thank you" to her, then guided Mathew toward the bedroom to get changed into his pajamas.

Dating his ex had been so much simpler back before he had a child. Back then, it felt like he was able to wander through wildflowers without a care in the world. Starting a relationship now felt like he was walking through that same field, but now it was riddled with landmines. One wrong step could ruin not only his life, but also that of his son and Dianna's.

It would be best to get a lot of these concerns out in the open and soon, but again, that felt like a very bad idea. He couldn't be selfish here. He had to let things happen at a pace that Dianna was comfortable with. Otherwise, he could risk losing her.

20

———————

Dianna

 ianna placed another cookie sheet in the oven and brushed some stray strands of hair from her forehead with the back of her hand. She still couldn't believe she'd blurted the information about her condition. It wasn't something she even spoke of freely with her family. It was something that she'd stumbled upon on her own and kept to herself.

In fact, she didn't even know if her family was aware that she had several of the characteristics of a person with Autism. She wouldn't be surprised if they brushed it off either. That's what a lot of people seemed to do.

From her experience, a neurotypical person usually viewed someone like her as a person with bad manners. She was blunt and could say things that hurt others—however unintentional. She'd learned from an early age how to keep her thoughts to herself, though public figures were praised for their ability to tell things how it was.

Somehow Tristan was different.

She'd been worried early on with all his talk about needing to help Mathew become something he wasn't. The way he wanted Mathew to conform to everything society wanted him to be.

However, lately Tristan had seemed to come to understand that Mathew didn't need to conform in the way he wanted him to. Were there certain expectations that everyone needed to follow as a society? Of course. Did that mean that Mathew needed to *constantly* seek approval from everyone? No. He needed to learn how to advocate for himself, and he needed to understand when there was a time when speaking was important and a time when he could decline to comment.

Those were the biggest issues she noticed with him besides his inability to cope when things went south for him.

She glanced up when Tristan materialized back in the kitchen. He didn't look nearly as happy and content as he had earlier. Though she wasn't as great at reading expressions as she wished she was. The tension in the room had elevated when Mathew got past the point of patience.

It got her thinking that maybe Tristan viewed those situations like they were threats—like he needed to contain whatever explosion was about to take place.

Tristan didn't say anything as he moved closer to her, step-by-step. He stopped about a foot before her and reached for her hands.

It was a gesture that she'd both loved and dreaded before she'd found herself in this relationship. Unnecessary touching was a pet peeve of hers. Now, she found she enjoyed any way he showed his affection.

Tristan rubbed his thumbs over the backs of her hands. "I don't think I'll ever get to be as good as you are with him." His voice sounded almost sad—like if he were an instrument, he was speaking in a minor chord.

Her brows creased. "It's not a competition."

A shadow passed over his expression. "No, it's not. But…"

"But what?" She tilted her head, giving her better access to view his face. "Are you upset I stepped in?"

"Of course not. I love that you're so good with him. And now that I know why, it just makes me feel…" He shrugged. "You know what? It doesn't matter. I'm glad you were able to diffuse the situation before he had a meltdown."

"It just takes a different approach. You'll get better at it."

"I've been at it for seven years," he said without humor. "How much longer do I have to practice before I start seeing results?" Tristan dropped her hands and smiled at her. His eyes didn't match the way the corners of his mouth quirked up. She'd seen that look before with her sisters but had never really understood what it meant until now. He was trying to put on a brave face even though he didn't feel like doing so. She could only remember a handful of moments when she'd had to do the same, and it had been incredibly difficult.

She should probably say something to comfort him. But the words escaped her. There was nothing she could tell him that would make him feel better other than what she'd already said. The oven dinged, offering her an excuse not to fumble over any wrong words she might say to ruin the evening.

When she pulled the cookies from the oven, she turned around to find him over by Mathew's artwork. He picked up a piece of paper and stared at it with a pointed focus. His eyes flitted to her, then back to the paper.

She grabbed her spatula and began removing the cookies from the tray. Whatever Mathew had drawn must have been…

Her head snapped up and heat burst from her chest up

onto her face like a volcano. She'd been drawing before dinner. And she'd left her sketch on the table.

Tristan's eyes locked onto her and he flipped the paper around, showing it to her. "I didn't realize you could draw this well." She'd only managed to block in his face before she completed his eyes. But just the pair of eyes was enough for him to know exactly what she'd been drawing.

Her blush deepened and she let the spatula clatter to the stovetop before she darted around the island and to his side. She grabbed the drawing and took a look at it. "It's not even that good."

He attempted to reach for it, but she spun away from him. Tristan laughed. "You can't be serious."

She shook her head. "Okay, well, it's not done."

"But it's me, right?" He laughed again, attempting to grab the picture.

Dianna stepped backward. "You weren't meant to see it."

"Why not? It's amazing." His features sobered. "Really, Dianna. You're very good. Have you ever considered doing it professionally?"

She clutched the paper tighter. "You don't think I should keep working for Shane?"

He chuckled and shook his head. "I'm beginning to see what you mean when you say you look at things differently. I think you could do both." Tristan slipped his arms around her waist and pulled her closer. His touch immediately melted the stiffness from her body. He dipped his head closer to her ear, his whisper sending goosebumps up and down her arms. "Have I told you that I think you're amazing?" He pressed a kiss to the sensitive area beneath her ear.

Dianna sucked in sharply and the paper slipped from her fingers. The fluttering in her chest seemed to be speaking its own language—one she couldn't understand. These flutters, the goosebumps, and every tantalizing thought that tripped through her mind only fed the thrill she experienced.

Tristan's warm breath was far more scintillating than she expected. Her whole body reacted to it, from her lightheadedness to her quaking knees. He brushed gentle kisses along her jawline before finding her lips. This kiss was sweeter than the first, a way for them to explore this new-found feeling they shared.

For the first time, she allowed herself to give in—to step outside of the box she had built around herself. It had taken more effort than she'd expected, chipping away the walls that protected her heart. It wasn't as hard as she thought it would be. But then again, being with Tristan felt a lot easier than she expected.

Dianna broke off their kiss, her heart hammering more than it should. She wrapped her arms around his neck and rested her cheek against his shoulder. It was suddenly making a lot more sense why her sisters were so happy in their relationships. What had appeared to be something not worth any amount of risk, was now something she valued.

Beneath her cheek, she could feel the quick thudding of Tristan's heart as it beat in time with hers. Was this experience something that would continue even after they got married?

Marriage.

Only a week ago, that thought would have made her laugh.

Now it sent fresh, excited tremors through her body.

But that excitement quickly waned, and she hid her frown into his shoulder. She really shouldn't be thinking about something so serious. They weren't from the same town. She couldn't assume that Tristan would want to stay here after the holiday. And to even consider the possibility that he would expect her to move to the city caused new waves of anxiety.

She'd never left Copper Creek. This was her home and the only place where she fit.

Tristan moved to take a step back, but she clung to him with a firmer grip. His arms moved around her, holding her steady. "You okay?"

She nodded into his shoulder. He was too perceptive. He'd know something was wrong if she didn't push past her darker thoughts. Though she wasn't ready, she released him and quickly turned toward the cookies. "I'm going to pack these up and put them in a container. Mathew can decorate them tomorrow."

"I'm sure he'll love that."

Tristan shifted behind her. When she chanced a glance over to him, she found him scooping up the paper she'd dropped. It wouldn't do any good to try to get it back. He grinned at her.

"I might have to commission you to draw one of Mathew."

"I haven't even finished that one."

He placed the paper on the coffee table. "I don't need one of myself. But I'd gladly take one of you or Mathew."

At first that warmth that continued to make an appearance had driven her anxiety through the roof. But the more that she experienced it with Tristan, the more she looked forward to it. Being with Tristan was like she had been transported to another world where even breathing felt different. What was absolutely surprising was that Tristan didn't even have to touch her to make it happen. He could give her a look or say something sweet, and all at once, it was there again.

Together they finished cleaning up. Side by side and not talking. That was something else she liked about him. He didn't feel the incessant need to fill the void with unnecessary words. She hadn't thought about it before, but that was something she had abhorred expecting in a relationship. Sometimes she simply liked to have her nose in a book or a quiet space to draw.

Her gaze locked onto Tristan's a few times as they worked. When they were done, Tristan jerked his head toward the living room. "You want to stay for a little while? Or do you have to get back for something?"

Dianna shook her head. "I don't have to get back for anything." Unlike that morning, this time she didn't want to leave. It felt like if she did, she'd be missing out on something.

Tristan held out his hand and tugged her toward the couch. "We could watch a movie, or you could draw some more."

"Do you draw?"

He gave her a funny look. "Why do you ask?"

"I just figured that since Mathew enjoyed it, he probably got his interest from someone else."

Slowly, he shook his head. "No. But now that you mention it, his mother liked drawing. They were only doodles, but that's how she spent her time when she had to wait for something." The tone of his voice shifted. She was getting better at reading him, and bringing up his ex wasn't something he liked to do. Great. She probably destroyed all the progress they'd made.

"I'm sorry," she murmured as he pulled her to sit beside him.

"Whatever for?"

"I know you don't like talking about her."

He draped his arm around her. It only felt natural to rest her head against his shoulder. His fingertips trailed up and down her arm and he didn't speak for a few moments, making it clear she was right in her assumption. Finally, he put words to what must have been on his mind. "It's not that I don't like talking about her. She'll always be a part of my life—one that has shaped who I am and who Mathew is."

"But it was a time that caused pain."

"Sure, but those moments are still meant to help us grow.

It's why I push Mathew so much. I know it's hard, but I also know he's capable of being what I know he needs to be."

She couldn't help it. That statement left a sour taste in her mouth. It wasn't up to Tristan to decide what Mathew should and shouldn't be. Tristan needed to guide his son, but he couldn't force Mathew to be something he wasn't destined for. She had a firm belief that every individual person had something special to add to this world.

But Mathew was young. He still needed that guidance and his father was doing a pretty good job at it, even if he was a little misguided. His love for his son couldn't be questioned, and that was more important than anything.

Dianna didn't know how, but she knew that Tristan would continue to grow just as Mathew did. They were both going to be okay.

"Does Mathew ask about her?"

Tristan went silent once more. Had that question been off-limits? Probably. Even though he said he didn't mind talking about her, it was clear he did.

"You don't have to tell me if you don't want to."

"No, it's fine." His voice was strained. "He's been asking about her a lot more recently, but I think it's only because he feels like there's something missing in our family." His arm tightened around her. "His classmates at school have two parents. It's only natural for him to wonder if she'll come back into his life or get replaced." He grimaced. "I'm sorry, that probably sounded a little heartless."

"I don't think it sounds heartless at all. You said she left when he was really little. She hasn't raised him. You've done that all on your own." She shifted so she could see his face better. "You can't replace something that was never there to begin with."

"But you can fill a void that should have been full in the first place." He gave her a pointed look that fueled the fire within her. He couldn't be suggesting that she was the one who could fill that emptiness, could he?

Every thought that ran through her mind told her she should push him away, tell him he was just moving too fast.

But her conversation with her sister had seemed to flip a switch. She'd spent nearly every single day with this family since their arrival. She'd seen good and bad, and she knew what she'd be getting herself into.

The fact that Tristan might actually want to invite her to be part of this wonderful family only spurred a sensation of excitement. She offered him a small smile. "You make a good point."

21

———————

Tristan

Several days passed with Tristan and Dianna falling into a comfortable routine. She'd come for the morning therapy, then they'd shift gears for the afternoon tutoring. Following that, they'd eat dinner together and then spend time in the cabin drawing, reading, or watching a movie.

He almost couldn't remember what his life had been like before he'd met her. Happiness was the biggest addition. Mathew seemed calmer and at ease. He was even willing to speak to people he hadn't been willing to before.

It had started with Shane, then one of the girls who worked at the country club. Then it snowballed from there. Tristan couldn't put his finger on it. There was something different about his son.

Mathew was happy.

That's what it was.

His son had found his place surrounded by the horses and the woods. Dianna probably had a lot to do with it too.

Since they planned on staying for the holiday, Tristan had done his Christmas shopping online. Dianna helped him wrap the presents. Everything was coming together for the season and he wouldn't want to be anywhere else. He and Mathew had always loved Christmastime and celebrating the birth of Jesus. And this year seemed extra special.

The weekend before Christmas, Mathew convinced them to go to town. Dianna had told him about the Christmas festival they held every year. There was a festival of trees, booths for people to sell last-minute Christmas presents, and the bakery made the best hot chocolate.

But the thing that Mathew wanted to do the most was go ice-skating.

Tristan held Dianna's hand as they wandered between the booths of homemade gifts. Mathew ran ahead to a table that had wooden slingshots, pocketknives, and various camping instruments. He picked up a knife, his eyes growing wide.

Tristan laughed and plucked the knife from his son's hand. "You need to be a little older for that one."

Mathew frowned. "But other kids—"

"You're not like other kids." He grimaced. That came out wrong. But it was too late. Mathew's features darkened and his cheeks turned red.

"You think I'm dumb."

"I never said that."

"But that's what you thought." Mathew folded his arms, his focus shifting from Tristan to Dianna. "Dianna would let me get one. Wouldn't you?"

She glanced at Tristan. "Actually, I think your father made a good point when he said you need to be a little older."

The shock on Mathew's face was just as volatile as the glower he'd given to his father. "I thought you liked me."

Dianna stiffened, then dropped lower as if making eye contact with him on his level would help. "I *do* like you. That doesn't have anything to do with your dad's decision. A knife is a weapon. There's a lot of responsibility involved with owning one."

"You think I'm dumb too," he accused. "It's because I'm different. That's not fair. Other kids my age get to have one."

Tristan chuckled, but it was laced with irritation. "I highly doubt that."

"It's true!" Mathew folded his arms, his voice getting louder. "I want a pocketknife."

Dianna released Tristan's hand. "Maybe you should look at the slingshot. That looks like a fun one, and we can practice shooting it out at the club."

"I don't want a slingshot. I want that pocketknife." The tension continued to grow. Now they were getting more than a few concerned stares in their direction.

The back of Tristan's neck flushed with heat and he stepped closer to Mathew, lowering his voice so only his son and maybe Dianna could hear. "You might not like it, but you aren't old enough yet to own a knife. It's not safe for you to have something like that. It's not my job to be your friend. My job is to keep you safe."

"You're only saying no because Miss Dianna said no."

Tristan scoffed. "I said no first. And it doesn't matter what Dianna says. You're my son, and I make the rules."

Mathew knocked a few things off the table and took off running. Tristan stared dumbfounded after his son, then shot a concerned look toward Dianna as she gathered the items that had been dropped to the ground. "I'm going to get him. I'll meet you at the ice-skating rink."

She nodded but didn't say anything. He muttered an apology to the vendor and chased after Mathew, his fury building with each step.

When he caught up, he yanked his son into a sitting position on the curb. "What in heaven's name was that?"

Mathew still scowled at him. "What?"

"We were getting along so well. What happened?"

His son looked away. "I want that pocketknife."

"Yes, I understand that. But that's no excuse for how you behaved. You can't act like that in public."

Mathew let out an exaggerated sigh. "Fine."

"Try again."

He groaned. "*What*?"

"An apology would be a good start."

"Why? You didn't say sorry."

Tristan dragged a hand down his face. "What did I do that requires an apology? I didn't make a scene and drop someone's belongings on the ground."

Mathew's eyes darted in his direction, then away. His voice softened. "You hurt my feelings."

Tristan let out a puff of air he'd been holding in his chest. He had a feeling that's what this was about. Carefully, he settled down to sit on the curb beside Mathew. "I didn't mean to hurt your feelings."

"I don't believe you."

"I didn't say you had to." He rested his elbows on his knees and peered up at the bright blue sky in order to gather his thoughts. One wrong statement could have his son running off again. "What I meant to say was that we have different rules in our family. If you were capable of showing the maturity required to own that knife, then I would have been happy to get one for you. But there are sometimes when you don't know how to control your emotions. People who get easily angry or upset need to learn how to regulate those emotions before they can own something like a knife."

Mathew didn't say anything. He still stared at the road in front of them, the frown on his face deepening. "That's not *fair*."

"I'm sorry, kiddo. Life isn't supposed to be fair." This wasn't the first time he'd said that, and like all the other times, Mathew made a face. "Come on, let's get back to Dianna. I'm sure she's worried about you."

Mathew continued to glare into the pavement.

"Mathew, I said let's go."

"I don't want to."

Tristan let out a sigh. So much for a good thing. It had been ridiculous to even think that things had changed for good. Of course Mathew would have regressions. He'd just hoped it wouldn't be until they were done with the therapy sessions here. He clasped his hands in front of him and peered down the street that had been blocked from traffic for the weekend. "I wanted to talk to you about something."

Mathew didn't respond.

"It's about Dianna and me."

This got a small reaction, though his son didn't meet his gaze. He shifted and his features softened a little.

"I love her."

Now, he looked up. "You do?"

"I do. And one day, I'd like to marry her."

Mathew's eyes rounded.

"But I wanted to see what you thought about it first."

He turned his focus back to the road. "Would she be my new mom?"

"Not if you didn't want it. But I'm sure if she said yes to marrying me, she'd like to be." Tristan couldn't get a read on him. In the beginning, Mathew had wanted Dianna to be part of the family. This outburst was the first time he'd shown any adverse reaction to Dianna. That was to be expected at some point. Eventually, the newness would wear off and Mathew would realize that Dianna would still have certain expectations whether or not she was in his life in a motherly capacity. Tristan glanced at Mathew once more. "If I asked her to marry me and she said yes, you're old enough to decide if you'd call her 'mom.'"

Mathew's brows were drawn together as if this decision would make or break the rest of his life. "I don't know."

"You don't have to know yet. I just wanted to tell you what I was thinking about."

"Okay."

"What do you say? Should we go find Dianna now?"

Mathew nodded. "I still want that knife."

Tristan chuckled. "I know. You'll get one, eventually, when you've been able to show you can handle it."

"That's going to be forever."

He ruffled Mathew's hair. "Sometimes it sure seems that way."

22

───────

Dianna

*D*ianna's heart raced, but it wasn't the calming kind. There were several different types of heart rates that Tristan had been able to stir within her. There was the kind that made her feel seen and heard—the one that made her think if there was such a thing as love, it was something she had for him.

Then there was the exhilarating kind that made her pulse race right alongside her heart and gave her bursts of adrenaline. Those were usually when she kissed him, and they made her stomach twist in a pleasant kind of way.

The third kind was happening now and she hated it.

Her palms were sweating and her heart hammered with a tempo that brought along with it the anxiety she had a tendency to experience. Over the years, Dianna had been able to figure out a way to control that anxiety. She avoided situations where it was exacerbated. It was the feeling she'd had when she disappeared that morning after the party. And right now, it was telling her that she should go home to avoid having to deal with Tristan when he came back.

There were some triggering words he'd used that rubbed her the wrong way. It was like he'd pricked her with several splinters, and they had just gotten under her skin enough that she couldn't pull them out.

Tristan didn't see Mathew the way she did. Granted, he would never truly understand his son and the things that triggered him. Which meant there was a possibility that he wouldn't understand her no matter how long they spent together.

Stop it, she admonished herself. Tristan wasn't like the other people she observed in town. If anyone would be able to relate to her, it was him. If she could just get past these niggling thoughts of doubt and fear, maybe she'd be able to find the happiness her sisters had found.

And yet, as she picked up the last of the pocketknives, she knew she wouldn't be able to stay in town. She needed to go home and reevaluate what she wanted in a relationship—if she wanted a relationship at all. Would future stresses and arguments turn her into someone just like his ex? She couldn't imagine leaving because of Mathew; that wouldn't be fair. But even she knew that this relationship was a little different. If she were to marry Tristan, she'd be accepting the responsibility of raising his child with him.

And their styles of parenting were vastly different—that much was clear.

Dianna wrung her hands together and inched back the way they'd been walking. She could call one of her sisters to pick her up, or she might be able to find someone who could take her toward her ranch if they were leaving. Already she was feeling sick to her stomach for wandering away. She really ought to tell Tristan that she needed to go home for a little while.

She only made it toward the beginning of the booths when she heard her name called out.

"Dianna!"

Her whole body froze, except her heart. That continued to bang wildly against the walls of her chest. They were supposed to go ice-skating. She could do that. It wasn't supposed to last too long. Maybe by the time they got off the rink, she'd be calm enough to get past this strange reaction she was having.

Dianna forced a smile and turned around, finding Tristan holding Mathew's hand. Tristan didn't seem to notice her unease, or if he did, he ignored it. He held up a slingshot. "Mathew decided to go for this one instead. I hope we didn't take too long." He looked down at Mathew and for all intents and purposes, his son seemed in better spirits. There wasn't any animosity between them—more evidence of Tristan's talent at being a good father.

The vise grip around her heart eased up a little. She shook her head and swallowed down the lump that had formed. "No. You didn't take too long. I was just..." She glanced to the side where a table had been set up with fudge. "I was just going to get some fudge."

"Mmm. That sounds good. What do you say, Mathew? Would you like some fudge?"

Mathew eyed Dianna, and that's when she saw something she hadn't seen before. He wasn't as open toward her as he used to be. The sparkle that they shared had dimmed. It couldn't possibly be due to the argument, could it?

Well, she knew better than that. Children were notorious for holding grudges.

Mathew broke eye contact first. "I just want to go ice-skating."

"Well, if Dianna wants—"

"Oh, I'm fine. I don't need the extra sweets." She tried to play it off, but even she could hear the strained tone of her voice. She was failing miserably at hiding that she felt off-centered now. It was like a weight had been placed on one shoulder and she had to use all her mindpower to compensate for the change. "Let's just go get our skates. I'll get some fudge later." She flashed Mathew a smile and was relieved when he offered one in return.

They got to the rink and there were no mishaps except for finding a pair of skates to fit Tristan. While the guy in the back started looking for those, Dianna took Mathew to the ice. He clutched her hand tightly, not speaking. That was fine by her. She'd far prefer to stay locked inside her mind with her thoughts.

"Do you love my dad?" Mathew's voice was strong and direct, and it had thrown her off guard. She nearly slipped on the ice and had to reach out to grasp the side of the rink.

"What?"

"Do you love my dad? I've heard him say he loves you. Do you love him?"

She gave him a side-eyed glance. "I suppose I do."

"How do you know?"

Dianna bit back a smile. "I don't really know."

"You don't know how you know you love him?" His features scrunched into a frown. "Aren't you supposed to know?"

She tilted her head, getting better at keeping her balance as they continued skating in a circle with slow, short steps. "I don't think anyone really knows the answer to that question. It could be a lot of little reasons or just one big one. And I think it's different for everyone."

"But you love him."

"Yes."

The look of pure concentration on Mathew's face was just the ticket to distract herself from her own spiraling thoughts.

"Why do you ask?"

He ignored her question and threw another curve ball at her. "Why aren't you a mom?"

She slowed and stared at him. "Why are you asking me that?"

Mathew shrugged. "You're a grown-up and you don't have kids."

"No, I don't."

"Do you want to be a mom?"

That was the question of the century. Even as he asked it, she couldn't say she knew the answer to it. She'd always thought it would be difficult to raise her own children. Working with other people's kids was different. She cleared her throat and focused on a spot ahead of them as she attempted to find her words. "I think I'd *like* to be a mother one day. But I guess I'm a little scared."

"Why?"

She let out a strained laugh. "You ask some pretty hard questions." Dianna gnawed on the inside of her cheek. She couldn't exactly tell him that she was scared she would fight with her children. Nor could she say that she was scared she'd end up having a kid who was simply difficult. If she knew him like she thought she did, he'd probably internalize those statements. He was far too bright to brush off answers like that. They stopped, and she crouched down to look him in the eye. "Have you ever been afraid of something and then when you gave it a try, you realized you didn't have anything to be afraid of?"

His brows pinched together. "I don't know."

"Hmm." She searched her memories of their sessions and

her eyes lifted once more to meet his. "Remember when you were scared to get Molasses to jump over that first bar?"

He nodded.

"Are you scared anymore?"

Mathew shook his head.

"See? That's what it's like for me. I bet that if I decided to become a mother, I would be really scared until I actually got to be one."

They stared at one another for a few moments, and then with a tone full of pure honesty, Mathew said, "I think you'd be a good mom."

Her heart stuttered and hot emotion seared the space behind her eyes. Voice cracking, she brushed at a single tear before it could reach her cheek. "Thank you, Mathew."

23

─────────

Tristan

Tristan would like to say it hadn't bothered him when he returned to the booth with the pocketknives to find Dianna gone. He wanted to believe that she had just wandered off because he'd taken too long with Mathew. It was understandable that she wouldn't want to sit around waiting.

But there was this teeny voice in his head that reminded him what it felt like to be abandoned by the person he loved. He'd loved Erika. She'd claimed to love him. But when things got hard, she left.

That wasn't love.

Dianna had wandered far enough that Tristan knew in his gut that she was leaving. He would have called her on it right then and there, but with Mathew watching and having just told him he was in love with her, he felt like he was up against a wall.

Something was wrong. He didn't know what it was, but he

could feel it right down to his toes. Dianna had some form of discontent, and if he didn't figure out what it was, then all of them might end up hurting.

He wrapped his skate laces around his fingers and pulled tight until his fingertips turned white. Right now he had the chance to collect his thoughts before he had to speak to her. It wasn't healthy for him to be comparing her to Erika, so he needed to stop that way of thinking immediately. Dianna was different, with completely separate quirks and struggles. If he could just figure out what was bothering her, then their little picture-perfect Christmas could resume.

Tristan lifted his head and watched as Dianna and Mathew scuffled across the ice, skaters passing them and giving them a wide berth. Mathew hadn't been ice-skating in a year or so, and he wasn't as steady on his feet as he probably wanted to be. It was just as well that Dianna appeared to have a similar talent for moving across the ice.

At least they seemed to be getting along. The tension that had hung in the air since Mathew's blow-up was worse than their first meeting.

Dianna smiled and said something to Mathew, who then responded. They still held hands as they skated. His heart warmed, breaking free from the concern and distress it had gone through when he couldn't find her earlier.

He'd overreacted. Tristan could see that now. She wasn't going anywhere. And if she had wanted to leave, she would have told him.

Tristan got to his feet, the skates digging into his ankles like they were supposed to. He glided across the ice with a grace that rivaled about half of the people skating. When he passed Dianna and turned around so he could watch her reaction as he skated backward, he wasn't disappointed. Her mouth fell open slightly and she let out a laugh.

"You've been holding out on me," she said.

He shrugged. "I like skating."

"You never said you did."

"Well, to be fair, I can't do it very often. Between work, Mathew, and the changing seasons, it's hard to make time for it."

Her eyes swept over him from head to toe. "You're obviously a natural. I guess I should have figured, seeing how Mathew is skating better than I am." Dianna's statement put a smile on Mathew's face that stretched from ear to ear.

While everything seemed to have settled down on the surface, he couldn't help but feel like this was the calm before the storm. Dianna caught him staring at her and she stared back just a moment longer than he expected. It unnerved him somewhat. Was she trying to tell him something?

He'd have to figure out a way to get her alone so they could have that discussion. Too many unknowns lingered in the air.

"*Dad.*"

Tristan jumped and glanced down at Mathew. "What, buddy?"

"Show Miss Dianna your tricks."

He chuckled and shook his head. "I don't think Dianna wants to see—"

"Yes, I do."

He lifted his gaze, finding her staring at him once more. Was it in his imagination? Or did a whole conversation pass between them in that moment?

Yep. Definitely in his imagination.

Dianna's smile was enough to make him throw aside his misgivings. "Alright. But just remember, you asked for it." Tristan turned around and tightened his body, crouching as he picked up some speed. He could feel them watching him, and it only spurred him to push himself harder. Once he got to the appropriate velocity, he leapt into the air and spun around like a cyclone, completing a near-perfect double axel jump. He landed a little funny on his foot enough to send a sharp pain up his leg, then stumbled a few paces to keep himself from falling on his face.

Several spectators clapped. He nodded to them as he made his way back to where Dianna and Mathew waited. His ankle pulsed with the throbbing pain, but it wasn't sprained or broken, and he'd be able to continue skating for a little while before it caused too much trouble.

"That was amazing," Dianna blurted the moment he skidded to a stop in front of them.

He held out his hand toward her and she eyed it with what could only be described as mistrust. He chuckled. "I'm not going to bite."

Dianna glanced at Mathew. "I don't think we should leave—"

Thank the stars his son knew what to do in this situation. Mathew nudged her forward. "Dad, teach her a trick."

"What? No. I'm terrible at—"

"Please?" His quiet word seemed to be the only thing that pushed her to accept his request. "I'll start you out with something simple."

Though there was clear hesitation in her eyes, she placed her hand in his and nodded. "Okay."

"First, we're going to go around the rink to get a good momentum going." They started around the edges of the inner circle. "See? The ice here is smoother because most of these skaters are using the outer area."

She clutched his hand and arm tightly, her fingers digging hard enough he could feel them through his coat.

"You're going to have to relax."

She let out a bark of laughter. "You can't tell me to relax when this isn't something I'm good at."

"Aren't you supposed to be the queen of helping people work through their issues?"

Her features stiffened.

Uh-oh. That was the wrong thing to say. He cleared his throat and tried again. "That is, what I meant to say was that you know all the tricks and ways to get through something when you don't think you can succeed. Isn't that right?"

"I guess," she hedged.

Now would have been the perfect segue into discussing where she was going when he'd caught her trying to make her escape. But something held him back. It didn't feel right to ask her when he was trying to smooth the feathers that had been ruffled earlier.

"Well, if you were working with Mathew—or another kid— and they were scared to do something, what would you tell them?"

She closed her eyes briefly. "I'd tell them to focus on their breathing or count to their favorite number."

"Which one works for you?"

Dianna glanced at him, curiosity flickering behind her eyes. "No one has ever asked me that before."

"I suppose there's a first time for everything."

"I guess you're right." Her smile returned and her grip relaxed a little. "I prefer to focus on my breathing. There's something about it that grounds me."

His mouth quirked up at the ends. "Okay, so *breathe*. Relax your body a little more and let me guide you through a few things. We're going to try to skate backward, and then I'm going to put you into a dip."

Her eyes widened, and immediately she stiffened in his arms.

Tristan chuckled. "*Breathe.*"

She nodded sharply and closed her eyes—something that showed a great deal more trust in him than he thought was possible at this point. He moved his mouth closer to her ear and said, "Okay, just stay relaxed and lean on me if you need to. We're going to shift so that your feet are gliding this way instead." He moved them into a position where he was propelling her ahead of him while she faced him.

Dianna gasped and her grip tightened once more.

"Don't worry, you're doing it."

Her eyes flew open and she stared around wildly. He nearly lost his momentum, which could have ended catastrophically. He didn't have professional training, but he knew enough to keep them afloat as long as she didn't put them in a precarious position.

"Now, we're going to turn again, but start gliding forward."

The more they skated, the more at ease she became. He pulled her around and in a flicker of movements, he was able to swing her into a dip. His face hovered over hers, both of them breathing heavily. One of her hands had come around the back of his neck and the other gripped his shoulder.

"Not bad," he said.

"I have a good teacher it seems." Her voice had softened like the rest of her body. Whatever tension had been coursing through her veins was now gone. He might have been able to equate it with this small moment. Or it could have been the talk she had with Mathew. Either way, he wasn't going to look a gift horse in the mouth.

Somewhere nearby a skater toppled and skidded across the ice. Dianna blinked, their moment frozen in time shattered. She scrambled to get upright, then adjusted her coat. "Thanks for the lesson. Maybe I can return the favor one day and teach you how to draw something other than a stick-figure."

The humor had returned to her features now, too. He grinned. "I'd like that." Before she pulled away entirely, his hand reached out, snatching hers so he could pull her close. Their faces were inches apart and their warm, white breaths mingled between them. "I love you, Dianna."

She blinked and a crease formed between her brows. "I know."

"No. I *really* love you. I need you to know that."

Dianna placed her gloved palm against his cheek. "And I love you."

Relief washed over him. "I think maybe it would be nice if we had some time one-on-one to discuss what this might mean for us. Our therapy sessions will be over next month and I—" His voice cracked as he recalled the very real apprehension he'd felt earlier today. "I'd like to figure out what options we have available."

She dropped her hand and looked away—a clear indication she wasn't expecting him to discuss this topic in the middle of the ice rink.

Tristan ducked his head and peered at her. "It's important we figure out where we want to take this—how far we want to take this."

"I'm not sure I'm ready for that."

He wasn't prepared for how much those words could slice through him like a hot steak knife through butter. "You're not?"

She shot a look in his direction. "I thought I was... but then I realized a few things today that made me... *I don't know*. How are *you* ready to discuss what I think you're wanting to talk about?"

Another stab at his heart.

"I guess I know what I want because I've had it before—"

She met his gaze. "If you had it before and it turned out as bad as it did, then you can't possibly believe that you want it again with me."

"That's not what I meant. I was in love before. It didn't turn out the way I wanted it to. But I still want to find that feeling again. And I have. With *you*."

"You can't be sure. No one is. What if I turn out as bad as your ex? Have you considered that? What if Mathew doesn't want me to be part of his life? I would never expect you to pick me over him. That would be ridiculous."

He dragged a hand down his face. This wasn't going the way he'd hoped. She was putting up walls faster than he would be able to get through them. He should have waited and just discussed these topics over dinner when she'd have enough time to let them sink in.

Maybe there was still a chance for that.

Tristan held up his hand. "Look, you don't have to say anything now. I don't want to do anything to jeopardize where our relationship is right now. Just agree to come to dinner with me tomorrow night. I'll get a sitter, and it can just be the two of us. Then you can tell me what you think, and I can do the same."

She snapped her mouth shut.

Good, he'd finally made the right choice. He'd been able to get her to consider his offer. Now he just had to figure out how to get through to her when they got to dinner. Luckily, he had an extra day to come up with a plan.

Not only that, but he'd have an extra day to discuss his plans with Mathew.

Dianna nodded. She scooted back from him, then glanced over in Mathew's direction. "I'm suddenly not feeling very well. I think this is all a little overwhelming and I'm feeling anxious, so I need some time alone."

He took a step toward her. She smiled, but it didn't feel all that genuine. Dianna held up her hand and shook her head.

"I promise I'm fine. But I think maybe I need to go home and lay down for a little while."

"Was it something I said?" He wasn't sure, but he thought he'd witnessed her hesitate. She shifted, her arms folded across her stomach. "Of course not. I just need some time to resettle my stomach. Do you think you could tell Mathew I'm sorry for not staying longer? I'll see him for our next session." She turned and skated toward the entrance of the rink.

He watched her go, feeling like an absolute failure. The latent fear that insisted on rearing its angry head came back with a vengeance. He should have just let sleeping dogs lie. She wasn't ready even though he knew he was. She was going to walk away from what they had because she didn't care enough to stay.

She was probably planning the exact way for her to break up with him at this very moment.

Tristan let out a heavy sigh. Hadn't he told himself he wasn't going to jump to conclusions? Well, that was exactly what he was doing, and he wasn't going to stand for it.

He spun around and headed straight for Mathew.

His son was staring off in the same direction he'd been looking. The frown was almost imperceptible. When had his son gotten so good at controlling that facial expression? "Where's Miss Dianna going?"

"She said she didn't feel well."

"She seemed fine to me."

Tristan shot a look over his shoulder. "Yeah. I guess everyone has different needs that we have to accept and respect."

24

───────

Dianna

Dianna paced in her bedroom. What was wrong with her that she couldn't even handle a simple relationship with a guy who was obviously smitten with her? Not only that, but he was also a great father to Mathew.

The biggest thing holding her back was how irritated she got with his views on how Mathew needed to change. On top of that, she wasn't sure she was ready to be part guardian to Mathew.

That was the only thing she could think Tristan might want to discuss with her. And there was no way she was ready to talk about *that*.

Had she entertained the idea a few times since their first kiss? Of course. What girl wouldn't? She hated to admit that she did a great deal more than simply consider it. She'd gone so far as to ask her older sisters when the best time for a wedding would be or if the time of year even mattered.

After bringing that up, the knowing looks her sisters gave her were the ones she avoided almost religiously. Each of her sisters who were involved or married seemed to act as if she were already engaged or soon would be.

Well, they couldn't be more wrong. If her anxiety had anything to say about it, she wasn't ready. She was absolutely terrified that Tristan was pushing her into something that she might not be able to handle.

Normally it took her months to come to a conclusion about something new. The only time she'd jumped into something without thinking was when she'd gotten hired by Shane. And the only reason she did that was because Constance practically dragged her into the office to have an interview.

She'd hated Constance for at least two weeks after that interaction. To be fair, Constance had this way of knowing what was best, even if Dianna wasn't sure.

Now, it felt like she was on that ice skating rink, but this time Tristan wasn't helping to hold her up. He was pushing her along faster and faster until the world around her blurred and she couldn't see straight. Her heart beat faster and her pulse howled like one of the wolves in the woods. She'd lost control of everything, and she didn't like feeling like she was teetering on the edge of something so dangerous.

Dianna should have known better. She'd been safe when she'd stayed at home reading her books. Her father's rule had helped facilitate that. Now she had no one to blame but herself. She'd let this happen when she'd allowed her curiosity to get the better of her and she'd kissed Tristan.

She sat on the edge of her bed and let her focus sweep through the room. She'd spent every day in this room growing up. It wasn't just the place she called home; it was her safe haven. It was the place she went to when the world became too much.

Taking the job with Shane had opened up a whole new world for her. She'd been able to help Mathew, and she wouldn't trade that for anything. She even looked forward to helping other children reach their goals through working with horses. And she'd come to terms with all of those changes.

So why was it so difficult to accept the change that was happening with Tristan?

That realization was what made this situation so much more difficult. If her head and her heart weren't in this together, then she wasn't ready.

That was the plain and simple truth of it all. How people managed to meet and fall in love in such a short time was beyond her. Apparently, Tristan was one of them.

She shot off her bed. Her mind was made up. She was allowed to feel cornered and do what she needed to in order to keep her head. And no one should make her feel bad about it.

Tristan wasn't due to arrive for about twenty minutes. She had enough time to saddle up and do a few laps with her horse before he got there. She needed the reprieve from her racing thoughts.

Dianna slipped out the front door, avoiding the kitchen where she heard some of her sisters preparing for dinner. The sun had long set and the moon shone bright over the snow. Christmas lights twinkled in the distance from the neighboring ranches. A cold breeze played with her hair and nipped at her cheeks. She pulled her coat tighter around her and shoved her hands into her pockets.

Christmas would be in about a week. Tristan would be due to stay for a little longer after that—unless they decided to stay permanently.

Her stomach fluttered with the thought. It wasn't unpleasant, but it also didn't sit well with her. If they stayed, she'd feel obligated to commit to something, which brought her right back around to feeling smothered.

Dianna let out a sigh, and the puff of warm air dissipated around her. She felt absolutely sick to her stomach. Between the guilt and the anxiety, she probably should have just called him and told him that she wasn't up for their date. But avoiding him would only start something she was even less prepared to deal with.

She wandered into the barn and stopped by her horse's stall. It didn't matter how long she stood there, running her hands down the animal's back or leaning into her strong body; Dianna couldn't shake this sense of foreboding that seemed to have latched on.

Normally, she could pull herself out of a funk like this. She had gotten to the point in her life where she knew what it would take to return to a peaceful state.

This time felt different. She couldn't put her finger on it.

"Hey."

She jumped, causing her horse to sidestep. Dianna faltered with her animal but managed not to stumble or topple over. Her wide eyes swung around, finding Tristan leaning his folded arms on the stall door.

"What are you doing here?" she demanded, a scowl crossing her features. "You're not supposed to be here for another ten minutes."

His brows creased. "You don't look pleased to see me."

Oh, if only he knew what was about to happen. However, this was not the right place for a discussion like that. The last thing she needed was to associate her favorite location with the conversation she knew she had to have with Tristan.

"It's not that. I just wasn't ready for you to show up." Dianna moved her hand along her horse's neck once more and offered Tristan a nervous smile. Something niggled at her—like she was making a mistake. But she'd gone over the whole thing in her head. Breaking up with him made sense. She'd run all the scenarios.

Tristan tilted his head, his gaze drilling into her and causing her to grow even more uneasy. Could he tell what she was thinking? He knew; she could feel it. And if she was right, why wasn't he saying something?

Maybe he was feeling the same way she was.

Even as the thought crossed her mind, she was surprised she didn't feel more relief with it, which only confused her more.

Head pounding, she tore her gaze away from him and let the awkward silence continue to grow. He'd been early; he could wait until she got what she needed out of her visit with the animals.

"You okay?"

She stilled, refusing to meet his gaze. "Sure, why wouldn't I be?" It was one of the first big lies she could remember telling anyone. If she were being completely honest, she'd tell him she hadn't been able to sleep and her appetite had all but disappeared.

"You're not quite acting yourself."

She allowed herself a peek in his direction. "Sometimes you might think you know someone better than you actually do."

"Is that what this is?"

She bit down on her tongue to prevent herself from saying something she might regret. If she wasn't careful with her words, she might get into more trouble than she originally thought.

"Dianna."

Glancing at him once more was the worst mistake of her life. His gaze captured hers, refusing to release her. He wasn't going to give up that easy. So much for postponing the conversation until later. She let out a sigh and faced him. "I'm fine. But there's something really important I think we need to discuss."

"I know. It's why we're going on our date." He glanced at his watch. "In about three minutes."

Dianna shook her head. "Actually, I think that might not be such a good idea."

He frowned. "Are you feeling sick?"

"In a manner of speaking."

"But you said you felt okay." He straightened, opened the stall door, and wandered inside. The stall wasn't very large in the first place. But with him taking up part of the space, she suddenly felt more claustrophobic than she had in her entire life.

Dianna sucked in sharply and moved backward, earning herself a confused frown from Tristan.

He reached out and grasped her hand. "Hey. I just want to make sure you're doing okay."

She couldn't help it. Something came over her that she hadn't experienced in years. She yanked her hand from his grasp and looked away. "You need to stop that."

"Stop what?" He chuckled, but it sounded strained and hollow. "Over the past few weeks, it's felt like you and me are meant to be together."

"You can't know that."

"Dianna." The hurt in his voice made her flinch. Just one more thing to feel guilty over. She'd made more than her fair share of mistakes, and she'd be paying for them dearly.

She took in a long, slow breath and let it out through pursed lips. "I've had a lot of time to think this over—this you and me thing." She fidgeted under his scrutiny. Why did this conversation feel so much harder than just resigning to stay in the relationship?

"What about you and me?" His voice softened though there was still an underlying tone of concern.

Dianna blew out a long breath and squeezed her eyes shut to ward off the strange sensations swirling in her stomach. These weren't normal. While pleasant, she couldn't ignore what her head had been telling her this whole time. A relationship right now wasn't going to work. Not with Tristan, not with anyone. His closeness made her want to wrap herself up in his arms and tell him to make her believe they could work. But that was her traitorous heart speaking. She knew better.

Didn't she?

Tristan's hand touched her chin. Her eyes flew open, finding his concerned gaze locked onto her. She could do this.

Dianna reached up and pulled his hand down to his side. "I don't think this is working."

Immediately his features tightened and he took a step back. "What?"

She swallowed hard, the lump in her throat constricting her so much she wondered if she was making the right decision. "I've had a long time to think about this, and I've realized I'm not ready."

"Not ready for what?"

A heavy sigh burst from her chest. "I'm not ready to fall in love. I told you this in the beginning. I don't even know if I want to have a relationship. I'm a mess, and the only thing that makes sense right now is for me to take a step back."

His brows creased and he rubbed the back of his neck. "You're not ready to fall in love."

"That's what I said," she muttered with exasperation. Why wasn't he listening to her? He'd been able to do so before.

"And you're not sure you want to be with me." His gaze flitted up to meet hers, cutting her off before she could add to their discussion. "I'm just trying to piece everything together."

His hands dropped to his sides and he cocked his head slightly. "But you do have feelings for me."

"I don't know how that has anything to do with what I'm trying to tell you."

"And you care about Mathew."

"Of course. But—"

"Then we're not breaking up."

"*What*?" She gaped at him. He wasn't allowed to do that, was he?

Tristan shrugged. "We're not breaking up."

"Don't be ridiculous. A relationship takes *two* people. If one of them wants out, it's dissolved. You can't just say you're going to keep on dating someone if they don't want to anymore. That's not how this works." Her heart rattled in her chest angrily while her stomach knotted deliciously.

He shoved his hands in his pockets, no trace of teasing in his expression. He was being absolutely serious. "From what I see, you *are* in love even if you don't want to be. Plus, you care about Mathew. Those are the only things necessary for us to be able to make this work."

"But—" she sputtered. "But I don't *want*—"

"I get that. Truly, Dianna, I hear you. But what you don't seem to understand is that I *know* you care about me. I've experienced your love. From your touch to the way you look at me. And I love you with all my heart. You can try to scare me off. You can push me away, but I am willing to wait as long as it takes. I'll give you space if you need it. But every now and again I'll keep calling, visiting, and asking you out."

"And I'm going to say no."

He winced, and that guilt slithered back into her stomach, replacing the pleasant feelings that continued to throw her off balance and make her question everything.

"Let me ask you something, Dianna." He pulled out his

hand and rubbed his finger and thumb together as if he needed to get something off them, but she'd seen this tactic before. He was having a hard time with this discussion, too. And if she was right about that, why was he so insistent on staying? Two miserable people shouldn't stay together.

"What do you want to ask me?" she rasped, hating the way her heart continued its acrobatics.

He glanced up at her and offered a sad smile. "Are you trying to break up with me because you truly don't want to be with me? Or because you're scared?"

She stiffened. "Does it matter? I'm making a decision I think is best for me."

"It matters to me," he said.

Dianna threw up her hands. "You're so infuriating. I just want to break up so I can breathe. I feel trapped. I don't want to be pushed into a corner."

He blinked. "Is that really how you feel about me?"

"I keep telling you this, and you keep ignoring me. Everything you just said, it's not romantic to me. You're bossing me around, making decisions for me that you think are best. I'm not your child."

"I know."

"Then stop trying to force me to do something I don't want. That's how resentment begins. So you really want to be in a relationship with someone who doesn't want to be there?" Her heavy breaths were the only sound between them, and they weighed her down like she had been attached to an anchor and dropped into the depths of the ocean. She was drowning, and the only thing that could possibly be causing this feeling was because she was *here*... with him. She needed out. Emotion caught in her throat and she let out a hiccup. "Can't you see this was never supposed to happen?"

"How can you say that?" His whisper tore through her, ripping her insides apart.

"I'm sorry, Tristan. I never meant for you to get hurt. I thought..." She didn't know what she thought anymore. She should have never allowed herself to develop feelings for him in the first place because now she wanted nothing more than to have him hold her. The tug-o-war with her heart and her head continued making things worse. "I'm sorry," she repeated.

Dianna brushed past him and ran down the aisle toward the house. Her eyes brimmed with hot moisture until they overflowed, and the tears stung her cheeks. If this was the right decision, then why was she feeling like she'd just lost the most important thing in her life?

She shot into the house and slammed the door shut so she could catch her breath as she leaned against it.

"You okay?"

Dianna yelped and covered her mouth with her hand, finding Grace standing in the darkened doorway of the living room, the lights from their Christmas tree making her appear as if she was glowing.

"What are you doing?" Dianna demanded, "You nearly gave me a heart attack."

Grace glanced over her shoulder. "Just putting a present under the tree. What are you doing? It looks like you've seen a ghost."

Dianna shut her eyes briefly. "I just broke up with Tristan."

Grace's brows lifted, but she didn't say anything.

"Don't ask."

"Wasn't gonna."

Dianna let out a shaky breath. "I don't know what I'm going to do."

A loud rapping sound on the door nearly caused her to

screech again. Her eyes flew wide and she stumbled away from the door. That could only be one person.

"You gonna get that?" Grace asked.

Dianna shook her head. "I don't want to talk to him."

"You probably owe him an explanation."

She glared at her sister. "I told him exactly what he needed to hear. Nothing more."

"Obviously, he *needs* more," Grace said when he knocked again.

Dianna shook her head. "I can't do it. Not right now. Not with the way I'm feeling inside." She spun on her heel and strode toward the stairs. If she opened that door, she probably would allow him to change her mind. While she *knew* this decision was the right one for her, the tension and flutters that accosted her were pleading for her to reconsider.

Too bad she was smarter than that. There were more important things than satisfying the needs of the heart.

25

Tristan

ristan paced on the porch. None of this made sense. It was true, Dianna had told him that she wasn't interested in a relationship when he first arrived, but everything after that had made it clear she was just as ready as he was. He couldn't wrap his head around what had gone wrong, and he wasn't going to leave until he did.

How could he go home to Mathew and tell him that everything was about to change... *again*? They'd picked up and come across the states to do Mathew's therapy, and he'd even had a few discussions about staying. Mathew seemed thrilled with the idea. He loved Dianna.

What had happened?

He stopped and knocked on the door again. She knew he was there. It wasn't like she escaped out the back door to avoid speaking to him. Normally, he wouldn't even bother. But already he felt like he was drowning, knowing that when the sun rose, his life would forever be changed.

Was it possible he'd read too much into what was developing between them?

No, he refused to believe that for even one second.

She'd been the first to kiss him.

She'd been the one to ask him if she could stay.

Irritation quickly infiltrated and poisoned the ache in his chest. Was she toying with him?

Losing all control, his thoughts shifted to Erika and how she'd disappeared when things got difficult. He hadn't thought that Dianna was capable of such duplicity. These darker feelings continued to spiral out of control with each flashback to his past relationship.

Tristan lifted his hand to knock once more when the door opened, revealing one of Dianna's sisters. He only knew Brielle by name. This one was younger than Dianna so that narrowed down what her name might be.

He glanced around her, shifting so he could get a better look inside the darkened front room. There were voices coming from the back of the house, presumably where the rest of the family was. Dianna's sister stepped out of the house and onto the porch. She closed the door quietly and leaned against it, her arms folded. "You must be Tristan."

His jaw tightened. "What letter of the alphabet are you?"

One corner of her mouth twitched upward. "G."

G. He couldn't remember what her name was. It could be Georgia, Genevieve or Gabrielle. But none of that mattered. He needed to speak to one person and her name didn't start with that letter. "I need to speak to Dianna."

"It's Grace."

He frowned. "What?"

"My name."

Tristan shook his head. "I need to talk to Dianna."

Grace glanced over her shoulder, then rubbed her chin before bringing her eyes to meet his. "Yeeeah. I don't think she's going to come down. She's got to be the most stubborn out of all of us."

That couldn't be true. Not with all the stories she'd told of her sisters. Dianna seemed like she fit into her family just fine. He cleared his throat. "I really need to talk to her about something important."

"She broke up with you."

He stiffened. "Boy, news travels fast."

She cocked her head to the side slightly and her lips spread into a wider smile. "If you're wondering... no. She didn't just come in and announce it to the world. I just happened to be in her way when she made her escape."

Escape. That word scraped against him like sandpaper, rubbing his already sensitive heart raw. Just like when she said she felt cornered or trapped... she didn't want to be in a relationship with him.

The heat and tight air in his chest deflated and his shoulders slumped. It wasn't hard to immediately start second-guessing everything he knew about this relationship. He took a few steps back and leaned against the porch railing. "Is that what she said she was doing?"

"What?"

"Escaping from me."

Grace snorted. "No. But she flew into the house like she was running from something terrifying."

"Is that supposed to make me feel better?"

"Does it?"

"No."

She shrugged. "Sorry."

Tristan shoved both hands into his hair and spun around to

face the dark yard. "What *did* she say?"

"I don't think I'm allowed to tell you that."

He huffed. The misery he currently drowned in would probably be better than hearing whatever Dianna had told her sister anyway.

"But I'll tell you what I know."

His whole body froze. Her shuffled footsteps wandered across the frozen wood planks of the porch and she rested her elbows on the porch railing, not looking up at him. "Out of all my sisters, I know Dianna better than the oldest ones, but not as well as I know the ones around my age. Keep that in mind when I tell you what I'm going to say next."

Tristan peeked at her. Her brows were furrowed and she wore a frown that mirrored his own.

"Dianna keeps to herself. Comfort. That's what I get from her."

"What does that mean?"

Grace lifted one shoulder and shot a look in his direction. "Dianna thrives when things are the same. She doesn't like change—which is why I think we were all surprised when she decided to start working for Shane. She just doesn't *do* stuff like that."

"I fail to see how that has anything to do with our relationship."

Her frown deepened. "Don't you have a kid who deals with similar stuff?"

"What? Hating change? We all hate change. Kids are just worse at dealing with it."

One brow lifted and she let out a soft laugh, shaking her head. "That's where you're wrong. My dad was *terrible* at accepting when my mom died. Then he was in complete denial as each one of us started maturing. I'm sure Dianna told you about his rule when it came to marriage."

He nodded, shifting his focus away from Dianna's sister. "She mentioned it. She also said that he changed his rule recently."

"Yup."

Tristan let out a heavy sigh. "With all due respect, I'm in the middle of trying to pick up the broken pieces of my heart. You'll understand if I don't have patience for your cryptic story-telling."

She let out a laugh. "Is that what you think this is?" Turning to face him, she leaned one elbow on the rail and set a stern gaze on him. "Dianna is *very* particular. She likes her things just so. When something big changes, it throws her off balance, and it can take her weeks or months to get through it. While that's happening, you have to understand that she needs her space to examine everything from every angle. Does any of that sound familiar?"

Confusion must have been plain on his face.

Grace let out an exaggerated groan. "She's probably more like your son than she is like you. She functions a little differently than you or I do."

Realization dawned on him.

She let out a sigh that sounded almost like relief. "See? Dianna will immerse herself in things so much that she will get in her own way because she can't focus on anything else. If she thinks it's a bad idea to date you for whatever reason, she's not going to suddenly change her mind. It can be a good thing, but in this case, it's bad. I'm sure you've noticed that she's almost obsessively passionate about certain things too. She's dedicated, and whatever she's good at, she turns it into something she can excel at."

"But she doesn't act like someone who's on the spectrum."

"That's *just* it. There is literally no single way to describe someone on the spectrum. They have different strengths and weaknesses than even other people who have the same diagnosis. Contrary to popular belief, some autistics are more social but have a harder time with change or emotional regulation. Some don't speak at all. There was this article I read once that even said people with autism experience deeper emotions depending what facet of their personality is affected. With Dianna, she'll probably come around. You just don't know when that will be."

Her words had the strangest effect on him. While he really wanted to hold onto his anger and frustration, he couldn't. Dianna was different. Wasn't that one of the reasons he liked her so much? More and more realizations fell into place, and he looked at Dianna's sister once again. "You sure seem to know a lot about her—about what it's like to be on the spectrum."

She sighed, tucking a strand of hair behind her ear. "I had a friend in high school. He shared a lot of the same tendencies as Dianna. I don't know if she's even realized it herself. She probably just feels like she's different."

"You haven't talked to her about it?"

Shaking her head, she looked away from him out into the yard.

"Why not?"

"I guess I didn't want to put her on the spot. I don't see her as being different. I didn't want to make her feel like she didn't fit in. I'd never want to alienate any of my sisters. And to be honest, I don't see it as a disorder. I see it as a unique way of thinking. Of being human." She rubbed her arms and shivered.

Tristan jumped and immediately removed his coat, placing it on her shoulders. "You shouldn't be out here in the cold."

Grace attempted to argue with him and refuse the coat, but he wasn't having any of it. They stood in silence for a few moments and he let the cold seep into his skin. It was like he was waking up—becoming more alert in regard to his current predicament.

"Maybe I'm not ready for a relationship."

He felt her eyes on him. Shoot. Had he actually said that out loud? Heat crawled up his neck despite the chilled air that whispered against his skin.

Tristan let out a strangled laugh. "How much do you know about my family?"

She shook her head. "Why would I know anything about your family?"

His embarrassment continued to worsen. "I just figured..." He sighed. "Never mind. My wife left me soon after we found out my son was on the spectrum. I thought..." He let out a sad laugh. "When I met Dianna, I thought maybe I had found someone I could be with—someone I could trust."

"You can trust Dianna." Grace's voice lowered, sounding almost upset. "She'd never do anything to hurt you."

She already had, but he wasn't about to bring that up. Somehow he felt like he was part to blame for all of this. Dianna was trustworthy; she just might not be meant for him. That realization hurt more than the actual breakup.

He pushed past her statement and continued. "I think I was so focused on what I wanted that I didn't see what she needed." His whisper was barely audible. The weight that rested on him felt even heavier. Everything was coming into a sharper focus, but he still wanted her. Nothing would be able to change his mind about that. Dianna was special. The only question that remained was whether he could actually step back and give her the space Grace had mentioned.

Tristan took in a deep breath and let it out slowly. "What do you think I should do?"

Grace snorted. "You can't seriously be asking me that right now."

"Why not? I think we know one another well enough. You haven't exactly held anything back up until this point anyway. Besides, I could really use the advice. This is the first time in a long while I have actually been in the dating pool, and we saw how well that went." He made a face. He'd really botched things up this time. "I still want her in my life, as strange as that sounds."

"It doesn't sound too strange to me." Grace reached out and touched his arm. "I think it's sweet. I hope one day I'll find someone who is as crazy about me as you are about Dianna. She's lucky she has you." She grimaced. "Even if she doesn't realize it yet."

"So you're saying I still have a chance?"

"Honestly? I have no idea. I haven't ever been able to predict the things she does. Her logic isn't anything like mine."

That didn't exactly instill any of the confidence he'd hoped it would. "Then it's the opposite. I don't have a shot at getting her back."

"I didn't say that either, and you know it. Geez, will you stop being so fatalistic? If you want her back, use what you have and take advantage of what you know. You've been working with her and your son for the last several weeks. There has to be something you can pull out of that magician's hat to help you out. In my opinion, nothing is ever lost for good. Dianna just needs to be reminded about that."

Tristan shook his head. "You didn't hear her. She basically said that I had suffocated her. I made her feel like she was being pushed into a corner."

"Then don't do that." She made it sound so simple. Like he knew what he'd been doing since the very beginning. Before he could point it out, she interrupted him. "Think before you speak. *Really* listen to her. Make her fall even more in love with you than she already is, and she'll come back to you on her own terms." She nudged him with her elbow. "It's not like you aren't going to be seeing a lot of her. She's still working for Shane out at the country club. Give her some space and see what comes of it."

She shrugged out of his coat and held it out to him. "Just do me one favor."

"What's that?"

"Don't tell her we had this chat. Something tells me she wouldn't be too thrilled about it."

He nodded. "Deal."

Grace headed for the door then paused, her hand on the knob. She glanced back at him. "Whatever you do, don't give up. It might sound silly, but the best things are worth waiting for. Worst case scenario—you go on a few dates with someone else while you wait." She disappeared inside before he had a chance to thank her. Somehow Grace had been the one to talk him off a ledge, and he didn't even know her that well. Her little speech was probably even better than anything Shane might have said to him. Could he do it? Could he stand back and watch Dianna work with Mathew without doing anything to further compromise his relationship with her? The better question was whether he could go on a date with someone else and not be thinking of Dianna for the entire evening.

That thought was laughable.

But maybe that was his only option. While he was willing to wait for her, he couldn't put his life on hold. She'd already broken up with him. There was only one way to go from here.

And that was up.

26

———————

Dianna

The quiet winter morning outside Dianna's window did nothing to quell the emotions that continued to run rampant in her body. She stared at her ceiling and pushed aside the thousand doubts that plagued her since she'd broken up with Tristan on Saturday.

Thankfully, though she did go to church with them, her family let her be on Sunday. But she could only claim to feel unwell for so long. With Mathew and Tristan leaving soon, it didn't feel right to skip work.

There was only one problem.

That meant she'd be seeing Tristan today.

Her stomach crashed and churned like the unsettled waves of the ocean. She'd been the one to break up with Tristan, not the other way around. There was no reason for her to feel anxious. This was what she'd wanted.

Dianna rolled over and glared at the wall. No one told her

that falling in love with someone would be this hard—this heartbreaking.

It was like her body had continued to be pulled in two different directions despite having two nights to sleep on her decision. She hadn't been able to find the peace she sought.

Someone knocked lightly on her bedroom door, but Dianna didn't move. Every muscle in her body ached. Her head pounded. Sometimes she wished she was anyone else. Then maybe she would be able to close her eyes and go back to sleep in order to avoid the inevitable.

"Dianna?" The door opened and Brielle poked her head through the door. "Cal stopped by and took a look at your truck. He said it was a simple fix and he'll have it up and running before you have to head over to the country club."

Still, she didn't move.

"Hey, you doing okay?"

The soft click of the door indicated Brielle had shut it before venturing farther into the room. "Are you still feeling sick?"

Dianna buried her face into her pillow. "I'm fine."

"You don't seem fine."

She let out a frustrated growl and sat up. "It's seven in the morning and I didn't have to be up yet, but you came in here to tell me about my truck. I'm grumpy. But I'm fine."

Brielle gave her a blank look. Then she lifted one brow and folded her arms. "You broke up with Tristan, didn't you?"

Dianna scowled at her sister. "I don't see how that's any business of yours."

"It's not. But it sure puts everything into perspective. And it totally makes sense why you didn't come out of your room much yesterday. For heaven's sake. What is it with you guys? Don't you know? There's a hazard when it comes to falling in love." She moved to the edge of Dianna's bed and bounced into a seated position. "I have a feeling it's why dad told us we couldn't date until the one before us was married. Can you imagine what it will be like when more than one of us is dealing with heartache?"

Stiffening, Dianna frowned at her sister. For some unexplainable reason, Brielle's words were more painful than the issues she was trying to stave off. "Not every relationship ends in heartache."

"I didn't say that it did." Brielle fell backward and craned her neck around to stare at Dianna. "But based on what I've noticed from Adeline and Constance, heartache comes right before you finally figure things out and realize you're making the worst mistake of your life."

Dianna huffed. "That's not going to happen."

"Oh? Because I've never seen you more miserable than you are right now."

"I'm only miserable because I'm not getting enough sleep." Dianna leaned back against her headboard. "And if you would have let me be, then maybe I wouldn't be so miserable."

Brielle laughed. "Deep down, you know that's not true."

Tossing aside her blankets, Dianna climbed out of bed with a huff. "I'm not going to have this conversation with you right now." Once again, she felt like she was being pushed around. This time it was her sister blocking her in and not letting her breathe.

She moved swiftly across the room, gathering the clothes she'd need for work, then escaping into the hall before Brielle could stop her.

Dianna knew what was best. It didn't matter what other people said about her. There was too much going on in her life right now to even consider adding or changing something. It didn't matter that she had feelings for Tristan. Why was everyone pushing her into something she didn't want?

Dressing quickly, Dianna's thoughts once again returned to how this afternoon would go. She didn't know if Mathew would ask her questions, and she wondered what—if anything—his father might have told him.

The ache returned to her chest. But that was natural. Hard decisions often led to having bad days. She'd get past this much like she had gotten through other hard events in her life.

By going for a ride.

Dianna grabbed her hat from the hook by the back door. She pulled on her boots and buttoned her sheep-lined coat before stomping toward the barn. The sky was overcast and dismal, much like her own attitude this morning. What she wouldn't give to start over—to make different decisions a few months ago.

If she'd never allowed Constance to drag her to the country club, then she wouldn't have accepted the position from Shane.

If she wasn't working, then she wouldn't have met Mathew and...

And she wouldn't have developed any feelings for Tristan.

Her heart twisted, angrily battling her head as she shoved thoughts of Tristan from her mind. There were more important things to do than to welcome someone into her life when she wasn't ready. Never before had she had this problem. Why wouldn't her heart just let things be?

She clambered into the barn and readied her horse. The wool blanket and saddle were flung on the animal's back, then cinched tight. Once the reins were adjusted properly, she climbed into the saddle and pulled the horse into the aisle.

Her horse whinnied and jerked her head, nearly rearing back on her hind legs. Dianna let out a soft squeak, her father's silhouette in the way of her escape. Her heart hammered and her hand flew to cover it as if that would be enough to quell the trouble that refused to give her peace.

"What are you doing in here?" she demanded once she could catch her breath.

Zeke chuckled. "I could ask you the same thing. Don't you have a job to get to?"

"I—well, that's not supposed to start until—" She clamped her mouth shut. "I don't have to be there for a few more hours. What are you doing here?"

He gestured around them. "Isn't it obvious? I want to go for a ride." Her father tilted his head as his gaze swept over her and her horse. "Seems to me we had the same idea."

She shifted in her saddle and glanced toward the exit. "Yeah. I thought it would be a great way to clear my head."

Zeke nodded, his lips pressed into a firm line. "Would you mind if I tagged along?"

"Don't you have stuff you have to do today?"

The first hints of a smile touched his lips. "I always have time to spend with my daughters. Especially if they're struggling with something." He nodded toward the stalls behind her. "Give me five minutes and I'll be ready."

THE ONLY SOUND they heard for the first twenty minutes of their ride was that of their horses' hooves crunching in the snow and the occasional snort. The trail started out narrow and finally grew wide enough for them to ride side-by-side.

Dianna's thoughts bounced around from her current dilemma to her father and what he had noticed. How much did he know? Had Grace or Brielle told him? She should have known better than to tell her younger sister anything. Grace had a nasty habit of spreading information to other people when she thought it was in the best interest of certain parties.

That didn't make it right.

"You're probably wondering why I asked to come along." Her father's gruff voice pulled her from the depths of her mind.

"Maybe a little."

"I know you were only about six when your mother passed so you probably weren't very aware of certain characteristics she possessed."

Her hands tightened on the reins. This wasn't what she had expected. She'd wanted to go for a ride where she could continue to analyze and confirm to herself how correct she was in her choices. Dianna glanced out of the corner of her eye toward her father but didn't say a word. He was the kind of man who didn't leave things unsaid. If he wanted to tell her something, he'd make sure he did before too much time passed.

"Your mother was the most generous and loving woman I have ever met. She was also the most analytical being on this planet." He chuckled, his focus remaining on the trail as they passed snow-covered shrubbery. "Sometimes she'd disappear to this other world where she got so hyper-focused on something I wasn't sure she'd ever come out of it."

Dianna stilled, her eyes swinging around to stare at her father.

"Did I ever tell you how hard it was to get that woman to accept me?" He shook his head and waved his hand through the air. "Of course not." Zeke gave her a sheepish grin. "I haven't been the best at sharing that sort of thing with you girls." Pain flitted across his face, and he looked away. She could almost feel his agony as if it were her own. "Your mother was supposed to be here to have these sorts of talks with you girls." His voice broke, and he removed his hat to run his hand through his hair. This was probably the most he'd ever talked about her mother with her that she could remember.

She squirmed in her seat, unsure of how she might smooth

the edges of this rocky conversation. "It's okay, Dad. We're doing fine. All of us are. Even Brielle."

Her father snorted and shot her a side-eyed glance. "That one is going to be the end of me."

Dianna bit back a smile. If only he knew what Brielle had been capable of over the years. "You'll see. Everything has a way of working out."

"Like how they're working out with that Wood fella?"

Her eyes widened and she tore her gaze away from him. Oh that was just great. Grace just couldn't keep her mouth shut. "I don't know what Grace told you, but—"

"She didn't say a thing."

Dianna risked another look in his direction.

"Yesterday, when you didn't come down for any of our meals, I had a feeling something was going on. We all knew you were getting close to that man and his son. Heck, that night you didn't come home—"

She gasped. "You knew about that?"

He offered her a smile. "There's very little I don't know about that goes on under my roof. When you didn't come home, your sisters were in a tizzy. I was the only one who played it cool."

"But why? I broke curfew. I was supposed to come home— certainly not spend the night with a ma—" Her face flushed despite the freezing air. "I didn't—you know—do anything—" She swallowed hard, this time unable to meet her father's studious gaze. "He was a perfect gentleman."

The silence was unbearable. Whatever he was thinking was probably far worse than what actually happened, and he hadn't even come to her and asked about it. The restraint he'd had was... unbelievable.

"Dianna." His soft voice wasn't enough to force her to meet his gaze.

She wrapped the reins around her hands and pulled them tight until she started to lose feeling in her fingers. This whole situation had gone from bad to worse, and all it had taken was for him to bring up her mother.

"Dianna, will you look at me?"

She lifted her gaze, hating the way her blush deepened.

"Do you think I would have stood by and let that man spend more time with you if I had thought otherwise?"

There was no way to put into words the shock she felt over his confession. She blinked and attempted to make sense of where this conversation had turned.

"Out of all of my daughters, I knew you would be able to fend for yourself. You know how to put up walls and stand your ground."

That didn't exactly sound as good as he was probably meaning for it to. From how he described her, she was a fortress and no one was permitted to enter. Mathew had probably weakened her defenses which had allowed Tristan to get close to her. That was the only explanation she could come up with. And even that made her cringe inwardly. Her eyes darted away, searching for a way to convert how he'd described her into something admirable, but she couldn't. No matter how hard she tried.

"But as with any strength, there comes weaknesses."

Dianna's focus shifted once more to her father.

"You are so much like your mother. I see her in you nearly every single day. It's not just the way you look. It's in the decisions you make and the foundation of your personality." He gave her a sad smile. "Your mother was so good at putting up barriers that I had to really work hard to knock them down. But once I did, it opened up a whole new world for both of us. I will always attribute the successes of this ranch to her analytical brain. Sometimes I thought she was magic with the way she could predict certain things."

"Why are you telling me this?" Dianna's features pinched. None of what he was saying seemed to fit with the things he was pointing out in her own relationship.

"Your mother loved deeply. She cared a lot about people and helping our ranch prosper. But sometimes she would stand in the way of her own happiness. When I tried to help her realize that, she would remind me that I was smothering her and she wanted to figure things out on her own."

Understanding dawned in Dianna's mind and she scowled. "So you think I'm making a bad decision in regard to Mr. Wood. You think I'm standing in the way of my happiness, is that it?"

He chuckled, holding up one hand. "Let me finish. Being with your mother was a learning experience. She could set her boundaries and need a certain amount of time to sort things out. And there's nothing wrong with that. I learned how to give her that space. But I'm only human. Sometimes I slipped up. Did that mean she walked away from what we had together?" He shook his head. "Granted, I think she was far too stubborn for that. And maybe you got a little of that stubbornness in you, too."

"I still don't know why you're trying to make me run back to Tristan. I made my choice. It's the right one—"

"It might be right for now. But you have to allow for the variables. Sometimes something that is right in the moment isn't necessarily right for the long haul."

She let out a groan. "So you *are* telling me that I'm wrong. What are you expecting? That I go apologize and tell him I want him back—" Just like that, her defenses shot up and her heart flipped. She was already worried about how their interaction would go this afternoon. There was no way she'd do what her father was suggesting.

"Relax. I'm not asking you to do any of that."

"You're not?"

"Sweetheart, only you know what is in your best interest. Only you can decide what you want from your life. The only thing I want you to consider is whether or not these decisions will make you happy five years down the road. Even ten years. If there is even a slight chance you will look back on this moment and realize you shut out someone who was perfect for you, then perhaps you could try to keep an open mind. Don't push someone away out of fear or frustration. Love is an amazing tool. You'd be surprised how much it can heal."

She stared at her father, completely baffled. Her shoulders slumped and the pressure in her chest deflated. He'd given her his opinion, then told her she needed to figure it out on her own. It was a small gesture, but that's all it took for her to feel seen.

27

––––––––––

Tristan

Tristan fidgeted with his keys. When they'd set up this therapy thing in the beginning, Shane had assured him that he could leave Mathew in Dianna's capable hands. It wasn't that Tristan hadn't believed his friend; he'd just been overprotective. Then everything had shifted and he continued to be present during their sessions because he wanted to spend time with Dianna.

He didn't think he'd be able to stay in the same area as her, not so soon after their breakup. So he'd told Mathew he had errands to run.

Dianna would be arriving any minute, and he wasn't sure how she'd react to him leaving. At this point he figured it could go either way. She might be upset, or she'd be relieved.

Mathew stood at the window, bundled up and ready for their walk to the arena where he'd get his session. Then they'd come back to the cabin for his schoolwork.

Tristan had called the sitter to come over in a few hours so he could be gone for most of the day. He kept telling himself this was what she wanted. Dianna didn't want to be smothered. She wanted space. As much as that pained him, maybe she made a good point.

"She's here! She's here!" Mathew spun around and glanced at Tristan. "When are you going to be back?"

He ruffled Mathew's hair and smiled. "I'll be back by dinner."

Mathew hurried to the door and yanked it open before Dianna had a chance to knock. "My dad is going away today. It's just gonna be us."

Dianna's surprised expression lifted to his and she blinked. "Oh?"

Mathew grabbed her hand. "Yup. He said he has some errands to run, but he'll be here before dinner. Are you going to have dinner with us?"

Tristan grimaced. He probably should have told Mathew in more detail what he meant when he said Dianna would be spending less time with them. He avoided her gaze as he dropped down to pull Mathew close. "Remember when I said that Miss Dianna wouldn't be spending as much time over here?"

Mathew frowned.

"Well, she's going to be busy and—"

"She's always busy. And she still stays." He spun around, pulling away from Tristan as he lifted his face to Dianna. "You said you liked spending time here."

Tristan risked meeting her eyes and immediately regretted it. Her large eyes were pools of pain and hesitation. Nothing had changed. But why would it? She didn't want to be with him. She'd said as much over and over again. She was probably wondering why he didn't just get the hint and walk away.

He had mixed feelings over such a notion. Grace had given him a sliver of hope. He'd grasped onto it so tightly he couldn't figure out where his longing ended and her suggestion began.

Dianna seemed to be frozen to her spot. He couldn't blame her. Mathew could be so direct sometimes.

Tristan took in a deep breath and rose. He placed a hand on Mathew's shoulder and gave him a small smile. "I'm sure Miss Dianna would love to stay, but she won't be able to today. Besides, Kimberly will be here in an hour or so. You've been wanting her to come back, remember? You said she promised to show you how to solve the Rubik's Cube."

Mathew shot a look in Dianna's direction, then brought it back to Tristan. "I guess."

Tristan patted him on the shoulder. "Go find your cowboy boots while I speak with Miss Dianna."

Mathew left without a word, leaving him with no buffer between himself and Dianna. She stood stiffly in the doorway. There were a thousand things he wanted to say and no way to form the words.

Shifting, he put his weight on one foot then the other. "I wanted to let you know that I was heading to town for the day—getting some last-minute Christmas presents. Mathew has his work set out for when you're done, and Kimberly will be here soon so you don't have to wrangle him all on your own."

There was a heaviness in the air between them. What he wouldn't give to tear it down and reach for Dianna to show her just what she was missing.

Instead, he let out a sigh. "If you need me to stay…"

She shook her head sharply. "Nope. I think we're good. I might even have one of the ranch hands come out and work with Mathew since we know he does so well with me."

He nodded. "Sounds like a good plan." Tristan turned

toward the interior of the cabin. "I'm leaving, buddy. Is there anything you want me to pick up for you?"

Mathew materialized. "I want some drawing pencils. Dianna said we could work on our drawing."

"You got it, kiddo."

HE SHOULDN'T HAVE DONE it. He should have walked right on by the florist and let her be. But now he was back in front of his cabin, holding a single rose. He was going to regret it, but the funny thing was that he didn't care.

In this moment, he was prepared to give her the rose. He wasn't sure why just yet. All he knew was that he wanted her to have it and he didn't expect anything in return.

The sack in his other hand dangled and bounced against his leg with the breeze that pulled at him.

Before he could reach for the doorknob, the door swung open, revealing Mathew with Dianna behind him. They were both bundled up and ready to head out into the snow.

Dianna sucked in sharply, but Mathew let out an excited, unintelligible noise. "Dad! You're back!" He tugged at the bag. "Did you bring me the pencils?"

"Sure did." Tristan's gaze locked with Dianna's. "But it looks like you have other plans in mind." They continued to stare at one another like they had before he left. Then he jolted forward. "I got you this." He shoved the single red rose surrounded with baby's breath in her direction. "I'll let you two get to it." Tristan brushed past her and headed inside. He didn't want her to overthink his offering.

Or maybe he did.

He just didn't want it to blow up in his face and end up having to explain why he got it for her. Tristan placed his hands down on the counter, his back toward the door. When it clicked shut, he released a breath that had been locked in his lungs.

There were two ways to look at this most recent interaction. He could pray this was a step in the right direction—that Dianna was pleased with his offering. Or the more likely scenario—she wanted him to just forget about her.

Tristan removed the items from his bags. He placed the pencils on the table next to Mathew's notebooks, then put away the few odds and ends. Then he moved to the window and watched his son and Dianna building another snowman. It appeared Kimberly had left. She wasn't inside the cabin. He'd have to ask Dianna why she left early.

Watching the two of them playing only served to ruin his current mood further. Anger, frustration, helplessness. He could no longer find the hope that had been in his heart the other day.

Grace had mentioned it might be a good idea to go on a few dates with someone else—get his mind off things while he played the waiting game. It felt wrong, somehow. But then she made a valid point. Distraction would be a good thing.

He spun around and pulled out his phone.

Shane answered on the first ring. "Just the man I wanted to speak to."

Tristan opened his mouth, then snapped it shut.

His friend chuckled. "I wanted to formally invite you to the Christmas Eve party I'm throwing at the club. It's going to be family-friendly, so bring Mathew. The whole town is invited, though I don't expect all of them will come."

"I—that sounds great." This could have been the perfect opportunity to bring up needing a date for the party. But then the door opened and Mathew came stomping into the cabin. Snow fell from his boots and he stopped long enough to wait for Dianna to enter.

"I'm sorry. You called me. What's up?"

Dianna shut the door, then hovered there, watching him.

Tristan turned away and lowered his voice. "Nothing. I mean, I don't remember. Just... we'll be there."

"Great. Oh, and Tristan?"

"Yeah?"

"I know we haven't discussed it officially, but I wanted to touch base with you about your stay. When do you plan on leaving? Of course you're welcome to stay as long as you would like to. However, I might need to move you to another location." He chuckled. "Unless you plan on staying even longer. Perhaps you'd like help finding a place to stay in town?"

The silence on the other end was deafening.

He froze, unable to form any kind of coherent sentence.

"You don't have to tell me right this second. Keep it in mind, and let me know when you figure it out."

Tristan dragged a hand down his face and nodded. But then cleared his throat, his voice squeezing out in a rasp. "Thanks. I will."

"Take care."

He hung up the phone and placed it on the counter, then turned to face Dianna. "Where's Kimberly?"

Dianna's brows lifted. "Oh, right. She got a phone call and needed to head home—something about a family emergency. She asked me if it was okay, and I told her to go ahead."

His chest tightened. "She should have called me. She can't just leave—"

"Tristan," she said. His name on her tongue did strange things to him. His head snapped around and he met her gaze. "It's fine. We didn't want to bother you. I knew you'd be back soon enough, and Mathew was well-behaved." She offered Mathew a grin. "You did amazing today."

Mathew beamed. "Does that mean you'll stay for dinner?"

She frowned. "Not today, buddy. But I'll see you again next week."

"Next week? I thought we had a couple more sessions before Christmas." Tristan moved forward. Was this another tactic to distance herself from him?

She folded her arms, standing her ground. "I wanted to talk to you about that. I've got some family traditions. If it's okay with you, we can start back up the day after Christmas."

It was just as well. If she wanted space, he needed to give it to her.

As hard as it was to agree, he nodded. "Sure. Whatever you need." It would be nice for her to notice how hard he was trying. But to point it out would defeat the purpose.

Her gaze darted to his, as if she was doing just that. "Thank you," she said quietly. "I guess I'll see you next week." She reached for the door, and he stepped toward her once more.

"Will you be going to the Christmas Eve party at the club?"

She glanced at him briefly. "I'm not sure."

"I hope so."

Dianna ducked her head. "Then maybe I will." She offered him a small smile. "Thank you for the flower."

28

Dianna

Christmas music drifted through the club as someone played the piano in the ballroom. Shane had spared no expense with the decorations. Much like the outside, which included a life-size nativity scene, the interior was overdone. There were wreaths, boughs with holly, and a huge Christmas tree decorated with ribbon and shiny ornaments in blue and silver that nearly reached the top of the twenty-foot vaulted ceilings.

It smelled like pine and peppermint, and Dianna knew the moment she stepped through the doors, she would regret her decision to come. She didn't know what she was thinking when she told Tristan she would.

And the second she mentioned it to Brielle, there was no going back. If there was one thing her older sister loved, it was spending time with men and flirting with them.

Dianna's other sisters had come as well—most of them,

anyway. Adeline was home with the baby. And Grace had opted to keep her company.

Brielle nudged her in the side. "Do you see him?"

"Who?"

Her older sister snorted. "You know exactly who I'm talking about. We can all see it, Dianna. You're the only one who seems to be in denial over this whole thing."

"I'm *not* in denial." But even as she said it, her focus swept through the room searching for that one person. Okay, so there was a chance she was in denial. Dianna shut her eyes and turned toward Brielle. "I'm not in denial. I just wanted to say hi, that's all."

Brielle laughed. "Oh, I'm sure that's all it is. You haven't been moping all week long because of the state of your relationship; you've just been in a bad mood." She patted Dianna on the shoulder and shook her head as she let out another laugh.

Dianna scowled at her. "I don't see you going out of your way to make any long-term connections. Nothing ever came from that kiss you and Shane shared."

Brielle sobered. "There's a *huge* difference between the two of us. *I* don't *want* to be tied down, and *you* do."

"Do *not*."

Her sister threw her hands into the air and let out a huff. "You know, there's nothing *wrong* with falling in love with someone. No one said you can't enjoy starting a life with that special person. It's not what I want right now, but that doesn't mean you shouldn't allow yourself to find your own brand of happiness." She turned away from Dianna, then scooted right up next to her and draped her arm around Dianna's shoulder. She pointed in the direction of a large fireplace on the other side of the room. "That man over there means something to you whether you like it or not. Something is telling you that walking away was a mistake, and you should probably listen to it."

Dianna's eyes landed on Tristan and her heart skipped. He was dressed like he'd been for the other party Shane had thrown for the adults. Just seeing him dressed like that brought back the memories of that night and the way she'd taken a chance when she kissed him.

Tingles, hints of the reaction her body had that night returned.

Teasing her.

Tantalizing.

"See," Brielle murmured. "I might not want to settle down for my own reasons. But that doesn't mean I can't see when my sister is completely head over heels for someone else."

Tristan glanced in her direction as if he could hear their conversation. Dianna's breath hitched and she pulled away from Brielle to face her. "It's not that I don't want to be with him." The confession escaped her lips before she had a chance to realize what she was going to say. Her face burned hot with embarrassment. She shifted again so her back was to Tristan and there was no possibility that he would see it. "I mean, I don't know if I want to be with him. I love him. I do. My feelings were never a question."

"Then what's holding you back?"

Dianna's jaw clenched. Her heart hammered irreverently. Brielle wasn't going to understand. No one ever did. It was like a vise had been clamped around her heart and her lungs, making it hard to breathe if she even considered moving forward with Tristan. Any step in that direction would cause her physical pain.

But that wasn't the worst part.

She felt the exact same way as she relived their breakup. Any time she thought back to that moment, she regretted it.

Dianna knew it wasn't normal. She wasn't *normal* in any sense of the word.

So now she was just *stuck*.

Stuck between two equally terrible feelings.

Stuck between two things that made sense and didn't at the same time.

Dianna let out a sigh. "I don't know."

"Yes, you do," Brielle shot back. "You know what's holding you back, just like I know what's holding me back."

She frowned and stared at her sister with a little more understanding. Brielle didn't want to be in a relationship for reasons she chose not to share. She might be scared or have her reasons, but she was confident in them. "Why aren't you interested in getting married?"

Brielle huffed. "Who said I wasn't interested?"

"I just thought... seeing as you don't date anyone for more than a few weeks."

Brielle studied her. It was as if she was battling herself regarding whether or not she should disclose any of this. As if she anticipated that Dianna would lean one way or the other based on her response. Then she let out a resigning sigh. "I'm not going to be defined by who I marry. Every guy I have gone on a date with expects something from me."

"You can't know that."

Brielle arched a brow. "First, it was that I was an easy mark. I *had* to get married if I wanted my sisters to have the same opportunity. Then there were those who were only in this for the thrill—the sneaking around."

"Shane doesn't seem like he fits either of those."

"He's the *worst* one."

Dianna's frown deepened with confusion.

"He's this bigshot who has to maintain appearances. He wants a girl on his arm to show off like some trophy."

Dianna arched a brow. That sounded a lot like what Brielle was good at. She was a charmer.

Upon seeing Dianna's expression, Brielle rolled her eyes. "I'm not a brainless piece of jewelry. I have dreams and desires. I want to make something of my life. There's no way I can do that with any of the guys here. I'd forever be in their shadow." She folded her arms and tapped her fingers there. Then her features softened and her voice lowered. "We all have different things we need in a relationship. Our personalities need to be fed in a way that makes sense. I've resigned myself to not finding a guy. I'll have my fun and when I get the chance to do more with my life, then I will." She laughed. "I'll probably end up as the crazy old spinster at the end of the road with a herd of goats to take care of. Who knows? But at least I'll be happy. *You* need to figure out what that is for you."

"But that's the problem. I don't know."

Brielle gave her a pointed look. "When you tell yourself why you can't be with him, what do you say?"

Dianna scowled. "That's none of your business."

Her hands came up and she laughed. "But you say it. You know what's holding you back. So let me ask you something else. Are you being held back for a good reason, or are you being held back by fear?"

Her arms folded tightly across her chest and she stepped back from her sister, not liking how easy it was for Brielle to poke her in her most vulnerable places. "Fear is a good reason."

Brielle shrugged. "You are allowed to have that opinion. But what would you tell that kid you've been working with if he said the same thing?"

And just like that, Dianna's arms dropped to her sides. Brielle's point had been made. She'd sliced through all of Dianna's defenses, making her look like a coward.

"Fear is what drives us, Dianna. Fear is what makes us *do*

more. *Fight* more. Go after the things that are worth *more.* There isn't a historical advancement that wasn't built on the backs of men who were scared. Do you think those Wright brothers weren't scared?" She didn't wait for an answer. "You bet they were scared. But with every failure, they persevered. We don't gain anything from hiding. Mistakes make you grow. Allow yourself to be uncomfortable for once in your life and reap the rewards."

Dianna's mouth fell open. She didn't shy away from new things as much as she used to. But apparently she hadn't hid it all that well either.

Brielle's focus shifted elsewhere, then bounced back to Dianna. "I'm going to find someone to dance with. Just think about it. Tristan isn't a local. If there is any chance that you will regret walking away from him, I recommend you think real hard about what would be worse. Taking a chance, or sticking with what you have."

"But he might not even want me after—"

Brielle gave her a small smile. "Guys are easy. I would wager he's just as miserable as you are. You were the one to break up with him. Set things right and give him a chance to tell you what he wants." She took Dianna's hand in hers, squeezed it, then wandered off.

Dianna glanced over to the fireplace only to find Tristan had disappeared. Her heart fluttered and her stomach flipped over. The club had grown more congested during the course of her conversation with Brielle. He could be anywhere.

Her gaze darted back and forth, seeking him out—not that she planned on doing what Brielle had said. She just wanted to have her eyes on him in case he headed her way. Then she could prepare herself for a conversation.

That's when she saw him. And it wasn't what she expected at all.

Tristan was chatting with another young woman. One of the girls from town. She smiled and laughed, and they glanced at Mathew who sat nearby with his favorite book in his lap. They were clearly making a connection.

Tristan was smiling, too. That smile he had reserved for her.

Dianna shoved that thought back to the depths of her soul. She didn't own that smile. Especially since she'd broken up with him.

The twisty, churning feeling in her stomach intensified and nausea overwhelmed her.

The realization hit her like a punch in the gut, and she hated it more than she despised anything else in her life. She'd been a coward. There was no other way to describe it. She'd done exactly what she tried to stop Mathew from doing. And that was getting in her head and stopping herself from finding joy in something.

She missed what she had found with Tristan.

She missed being a person Mathew could count on as more than just a teacher.

Brielle had finally been able to break through the strange walls she'd built around herself and explain things in a way that she couldn't logically argue with.

And as much as she hated it, she couldn't walk away from it either.

For as far back as she could remember, she couldn't pin down a single moment when she'd experienced jealousy. Sure, she'd envied certain people and their abilities, but with a sort of admiration. She'd been able to stand back and acknowledge that these other people were capable of things she was not. She could accept they had strengths where she had weaknesses and the other way around. She was even capable of analyzing certain scenarios and understanding where she fit in all of it.

Right now was not that kind of feeling.

The knots that had formed were hot and tight. They overwhelmed all of her other senses somehow. All she wanted to do at this very moment was storm across the room and push that woman aside. She wanted to face Tristan and demand to know why he wasn't coming to *her*. Why wasn't he fighting for *her*?

There was a part of her that knew these thoughts were illogical. They had no place in her heart or her mind. And yet they existed all the same.

It was a pretty good thing that she wasn't immature enough to do any of that. She was strong and independent, and when Tristan was ready to talk to her, maybe—maybe she'd bring up the possibility of trying again.

But what if he told her no?

Well, then she'd do the respectable thing and accept his response. And immediately hurry home where she could eat an entire pint of ice cream and hate how she'd let him slip from her fingers.

Tristan glanced toward her, and their gazes locked like they had several times before. She stood frozen, unable to move, unable to tear her eyes from his. He'd caught her staring.

At this point she shouldn't even care. She lifted her chin and flashed him a smile she didn't feel like giving. Although by the feel of it, her smile probably came across as something closer to a grimace.

That's it.

Dianna turned and headed for the bar. If she was a drinker, she'd grab something with a little bite to it. Too bad. She could use something to help her relax. Instead, she got her usual seltzer water and headed for the back door. Tristan could flirt with the new girl. She still had some time. It wasn't like Tristan was leaving tomorrow. They had a few more sessions at least. That was more than enough time to wrap her head around the epiphany she'd just experienced.

She'd been the first to kiss him. She could be the one to tell him she was wrong.

Dianna took a deep breath and let it out, a puff of warm air escaping into the dark night. Her skin was so flushed that the Christmas Eve weather was almost a boon to her. She leaned against the banister of the porch railing and stared out at the faint barn lights that glowed in the distance. Being out here for only two minutes was all it took to help her think more clearly —without all the noise and distraction of the guests.

Brielle was right, though Dianna wasn't willing to admit it outright. She'd never hear the end of it.

But Dianna would do something to win Tristan back. She'd be brave and tell him she was wrong.

"I know I'm probably the last person you want to see right now."

She gasped, her glass dropping from her hand and over the edge of the porch. Dianna leaned over just as she heard the shattering sound below. Tristan moved next to her, leaning over as well. His warm hand was right next to hers, their pinkies barely touching. Dianna focused on his touch, hoping it would steady her, but it only served to start the engine of her heart again.

Tristan grimaced and glanced at her. "Do you think Shane will be mad?"

Dianna couldn't help it. She let out a soft laugh. The situation was far from funny, but she didn't have any other option at her fingertips. If she didn't laugh, she might end up crying.

Just like before, his eyes landed on her with such fierceness she felt locked in place.

Now.

She had to act now or risk losing the most important person in her life.

29

Tristan

"You look—"

"I have to tell you something—"

They both stopped and exchanged smiles.

"Ladies first," he offered. The worst thing he could do in this moment was come on too strong. He needed to show her he loved her without making her feel like he expected anything in return. He'd thought about it over and over and over—all of the things he had done wrong and all the things he could have done differently.

Dianna shook her head, her gaze dropping to where her hand touched his. Did she want him to move? She hadn't pulled away even though she had plenty of room to do so. Maybe this time it was okay.

She glanced at him momentarily. "You can go first. I insist."

This felt like a trap. But at the same time, he knew in his soul he needed to speak up or forever regret what he could have done. Speaking with that other young woman was proof enough to him that he'd lost out on what he wanted. There was nothing wrong with her. She was pretty and carried on a conversation better than some of the people he'd spoken with while living at the country club.

But she wasn't Dianna.

He swallowed hard. "Would you like to go for a walk with me?"

Her features pinched. She glanced out into the darkness, to the building, and back to him. "But Mathew—"

"Brielle offered to watch him."

"She did?"

"Yes," he drawled, "should I have said *no*?"

Dianna shook her head again. "No, I'm just surprised is all. She's usually very *self*-oriented. She usually only does things if they're going to help herself." Dianna made a face. "I'm sorry, that probably really sounded bad."

He moved his hand, placing it over hers, and she lifted her large, innocent eyes to meet his. "You know what? That doesn't always have to be a bad thing. People should be able to stick up for what they want without feeling guilty about it."

She stiffened, though he couldn't tell whether it was due to him holding her hand or the words he'd said. Speaking to Dianna now was utterly terrifying. What he wouldn't give to know what was going on in her head at this very moment.

He needed to start with the basics—ease into it.

"You look pretty tonight."

"Thank you." She took a peek at him out of the corner of her eye. "You clean up nice, too."

He chuckled. "Do you ever get the feeling that we never really get past that awkward stage from when we were teenagers?"

A wry smile touched her lips. "Somehow I think my child-hood differed from yours by a great deal."

"You're probably right." Tristan shifted his focus to the vast property that surrounded the building. It wasn't better than taking in her beauty, but looking at her did a number on his nerves and he needed to be on his A-game. "When I was a teenager, the most important thing was finding a date to prom."

"Yeah. I can't say I had a similar experience."

He looked toward her. "No, I don't suppose you did." He took a chance and wrapped his fingers around hers. If she didn't pull away, he'd continue. Tristan waited for what felt like an endless moment, but Dianna didn't move. Maybe that was a sign for him to keep going, or maybe it was just wishful thinking.

"Anyway, the hardest part about any of that was asking the girl to go to the dance—especially the first year." He chuckled, but the sound was strained. His focus remained on their hands. It felt surreal to be here again, close to her, talking quietly and holding her. He had to force himself to get back to the subject at hand. "There was nothing worse than being turned down by the girl of your dreams."

Inwardly, Tristan grimaced. He probably shouldn't have said it that way. Dianna might interpret his statement the wrong way. He didn't blame her at all. When he glanced in her direction, he'd expected her to be upset, but instead she looked thoughtful. Her eyes flitted to meet his and she gave him a small smile.

"I suppose I never thought about that side of things."

"How do you do that?" he blurted the question, effectively destroying the ambiance.

"What do you mean?"

"How do you manage to surprise me at every turn?"

Her cheeks warmed and she looked away. "You don't have to

say those things to me. I haven't been all that great to you lately."

His brows creased and he faced her, taking both of her hands in his own. "How can you say that? I think you're amazing." When she didn't look up, he tipped his head, angling it so she didn't have much of a choice but to drag her gaze to meet his. "Despite everything that has happened, you have stuck around. You continue working with Mathew. You're there for me. Do you realize how much I respect you for that?"

She didn't answer. But at least she was still looking at him.

"I mean it. There is so much about you that I admire. I don't know if you ever realized this, but there are no simple reasons why I fell in love with you." Here it went. He was going in deep with this one. There was no turning back, even if he wanted to. Tristan only prayed he was making the right choice and that telling her this would only help their relationship get back on the right track.

Tristan let out a heavy sigh. "Yes, I love certain things about you. Like the sound of your laugh and the way you make me feel when you smile at me. But my feelings go so much deeper."

"But we still barely know one another."

He gave her a crooked smile. "And there's the irony, I suppose. I figured I would never find someone I wanted to bring into Mathew's life after Erika left. I didn't think anyone would be able to care for the two of us, let alone handle the ups and downs we deal with when it comes to Mathew's... quirks." Tristan chuckled. "To be clear, my feelings for you don't hinge on how good you are with him either. While you seem to be the 'Mathew Whisperer,' that's a very small part."

How could he bring up every single thing without making her feel like he was putting her on the spot? Ultimately, he needed to assure her that her feelings mattered too, and he wasn't going to push her into something she wasn't ready for.

He bit down on the inside of his cheek to keep himself from speaking. He needed to know she wanted to join the conversation at hand.

When she didn't talk right away, his heart stuttered. He hadn't given her enough space or time. Hadn't he told himself that was the most important thing right now if he wanted to get her back? He'd done it again. He'd messed up an opportunity that God had seen fit to place at his feet. How could he have squandered something so wonderful? He tore his focus from her. Hopefully, she wouldn't see the disappointment he suffered with. If he was lucky, she would also miss the desperation in his eyes he was sure had been brought to the surface.

"Are you sure?"

Tristan's head snapped up and he studied Dianna hard. "Am I sure about what?"

"All that stuff you just said. How do you know?"

A sad laugh bubbled from his chest and he tightened his grasp on her. "You forget I've been around the block before. I know what I want, and that's you."

"But don't you see how backward that is? You thought you wanted your ex. And now you want me? Who's to say I won't turn out just like her?"

He brought her hands to his lips. "You are nothing like her. I knew it from the very first moment I laid eyes on you. Besides not being the type to walk away from a child and being there for the long haul, you know your place in this world. You probably had that all figured out since you were a child. I have never had a woman put me in my place nearly as many times as you seem to be comfortable with."

She made a face. "I'm so sorry."

"Don't be. You're right."

Dianna blinked.

He chuckled again. "I bet you didn't think you'd hear me say those words, did you?"

She shook her head.

"Yeah. I've had some time to think about some of your soap boxes, and I have to say you make several good points. It's too bad that people have this view of those with disabilities. The statistics are amazing. So many people don't even know how to interact with someone who simply thinks differently than they do. I'm not saying that the world is ready to change its ways immediately, but I do think something has to happen to help the new generation navigate their futures." He took a step toward her. "As a father, I'm guilty of trying to prepare my son for the current state of the world. When I should also be trying to educate the world in preparation for children like Mathew."

To say she had a shocked expression would have been an understatement. On this topic specifically, they had always butted heads. It was different being the parent than it was being an outside voice. But after speaking with Dianna's sister, he came to realize that Dianna wasn't offering her opinion as a typical person.

She was atypical in every sense of the word.

And he loved that about her more than she would ever know.

Tristan cleared his throat, forcing himself to drop her hand and brought his up to rub the back of his neck. "You know what I realized today? I'm never going to find someone as good as you. It would be a miracle to meet that kind of person twice in a lifetime. I had you and for whatever reason, I lost you. But I'm not going to let that stand in my way."

Her eyes widened, causing him to second-guess the path he'd started down.

"I need you to know that I don't want anyone else but you. I could say my reasons stem from Mathew's needs and knowing just how good you are with him... but that'd be a lie. If I were completely honest with both you and myself, I'd have to say I'm being selfish. I want you in *my* life. And I'm willing to wait as long as it takes. I don't care if it takes a month, a year, or ten years. I'm not going anywhere."

The shock was less noticeable now, but there was something else. It ran deeper, and he wasn't sure what it was exactly. She almost looked like she was about to cry. Her eyes were red-rimmed. But then she looked away.

Well, at least she wasn't running. She could have argued with him, too, but she didn't do that. And she didn't pull her hand from his grasp. Did that mean she was considering his words? His chest burst with a warm surge of hope. This was a dangerous game.

No, not a game.

This was his life. It was real and it could be ugly or painful, but it could also be filled with charity and faith. He only had to be patient.

Tristan released her hand and took a step back. "I'm going to be ready whenever you are. I'm planning on finding a place to stay in town. I'd also like to speak to you and Shane about continuing Mathew's therapy for as long as it suits you. I won't pressure you into anything you're not ready for—"

"I love you."

His voice died in his throat. He had to be hallucinating. There hadn't been a doubt in his mind that he'd overstepped based on her expression. Then again, she was a queen at keeping her emotions hidden. Dianna was the type of person who only allowed certain people past her defenses, and he'd been lucky enough to be one of them when they'd gotten close.

"I love you," she repeated as she stepped toward him, closing the gap he'd created. "But I'm scared." She reached for his hand and laced her fingers between his. Her voice lowered so much he almost couldn't hear it over the sound of *Jingle Bell Rock* playing inside. "I'm terrified that if I let myself start on this path and it turns out to be the wrong one, that we'll get hurt and it will be all my fault." She peeked at him. "It's a pretty stupid fear, isn't it?"

His hand tightened on hers. "That's a completely reasonable fear." He couldn't deny it hurt a little to know she was more worried over the relationship failing than she was about the happy moments they might share. But then Mathew could fixate on the hard stuff occasionally, too. Tristan placed his free hand against her cheek, relishing the way she leaned into his touch. "But I'll let you in on a little secret. I can't think of a single person who hasn't experienced that worry at least once in their life. It might not matter to you that other people go through this every single time they start a new relationship, but let me assure you, it's more common than you think."

For the first time since his confession, she gave him a genuine smile. "You know, even though you might think that I've got some worthy qualities, that's one that I know I don't have."

"What's that?" Amusement crept into his voice.

"Your uncanny ability to make me look at things in a different light. How you go out of your way to make me feel better about something. Even my family can lose their patience with me. But not you." She pressed her lips together and bit down on them. "I love you."

"So you said." He chuckled.

"Yeah, well, I wanted to make sure you know before you go chatting up the girls at this party."

His mouth dropped open. "What?" A shocked laugh escaped his lips.

"I saw you talking to that girl earlier." Her face blushed a shade brighter than he'd ever seen. "And I'd be lying to you if I said it didn't make me feel a little bit jealous."

This news surprised him in a way that probably shouldn't have been so enjoyable. If he was any other guy, he might use this moment to fuel that jealousy. But he knew better. Relationships that lasted needed to be built on a foundation of mutual trust and respect. "The woman I was speaking with is the daughter of a family who has an apartment over their garage. I was discussing the possibility of renting it."

Dianna's eyes widened and she bit back an embarrassed laugh. "Really?"

He squeezed her hand. "Really. I told you. I will wait as long as it takes for you to be ready. And when you are, I'm going to ask you to marry me so fast it's going to make your head spin."

That was probably too much information for the moment. But it was out in the open now. She knew his intentions and for the time being, she couldn't use any more excuses. She either wanted him, or she didn't.

Tristan had a good feeling about it now. The way Dianna would meet his gaze. The way she smiled at him.

Her confession.

All of those hints were enough to build up his confidence. If he had to, he'd return to the cabin tonight without so much as a promise to see her again.

That was how much he trusted her after this conversation.

"Well then, what are we waiting for?" Dianna grinned.

Tristan laughed and effortlessly picked her up, swinging her in the air before he set her on her feet. Words would never be enough to express the way he felt at this very moment. So instead of a long flowery speech, Tristan slipped his hands around the nape of her neck and pulled her closer. All the kisses they'd shared before paled in comparison to this next one.

When his mouth closed in over hers, he made sure every single nuance regarding how he felt about her would seep into her core. He kissed her sweetly, softly, then with a more fevered passion. This kiss had to show her everything that was in his heart and more. She needed to trust that he was giving his whole self to her—mind, body and soul.

Her hands pushed into his hair, and her eyes fluttered closed. She came alive beneath his touch, refreshing the memory of their first kiss and every single one since.

He had hope for a life together with Dianna.

30

Dianna

Dianna had invited Tristan and Mathew over to her family's home for Christmas Day celebrations. All her sisters had adored Mathew, and he was spoiled by their attention. It only took a few hours for him to warm up to them, which had surprised both Dianna and Tristan.

The week between Christmas and New Year's Eve, she spent nearly every waking moment with them. The funny thing was that the more time she was in their company, the more it simply felt right.

All her fears and concerns had managed to disappear. She couldn't figure out why exactly, but she was definitely more relaxed about everything. Occasionally, she berated herself for the silly reasons she'd had when she broke up with him in the first place. While she would never admit that she was one-hundred-percent wrong, she could see now that her overreactions hadn't been necessary.

The funny thing was that her new outlook seemed to help her work with Mathew even more successfully. While he worked on one of his drawings, she sat beside him with her own paper and pencil, sketching out his studious features. He hadn't noticed who she was drawing yet as he kept his focus zeroed in on his own paper.

The cabin was quiet but cozy. A roaring, crackling flame danced in the fireplace. Snow had started falling about an hour ago. This was shaping up to be a wonderful New Year's Eve, and she couldn't wait for tonight when she could ring in the new year in Tristan's arms.

Mathew glanced up and his eyes zeroed in on her picture. His eyes widened and bounced up to meet hers. "Is that me?"

"Sure is, kiddo."

"Do I get to keep it?"

She laughed. "If you'd like to."

He nodded vigorously. "I want to hang it up in my room."

Dianna continued sketching. "I think that's a wonderful idea."

They were silent for a few more minutes. Tristan had gone outside to find more firewood so they were completely alone. Mathew shifted in his seat and put his pencil down. "Are you going to marry my dad?"

She froze. Besides Tristan's long speech the other week regarding how much he cared about her, they hadn't really discussed the future all that much. She could assume that was where this relationship was going, but that could turn into a grave mistake. It was best to sit back and let nature take its course.

But this was Mathew she was talking to. He wasn't known for his patience.

Dianna didn't meet his eyes as she used her thumb to smudge a part of his hair. "I don't know." It was an honest answer, and it shouldn't have caused her any grief whatsoever. And yet it did. The pain was only a twinge. And it wouldn't do her any good to linger on it. Besides, after what she put Tristan through, she couldn't expect him to throw caution to the wind and ask her to marry him. He probably thought she'd turn him down and leave him high and dry just like his ex had done. It didn't matter if she'd never shown signs of such betrayal. Tristan was allowed to err on the side of caution. But that didn't stop her from hoping one day he would ask her to be his for the rest of their lives.

"Why not?"

She was yanked from her thoughts with such force she had to recall what Mathew had asked of her. It took a little longer than she expected, and he frowned at her while he waited.

Right. He wanted to know why she didn't know if they would get married.

"I'm not sure if your dad is ready to move to the next step of our relationship."

"He is." Mathew's statement was so quick and ready, that she had to wonder what they'd talked about when she wasn't around. "Do *you* want to get married?"

She bit back a smile. "Boy, you're chock full of questions today, aren't you?"

He shrugged. "I just thought it'd be nice if I got what I wanted for Christmas."

Dianna knew she would regret it the second the words escaped her throat. "And what's that? What did you want for Christmas that you haven't received yet? From what I remember, you got plenty of presents."

"Yeah..." he drawled, "but I didn't get what I wanted most."

"Which is..." she prompted with exaggeration.

"A new mom."

Just like that, her whole body flashed with hot and cold

sparks. Her extremities went numb and her heart pounded erratically. "And you want *me* to be that for you?"

Mathew looked her dead in the eyes. "Don't you want to be my mom?"

A bark of laughter was the only sound she could muster. "What?"

He shrugged and turned his attention back to his picture. "I like you. You like me. And my dad likes you. Why wouldn't you want to be my mom?"

She leaned closer to him. "Buddy, it's not as easy as all that. Both people need to *want* to get married first."

"My dad does. I think he wants to ask you, but he's scared."

Dianna nearly choked on her beverage. Before she could say another word, the door opened and Tristan wandered in, dusting himself off from the firewood he'd gathered. He flashed them a smile from the doorway, and she returned it.

Tristan wanted to ask her to marry him. When he'd brought it up on Christmas Eve, she hadn't believed him. In fact, she'd thought he was just saying that to make her feel good. But the thrill that coursed through her veins at Mathew's confession was enough to set everything inside her on fire. If he were to come over to the table and ask her at this moment, she already knew the answer.

That was how her brain worked. When she knew she wanted something, she was all in.

And looking around the cabin at Mathew and Tristan only solidified those feelings. This could be her life, and it was one that she wanted.

But if Tristan was too nervous to do anything about it, she might just have to do something about it all by herself.

DIANNA AND TRISTAN each held one of Mathew's hands in theirs as they wandered toward the country club. They promised Mathew that he could stay up until the ball dropped if he took a nap.

When that kid wanted something, he made sure to make it happen.

She grinned down at him, loving that they shared so much in common. It was as if God himself had sent Tristan and Mathew into her life because he knew how much they all needed one another. They fit like the pieces of a puzzle.

Feeling a pair of eyes on her, Dianna glanced up to find Tristan smiling. She laughed. "What?"

"I love you," Tristan said.

Mathew craned his head around, his focus bouncing from his father to Dianna. "Aren't you gonna tell him?"

Dianna's insides froze and she met Tristan's curious gaze with a fresh wave of nerves. She hadn't told Mathew she had made special plans for the night. How did he know?

"Miss *Dianna*." He sighed. "Aren't you going to tell my dad you love him too? That's how it goes, right? You have to *communicate*."

Both Tristan and Dianna laughed, the tension in her body broken. "You're right, bud. That's exactly how it goes." She leaned over him and puckered her lips. "I love you," she murmured just before Tristan brushed his lips against hers.

Mathew beamed. "I knew it."

"Knew what?" Tristan chuckled.

"You'll see."

Before they could pin him down and get him to explain himself, they arrived at the country club and he disappeared inside. Tristan faced her, his hands clasping her tightly. "I love you so much."

"I love you, too." It got easier and easier to say those words.

She almost couldn't remember what it was like before she'd found her sense of equilibrium.

"There's something I want to talk to you about before I move out in two weeks."

She tilted her head. Maybe she wouldn't have to do anything after all. Tristan could take the reins and she could enjoy the ride.

"I want your opinion on something."

Confusion marred her features. "Okay."

"I'm writing a book."

Her eyes widened. "You are?"

He nodded and laughed. "Don't sound so surprised. It's nothing special—just a lot about our lives with Mathew and the things we've done to make his life and ours easier. I thought that it would be a good jumping-off point for your future— perhaps a future we might share."

Dianna's mouth went dry. This was a very strange way to go about a proposal. She felt like she'd been hit up against the side of the head with one tidbit of information only to be slapped on the other with more of the same and yet a different topic.

"You are absolutely incredible with Mathew. So much so, that I thought you might be interested in teaching others how to do what you do. I'd love for you to collaborate on my book and maybe start a training program to help inform the public about what it means to be on the spectrum."

Every word he said was like liquid gold. She'd never thought about doing such a thing, and now she hated herself for not coming to the idea on her own.

"But if you don't want to—" he started.

She clutched his hands almost too tightly. He grimaced, and she relaxed her hold on him. "I think that's an amazing idea. I'd be honored to be part of it with you."

A smile split Tristan's face and he pulled her in for a long, warm hug. When he pulled back, he still wore that grin. "You are the best thing that has ever happened to me. I hope you know that."

She lifted a shoulder. "I think I've been told that before." More specifically, by him. She jerked her chin toward the entrance. "Come on. Let's join the festivities before it gets too late and all we have left is the countdown."

He wagged his brows. "Maybe that's all that I need from tonight."

She blushed. He had no idea what she was up to. Boy, would he be surprised.

As the clock ticked closer to midnight, more and more people seemed to materialize. The whole club was filled with not only locals but people from nearby cities. Dianna even overheard a conversation about a guy who was just passing through and thought he'd stop by to see what the party was all about.

Shane's business reputation and what he had created here was already bringing people to their small town. It was exciting, thrilling, and even a little terrifying. New people meant her circle would be expanding.

Tristan put his hand in hers and squeezed.

Dianna looked down at where their fingers intertwined and her thundering heart shifted gears from anxiety to something far more palatable. She glanced up, finding his warm gaze on her. She leaned into him, resting her cheek against his shoulder.

If anyone had told her that when she met him, this was how her life would be a few short months later, she would have called them crazy. Change was a bitter pill to swallow, and she'd perfected the way she lived her life in such a way that prevented much of that from occurring.

Yes, she taught Mathew that change was important. It was one of those better-said-than-done situations. And now she realized she'd only done herself a disservice by hiding behind her drawings and her books.

Tristan released her hand and wrapped his arm around her before pressing a kiss to her temple.

This just felt... *right*.

The New Year would be welcomed with open arms in less than five minutes.

Her skipping heart rate danced to the beat of the music, and with each passing second, it seemed to do its own countdown.

Five, it took a thundering step forward.

Four, there was no room for hesitation now.

Three, she'd found so much more happiness than she could have ever dreamed possible.

Two, it was now or never.

One.

Dianna faced Tristan and held both of his hands in hers. His focus was on the television screen playing the recording of New York Times Square when his gaze flitted down to meet hers. He gave her a confused and yet curious smile.

Dianna tilted her head. "Hey."

"Hey," he murmured.

"I wanted to talk to you about something."

That got his attention. She saw it in the way his gaze flitted around the room. He shifted his weight and it almost looked like he was trying to find an escape. She tightened her hold on him and tugged him closer to her.

"Don't worry, it's nothing bad."

The crease between his brows deepened and his eyes made it clear he was recalling the last time they had a one-on-one talk. The one where she broke up with him. Tristan let out a strained laugh. "I wanted to talk to you about something, too. But maybe you should go first."

She hesitated. Had Mathew assumed wrong? What if Tristan *wasn't* interested in taking another step forward in their relationship? They were here with all their friends, and she could very well make a total fool of herself.

Her stomach knotted uncomfortably and her palms grew clammy.

No.

She wasn't going to allow her fears to talk her out of this one. She'd planned on laying it all out on the table so he was aware of where she stood.

"Alright, folks, the countdown begins in one minute!" A voice called over the crowded room. Cheers erupted, but it was almost like they were somewhere else, surrounded by lightly falling glittering snow.

The sounds around them were muted and all she could hear were the irregular beats of her heart and her breathing.

In and out.

She could do this.

"Tristan, I—"

"I love you," he interrupted.

Dianna chuckled. "Yeah, I know."

"And I meant what I said. I will wait as long as it takes."

"It's fine, Tristan. I have no intention of changing what we have." Well, that wasn't entirely true. She let out a soft laugh. "Actually, I am, but not in the way you might be thinking."

"Before you say anything—" Tristan dropped her hands and patted his coat pocket, then froze and looked at her. His hands dropped and he took ahold of hers. "Actually, you can go first."

She nibbled on her lower lip. This was harder than she had

thought it would be. He was going to think she was crazy. She just knew it. Typically, guys were the ones who—she shoved the thought aside. They lived in a modern era. Who said she couldn't?

The crowd around them shouted. "Ten!"

"Tristan, I love you more than I thought possible." Her voice shook slightly, and Tristan tightened his hold on her.

"Nine!"

"And I love Mathew, too." She prayed she'd be able to help him see what he meant to her, but right now words seemed like an insurmountable obstacle.

"Eight!"

"I thought I wanted predictability."

"Seven!"

"But you've made me see I can have so much more." Boy, she probably sounded like a loon.

"Six!"

"I guess what I'm trying to say is..."

"Five!"

"...I don't want to live a single day..."

"Four!"

"...without you in it." She met his steady gaze with one of her own and a burst of courage propelled her forward.

"Three!"

"I want to marry you, Tristan."

"Two!"

He didn't even hesitate for a second. "Yes!"

"One!"

She gaped at him. The crowd around them went wild; streamers flew in the air as if in slow motion. He swept her into his arms and pressed a firm, claiming kiss to her lips. Wait a minute. Were they engaged?

Her legs went numb, but that was completely fine as he

managed to hold her up. Her whole body vibrated with joy and electricity. Both of her hands landed on his shoulders and she kissed him back, giving everything she had to offer. And he was accepting it with every ounce of his being. They had become one, connected by something far greater than themselves.

"I *knew* it." Mathew's accusatory voice yanked them from the euphoria they found themselves in.

Tristan pulled back, but he continued to hold her close to his chest. They both looked down at Mathew staring up at them with a wide grin plastered on his face. Dianna bit back a laugh and dipped her face closer to Tristan's shoulder.

Mathew looked from one to the other as if he were completely unaware of the celebrating going on around him. "Does this mean you're going to be my mom?"

Chills ripped through her body and she looked up at Tristan for a moment before returning her gaze to Mathew. "If that's what you want."

"I knew it," he repeated. "I just knew I was going to get a mom for Christmas."

Tristan laughed. "It's not Christmas anymore, kiddo."

Mathew shrugged. "It's a late Christmas present, then."

Dianna and Tristan pulled apart just enough to allow them to crouch down. Mathew didn't need an invitation. He launched himself into their arms.

So this was what complete felt like.

EPILOGUE

One month later

Tristan

"There's really not much we have to pack. It's not like we were expecting to stay." Tristan gave Shane a pointed look.

Shane laughed and clapped Tristan on the back. "Well, I can't say I'm disappointed. It will be nice to have a familiar face around here. You know, not a local."

"The locals aren't so bad." Tristan's gaze drifted toward the cabin where Dianna played in the snow with Mathew.

"You said you hired Grace? How is she doing?"

Shane rubbed his jaw and glanced back toward the main building. "Hard to say. She started about a week ago. She's quiet. I'm not sure she's going to be a good fit."

Tristan's brows furrowed. "Oh?"

"Yeah. We have a few clients scheduled to arrive next week, and I was going to have her be assigned to one of them. But I might have to reconsider. The client in question seems a little rough around the edges."

He gave Shane a wry smile. "You know better than anyone that the Callahan women are forces to be reckoned with. Just because Grace is the youngest and she's the quietest, doesn't mean she can't hold her own. Think about it. She had to stick up for herself in that household."

Shane arched a brow. "True, but she just turned twenty-one. Do you honestly see her being willing to put her foot down when the client doesn't want her help?"

"Exactly what kind of client are you describing? I thought you focused on helping kids like Mathew here."

"I do. But equine therapy has the potential to help so many more demographics. I don't want to turn anyone away who might need help."

"What kind of client are you assigning to Grace?" Tristan shot a look in Dianna's direction. He got this sense that Shane was worried about something serious. If there was even a chance that Grace wasn't going to be able to handle it, Dianna wouldn't be afraid to step in and have a word with Shane. "You're not suggesting that this client could be dangerous."

"No. Of course not."

"Then why do you seem so nervous?"

Shane blew out a long, slow breath. "He's a US Military veteran."

"Oh. I heard about that. Weren't you doing some kind of group session thing? Why would you have to assign him to Grace?"

"Because he doesn't do well around other people."

That's when all the pieces came together. Tristan's mouth dropped open and his brows pulled together. "And you thought the best person to set him with would be Grace? She's barely trained. What were you thinking?"

"There's no one else I can team him with. This guy doesn't trust easily. Anyone I could assign him to would be a hard sell anyway. I thought that Grace's meek attitude might be something that would help him relax a little."

Tristan dragged a hand down his face. Shane was right to be concerned. This didn't sound good at all, "If he doesn't like people, then why is he even coming out here to get therapeutic services?"

"It was court-ordered."

For the second time, Tristan felt like he'd been slugged in the chest. "You can't be serious. A court-ordered therapy? You realize people who don't want to have therapy aren't the most amicable in the first place."

"That's what I'm saying. I don't know what I should do in this situation. Everyone else I have on staff can be argumentative. Have you met your fiancée?"

Tristan shot another look at Dianna.

Shane was right.

From the very beginning, Dianna had fought him on certain aspects. Pairing her with a client who wasn't very willing to listen could be disastrous. He rubbed the back of his neck and returned his focus to Shane. "You want a suggestion?"

"Of course."

"I wouldn't tell Zeke Callahan any of this."

Shane chuckled. "Wasn't planning on it."

"Dianna is pretty good at this therapy business. She'll be a good resource for Grace if things get difficult."

"Truer words, my friend. Truer words." Shane peeked in Dianna's direction. "You got a good one. You're a lucky man."

"I couldn't say it better myself."

At that moment, Dianna gave him a dazzling smile, then

started running toward Tristan, holding Mathew's hand. Before he knew it, they were both tackling him to the ground in a snowy hug. And he knew without a doubt that his son's Christmas wish had come true. Mathew has a mom who cares. And he has the most beautiful woman he's ever seen... by his side for life. It was going to be a good year indeed.

~

Hello reader,

I hope you enjoyed Dianna and Tristan's love story!

Coming up next with the Callahans...

Grace Callahan knows horses inside and out—but being a new therapist at the Equine Therapy Center has her feeling like an imposter. When her first client turns out to be a brooding, stubborn military vet who doesn't believe in therapy, she's not sure who's in for the tougher ride.

Riley Scott's army career is over, and he's not interested in talking about it. But working with Grace and her gentle horses might be the one thing that breaks through his defenses... and his heart.

Can these two opposites find healing—and maybe even love—before they push each other too far?

Look for *Trusting a Cowgirl, Callahans of Copper Creek Book 4* at **nataliedeanbooks.com** and other retailers.

ABOUT THE AUTHOR

Born and raised in a small coastal town in the south, I was raised to treasure family and love the Lord. I'm a dedicated homeschooling mom who loves to travel and spend time with my growing-up-too-fast son.

When I'm not busy writing or running my business, you can find me cleaning house, cooking dinner, feeding our three rescue cats, trying to make learning fun and coaxing my son to pick up his toys. On less busy days, you may also find me paddling down a spring run in Florida, hiking a mountain trail in Georgia (on the rare vacation to the mountains), or enjoying a book.

If you love Natalie Dean books, you can be notified of new releases by signing up to my newsletter at nataliedeanau thor.com, where you will also receive two free short stories for signing up. Just click on the "Free Books" tab at the top and you'll be on your way!

Also, as previously mentioned, I've opened my own online bookstore and I'd love your support! As of June 2024, I'm selling my ebooks at Natalie Dean Books. By late summer or fall 2024, I should have audiobooks, regular paperbacks, large print paperbacks, dyslexic print paperbacks and signed paperbacks all available. At the request of my loyal readers, I'll also be adding merchandise, such as glasses, cups, magnets and more. So come check out my small mom-owned author business at nataliedeanbooks.com.

You can also scan the QR code below to be taken to the home page of Natalie Dean Books.

facebook.com/nataliedeanromance